PLAY THE LAST TRACK

Editing and Proofreading by Laura @ Hummingbird Editing

Book Cover by Rebecca Parker @ Booked For Design

Second edition 2026

CONTENTS

For Ash, because Katie & Flynn would've stayed side characters
if it weren't for you.

Content Warning

Readers should be advised that Play The Last Track includes mentions of physical abuse, emotional and mental abuse, and cheating. While it happens off page, some readers may still find it upsetting. If any of these warnings trigger you, please read with caution.

PROLOGUE
KATIE

"Who am I supposed to talk to? Eight hours stuck next to a stranger."

"You will be fine." Ivy laughs as she leans back into Scott's chest. The sight only makes my scowl deepen.

Ugh.

My best friend and her fiancé are absolutely sickening.

Well, not really. The two of them are perfect together. Made for each other. Fate brought them to one another, and I promise you, I'm not even a little bit jealous.

Okay. Maybe, like, ninety-five percent happy for them and five percent jealous.

Ten percent jealous, ninety percent happy.

Fifteen percent, but that's really it.

I used to be happy. I used to have someone to lean on when I was tired. Someone I would sit next to on flights. Someone I looked at with that kind of love.

I think.

That's been my problem the last few months. I think I was in love, but I'm not certain.

Grant says he was certain. He says he was in love with me. That he wanted to spend the rest of his life with me. He tells me all of this over and over again.

But he doesn't show it. I don't think he ever has.

The longer I went just hearing those words and not feeling them, not seeing them, the more I think I fell out of love with him. Or, maybe, I just woke up to what I settled for.

Ugh.

"Can't we all just sit in coach? That way, you can sit next to me and Scott. Everyone wins." I beg my best friend, but it's completely futile. The tickets are paid for, and we've checked in.

Still.

"My knees and my back will pay for it," Scott mumbles. His face is pressed into Ivy's neck as he tightens his arms around her waist. My heart clenches. See? That's loud love.

I groan and mumble, "Old man."

"It's eight hours, and then we will be in Rome. Watch a movie and have a nap," Ivy says.

"Scott, swap seats with me. I need entertainment, and Ivy will gossip with me. I have to tell her about the mess Doug and his cronies made in the bar the other week." I clasp my hands in front of my chest, hitting him with my best ever puppy dog eyes. "Please."

"Not a chance, Murphy," Scott replies instantly. He doesn't even look up. Dammit.

"Don't worry, Rockstar. I'll keep you entertained."

A shiver rolls through me, and I have to work not to let it show on my face. I look up. Standing over me, broad shoulders stretching a crisp white T-shirt to breaking point, and a smile that would make even the devil fall to his knees, is Flynn Reed.

Tight end to the Boston Broncos and Scott's best friend.

And my secret, totally off limits, but definitely in my dreams, football crush.

Fuck, yes.

Chapter One
Flynn

Four Months Later

I DON'T KNOW WHY I come here.

The ground is sticky. The music is loud. The food is so greasy, I'll have to do an extra lap or two during my morning run to work it off. The leather seat of the booth I've tucked myself away in is at least minimally comfortable, and the table is wiped clean. There is no round green lamp hanging low from the ceiling over my table, like most of the others, so I'm shrouded in darkness. It could be worse.

I could be sitting at the bar, practically front row to the douche parade going on.

A group of men on the other side of the bar starts yelling out a countdown. I look up in time to see the one in the center of them slamming a shot glass down onto the bartop. He opens his mouth, showing that he's swallowed all the liquid, and his friends cheer. I roll my eyes and shift in my seat, settling back into the booth. Before I look back down at my screen, where I have the tape from last year's game against New York up, I see a flash of blonde hair.

That's all it takes. A single flash completely distracts me.

Katie Murphy stands in front of the group of men, hands on her hips, and hair falling down her back in delicious waves. My fingers twitch as I remember what it felt like to run my fingers through those strands. Adrenaline rushes through me, and I take a deep breath, leaning further back into my chair to try and see more of her.

The bar is in the center of the room. As a patron, you can be served from three sides. The fourth has a small gap that the staff use to go in and out, and a glass washing area. The middle is an island, fridges packed with beer under the countertop on all sides and shelves stacked high with liquor bottles.

I can see her blonde hair through the gaps between the bottles. I shift to the left and catch a glimpse of her profile. Long lashes, soft skin, perfect lips.

She's smiling at the men, laughing at their jokes. Damn, if that doesn't make me a little envious.

I continue watching her through the gaps as she moves. Her hands stay on her hips as she speaks to the group in front of her. There are at least five of them. They all lean over the bar as if they're itching to jump over it and get closer to her. The one in the middle, the shot-taker, laughs loudly, and I see Katie take a step back and away from them.

The hairs on the back of my neck stand up.

"Justin," I call out to the glass washer as he passes me, a stack of glasses higher than his head balancing in his hand. He stops at my call, spinning on a heel.

"Flynn. Hey, man. Didn't see you there." He picks up the empty glass in front of me and gives me a grin. He's only a kid, but he's a good one. Ivy told me he plays for his community college team. Whenever I come in and he's here, you can tell he's dying to ask about football, but he hasn't yet.

"All good, man. Hey, can you get Katie for me? I need to pass on a message from Ivy." Another loud cheer comes from the group Katie is still serving, and my stomach clenches. I add, "It's important."

"Sure. One sec," Justin says, walking toward the bar.

He places the glasses in the dish area before heading over to Katie, tapping her on the shoulder. Another swish of blonde hair, and the collective moan coming from the group lets me know she's walking away from them. Pressure releases in my chest, and I breathe out slowly to calm my nerves.

I run my fingers through my hair, messing up the strands in an attempt to bring life back to it. After being trapped under my cap during my workout, it's giving me definite hat hair.

"What do you want?" Her sharp tone sends a jolt of excitement through me, and I can't help the smile that tugs on my lips.

"Just wanted to compliment the chef. Food's been great tonight," I say as I sit back in the booth and let my eyes wander down her body. I know what lies under those tight black jeans and that long-sleeved top. I know what noises she makes when I kiss a particular spot on her neck. I know her. I think about her.

Yet, after that night, she can't stand me.

It's killing me that I don't know why.

Months ago, on a flight over the Atlantic, I sat next to Katie Murphy, and she kept my attention for longer than the eight-hour flying time. We spent three weeks in an Italian villa with our loved-up best friends, smiling and flirting with one another. One night, after a few too many wines, we fell into bed.

I think that night changed my brain chemistry.

Katie Murphy, with her golden hair, her long legs, and her infectious, witty smile, has been on my mind since. Forget the girls I used to take home after a game to burn off extra adrenaline. Forget the failed dates I tried when I got it into my head that traditional dating might be a good idea again. This woman infiltrated every inch of my damn brain.

"You're full of shit, Reed. Go away." She tuts, picking up the plate in front of me.

"How was your day?" I say as I slide out of the booth, swiping my phone from the table and following Katie toward the kitchen. I'm not so bold as to follow her *into* the kitchen, but I watch through the service window as she places the plate into the dish pit.

She glances over her shoulder, rolling her eyes when she realizes I've followed her. I grin, calling out through the window. "You didn't answer me."

"It was better before you came in here. Go home, Reed. I don't have time for this today." When she comes out of the kitchen, she shoves me out of the way so she can pile the plates of food that just got put up into her arms. She carries them over to a table, and I stay a few steps behind. Her smile falls, quickly replaced with a scowl when she turns around to see me still hovering.

"Come on, Katie. Give me something." I place my hand on my heart. "Then, I promise I will leave you in peace."

"You promise?" The words drip with sarcasm, and Katie doesn't look up at me as she moves past. I don't step back, so her shoulder brushes my chest as she does. She tries to hide it, but I don't miss the shiver that runs down her spine. The image of her, bare and willing, and under me as I run my hands down the contour of her back and over the curve of her hips, floods my mind. My dick twitches, and I silently scold him.

"I saw Scott at practice today." I follow her back to the bar. She reaches around the bartop and picks up a pile of coasters, playing with them. Finally, she looks up at me.

Crystal clear, white sand, and clear skies kind of eyes stare back at me. Bright, gleaming, and blue. So, so blue. Blood rushes in my ears, and I can feel my pulse start to race.

"I would hope so. You play for the same team," she replies.

"He said Ivy wants to have family dinner this Sunday. After the game."

"You're not part of her family. Why are you going?"

"Oh, come on, Rockstar. Don't be like that." I step forward, closing the distance between us.

"Don't call me that." I watch her throat closely as she swallows hard.

I step even closer, bending my mouth to her ear. "Why? You like it?"

She scowls. The force of her eye roll looks like it hurt, and I laugh, pulling away from her and giving her space. She steps back into the bar and closes the swinging door that blocks off the entrance. It's normally kept open, so the staff can move in and out with ease.

"I'll see you Sunday," I say, leaning over the bartop a little and tapping out a gentle rhythm with my fist. "See ya later, Rockstar."

I walk away and urge myself not to glance back, not to get lost in the blue of Katie Murphy's stunning eyes. Just as I reach the door, pausing as I wait for the large group of guys that were crowding the bar before to filter out, Katie calls out.

"Stop calling me that!"

The smile that curls over my lips is unmatched. She may hate me after our night together in Italy, and she may not want to tell me why, but I get under her skin. Boy, do I love it.

The group of shot-takers lingers on the sidewalk outside the bar.

"Where do they find the staff for this place? It's like a walking runway show in there," one of them slurs. My shoulders tense.

I pull my cap from my back pocket and shove it down over my head.

"The blonde one is a smokeshow," another says. My shoulders tense, and I flick my gaze up. The only blonde in there tonight is Katie. The guy who took the shots, the one practically trying to jump the bar to get her attention, stands in the middle of his friends. He wears a polo shirt that he's tucked into his chino pants. The same chinos are cuffed at the ankle. My gaze drops, and I internally gag as I take in the boat shoes he's wearing. What a douche.

I shake my head and shove a hand into my pocket in search of my keys. Sadly, the douche keeps talking.

"She looks like she'd take it hard, however you wanted to give it to her, and she'd say thank you at the end." My blood begins to boil. The edge of my vision tints red. "I bet I could have her over the hood of my car after a glass of wine or two. Easy."

My resolve snaps.

Before I know what I'm doing, my fist is flying through the air and connecting with the douche's nose. A sickening crunch echoes. There's a beat where he looks at me like I'm insane before he pulls an arm back, and his fist heads straight for my face. I dodge it, grab him around the waist, and take him to the ground.

The next thing I know, my knuckles are split open, I'm being pulled off the douche bag by his equally douchey friends, and I've done enough damage to the guy's face that he's most definitely going to have a black eye.

"Who the fuck are you?" he demands.

"Your worst nightmare if I catch you drinking here again," I growl.

"What is your problem, dude?" He shakes off his friends and steps into my space. I have a few inches on him, but I have to give him props for trying.

"Have some respect." I shake out my hand. "Don't speak about a woman like that. Especially not that woman."

"Whoa." He sways a little as he holds up his hands. "I didn't know she had a boyfriend. I was just making a comment."

"A disrespectful one. Get the fuck out of here," I growl. "Now."

The douche in the boat shoes looks like he wants to argue, but his friends pull him away. They yell and shout their distaste for me as I watch them go, standing in front of the entrance to Pat's with my arms crossed over my chest.

Fuckers.

I shake out my hand again. Goddamn, that went too far.

I bend down to pick up my cap that fell off during the scuffle, and when I look up, I see the camera pointed my way from across the street. It flashes a few more times as I shove the cap on my head again and walk down the sidewalk toward my car.

Fuck, fuck, fuck.

***

I flex my hand, opening and closing my fist. The skin across my knuckles tightens, and pain shoots through my nerves. It's angry and red, and the open wounds haven't even started to heal over. I sigh, pulling the bandage tape from my bag and tugging at the end. A little clumsily, I wrap the tape over my knuckles and around my hand. I tear it off, tucking the end away to secure it.

I flex again, feeling my range of movement. Restricted but good enough.

I look up, scanning the room and looking around at my teammates. No one is paying me any attention as they duck in and out of the locker room, getting ready for practice. I flex my fingers for the third time before shaking my hand out and getting to my feet.

I was an idiot to have gone out last night. My head is pounding, and my stomach turns at the idea of the next four hours of running drills and catching a ball. The image of the guys across the street, snapping pictures, haunts me.

And I busted up my fucking hand.

Goddammit.

I turn into my locker, pretending to prepare my pads and practice jersey before slipping it over my head. I squeeze my eyes tight as I block out the dumbass decision I made last night after leaving the bar. I didn't even drink that much. A beer with my burger, sitting in my favorite corner booth with my head bowed and my eyes trained on the film tapes I had saved on my phone.

A few glimpses at Katie. A little flirting.

That's all I wanted from the evening.

But when I heard the way that guy was running his mouth, I just snapped.

Fuck.

I am so screwed.

I snatch up the gloves sitting on my seat and storm from the locker room. As I move through the tunnels, I feel the familiar mask slip over my features. I smile and nod to everyone I pass. I laugh as one of the social media girls asks me my favorite band at the entrance to the practice field. I answer, flashing a cheeky grin and throwing a wink to the camera before stepping onto the grass.

Football is everything to me.

This.

The field. The team. The game.

I thrive on the energy it gives me. I study my game tape and my playbook like they're the most interesting things in the world. I eat well and I train hard. I play hard. I want to be great.

I am doing everything I can to be great.

I shake out my wrapped-up hand and flex the fingers once more before slipping a glove over the bandage as I approach Scott, standing in the middle of the field.

"Hey," I say as I get closer. He jerks his chin up, not breaking his focus as he takes the ball held out by one of the assistant QB coaches and throws it down the line. A running back, one of the rookies, is there to catch it. He does so effortlessly, tucking the ball into himself as he side steps a defender and goes for a touchdown.

It's clean, smooth, and exactly what the playbook outlines.

I shake out my arms, then my legs, trying to loosen my muscles. Scott glances at me before taking another football and spinning it on his palm. I stretch out my legs, leaning to one side and then to the other. Rotating my arms, I groan at the way my hand throbs with the movement. I sink into a squat, stretching my hamstrings out.

"You look like shit," he says before throwing the ball down the line. I swallow the guilt clawing up my throat and plaster my best smile across my face.

"So sweet to me, Harvey." I clap a hand to his shoulder. He grunts and shrugs me off.

"Warm up," he grumbles, twisting another ball between his palms. "Let's run some plays."

I hesitate for only a moment, letting my grin slip just a little as I think about my bruised and battered hand. Before I can talk myself out of it, Scott calls the play, and I'm sprinting down the field.

My legs burn under me, but I ignore it, pumping them fast as I keep the ball in my sight. It sails through the air, and if I get there, it should tuck into my waiting hands just as I get into the end zone.

I'm a step or two off. My fingers tip the ball, and I slip, unable to grab it as pain shoots up my fingertips and ripples through my injured hand.

Fucking hell, that hurts.

I catch the ball on the bounce and slow down. I look up to see Scott glaring at me from thirty yards away. I drop his gaze and toss the ball to the side, jogging back over. I position myself to his left, crouching on the line.

"Again," I grunt.

I sink into my zone. My knuckles are probably rubbing raw against the bandages, and my glove won't be helping, but I can't bring myself to care. The look on Scott's face when I fumbled that pass, an easy fucking pass, was a punch to the gut.

So I block it out.

Last night. Katie. The comment. The asshole. The punch. All of it.

I focus on football, and the next pass that flies through the air, I catch it.

CHAPTER TWO

FLYNN

Behind closed doors, I'm a creature of habit.

Football can be glamorous. The world is loud, bright, and big. *Overwhelming.*

But to me—to who I am to the public and the fans—I'm unfazed by it all. I smile and make jokes. I laugh on the sidelines and wink at the camera. I am the loud, the bright, the big.

Flynn Reed.

Number forty-nine. Tight end for the Boston Broncos. The charming, cheeky one.

I don't mind it. Keeping up the act and the persona has become part of the job. When the social girls need someone for their content, they come to me. When the team needs a player for press days, I'm their guy.

I'm honestly happy to help out and step up.

I plaster a smile on my face, and I do whatever they need. I've done it since they drafted me right out of college, eight years ago.

When I get through my front door, in the safety of my own home, I get to drop the smile.

I toe off my sneakers just inside the door and flip the light switch on the wall next to me. The lights over the displayed records hanging on the wall illuminate, and there is a pile of books I haven't found a place for stacked along the corridor below them. The dark wood paneling of the stairs seems to seep into the deep forest green color that I chose for the entryway. It's moody, but it's home.

I hoist my bag up further on my shoulder as I take two stairs at a time to the upper floor. Dropping the bag inside my bedroom, I rip off my hoodie and hop on one foot and then the other to tug off my socks. I throw them toward the hamper.

In the bathroom, I carefully unwrap the bandage covering my knuckles.

Just as I had suspected, the skin is red raw and chaffed. I turn on the faucet in the sink, leaning down a little to run my knuckles under the clean water. I hadn't bothered showering at the stadium, not wanting to risk anyone seeing my hand. The open cuts sting, and I let out a hiss.

"Goddammit," I groan, shaking my hand out.

I swipe the hand towel from the railing and press it gently over my skin. There isn't much point in drying my hand off when I'm about to get in the shower. Still, I dab the dry towel over my damp skin before setting it back on the counter. I wander back into my closet, pulling my T-shirt from over my head. I strip off my shorts and my briefs. All get tossed into the basket as well.

Back in the bathroom, I turn on the shower and step under the spray. The water burns my skin, steam billowing out in waves. When the water trickles over my knuckles, they start to sting again, but I ignore them.

So stupid.

Punching the guy was so, so stupid. I am an idiot. A fucking idiot.

I should call Hollie. Tell her what happened, so she's prepared. If she finds out through some fucking article because this blows up, she'll kill me in my sleep. She's barely five foot, but is a force to be reckoned with, and a loyal friend after all these years. She functions as my manager, agent, and publicist, with an experienced team behind her. I guess she needs it with me. Despite that, she still scares the hell out of me. The fight is a haze of raised voices and unintelligible insults, all but that one comment that made me see red and snap. The bright flash of a camera's bulb, though? That memory is loud and clear.

Yeah, I need to call Hollie.

I add the task to my mental to-do list for this evening before running my fingers through my damp hair and lifting my chin, letting the water spray over my face. I close my eyes. The image of a woman is so clear, so prominent in my mind, that I feel like I could reach out a hand and touch her.

Blonde hair. Soft curls. Thick, long strands begging me to touch them.

Blue eyes. Sparkling and bright. Shining at me with amusement and wonder, and a little bit of lust.

Firm body, long legs, and curves in all the right places.

I groan and shake my head, but the mental image doesn't disappear, doesn't fade. I open my eyes and stare at the white subway tile of my shower wall. Picturing her is a nightly habit. And a morning habit. And afternoon.

Our night in Italy was months ago. Yet, I still remember the soft moans and the way she moved her hips. I still feel the way her nails dragged down my back when I made her come the second time, and the sound of her muffled screams during the third. Katie Murphy is everywhere now.

It doesn't help that I've been frequenting the bar she manages more and more. So much so that I'm running out of excuses as to why I keep coming in to eat alone.

Not that she asks. She communicates in sarcastic comments and eye rolls.

It's killing me that I don't know what happened.

One moment, we're sitting under the stars and sharing secrets. We're drinking wine. We're having the night of our lives with multiple orgasms. We even had a snack break and then went back at it. We were laughing, smiling, and flirting. I could tell she liked me. I liked her too. Still do.

The next day, we couldn't keep our eyes off each other. Then, after dinner that night, I knocked on her door, hoping for a repeat, and she told me fuck off.

I have no idea what I did or what changed, and I cannot let it go. I cannot let *her* go.

The water runs hot down my back as I bow my head again. Don't get me wrong, her sarcastic replies to my consistent pestering get my dick hard, but I want nothing more than to earn back her smile, her laugh.

I want, no, I *need* to know what the hell I did to make her hate me so much.

I shut off the water and take a deep breath. My hand hurts like hell, but I'll just have to get used to it and get over the pain.

I towel off, drying my hair just enough that it isn't dripping on the floor anymore, and wrap the towel around my waist. Step by step, I go through my skincare routine. No one can judge me for wanting to look after my skin. I sweat under a helmet and get tackled to the ground, into the mud, on a regular basis. If my wanting to ensure my skin is clean and clear is a crime, someone sue me.

After hanging my towel back on the railing, I walk into my wardrobe and pull on a pair of gray sweats and an old T-shirt from college. I rotate between a few these days. They're soft, and after a hard day, I just want to be as comfortable as possible.

Like I said, creature of habit.

I head downstairs with a plan to watch something other than game tape while I dig for something to cook for dinner, but barely make it into the kitchen before my phone rings.

Hollie's name flashes across the screen, and my stomach rolls over.

Oh, fuck.

"Hey, Holl—" I begin.

"You asshat. You absolute fuckwit. What the fuck were you fucking thinking?!" Her voice is high-pitched and screeching down the line.

Shit, shit, shit.

Those pictures I should've called her about last night and put off instead have most definitely leaked.

"—in a contract year. Are you stupid? I actually think you must be fucking stupid. No one is this dumb. It was outside a bar you frequent. That Scott frequents. Did you honestly think there wouldn't be some sort of paparazzi waiting to catch a glimpse? You just gave them the pay day of a fucking lifetime."

"Hollie, calm down," I try weakly. I regret it as soon as I say it.

"Oh. Yeah, sure. I'll forget it." There's a pause, and I hold my breath. "I'll forget *you* in a minute. Are you kidding me, Flynn? A fight? A fucking punch for punch, tackle the guy to the ground, and most definitely do some damage type of fight?"

"I can explain."

"Go on then. Explain this mess."

I take a deep breath. "They were drinking pretty heavily at the bar. I left, and just happened to be following them out. They were making comments about Ka—the staff."

"So you punched him?"

"I fucked up. I know."

"You more than fucked up, Flynn. The team called. They want answers." She sighs. "Okay, first things first. Are you okay? Did you get hurt?"

I look down at my red, aching knuckles. "No."

"Good. That's good." There's some rustling on the other end of the phone, like Hollie is pulling notes in front of her or something. "A sports gossip blog is circulating the pictures on their socials, and TMZ has now picked up on them. There's a video on Instagram, too, but I am working on getting it taken down. You certainly know how to make waves, Flynn."

"What did the team say?" I hit the speaker button on my phone and put it on the counter. If I don't start doing something with my hands, I'm going to start spiraling.

"They're pissed. Obviously. They didn't outright say it, but they mentioned that your contract is up at the end of the season, and we should really, really be considering other options if you're set on going down a destructive path. The bottom line is, we need to clean up your act and keep your nose clean until the ink dries on your extension."

"Yeah," I breathe out, pulling a box of dried pasta from the cupboard and two chicken breasts from the fridge.

"You do want to keep playing with the Broncos, don't you?" she asks quietly.

I pause, the pot I just pulled from the drawer hanging by my side. That shouldn't even be a question. I shouldn't even be considering another path. Obviously, I don't want to resign. Right?

I want a ring. I am chasing a ring. The Broncos are my best chance. Right?

I shake my head, trying to clear away the thoughts as much as possible. "Yeah. Of course."

"Well then, we need a game plan," Hollie says. "A good one."

"I could publicly apologize?"

"No. We have already paid the guy's emergency bill, and he's happy with season tickets to stay quiet on the matter. We need something more obvious. Something the press can sink their teeth into, in a good way. Something that helps paint you in a better light, a softer and more relatable light."

"Whatever you say goes. Just let me know where you need me to be and when."

"Mmm," she hums through the phone, and the sound makes my stomach churn. She's already got a plan. That's her *I already have a plan* hum.

"What?" I ask.

"Nothing ... nothing, I just ..."

"Spit it out, Hol."

I hear the smile in her voice when the next words come down the phone. "We need something more ... long term ..."

"You obviously have something in mind, so spit it out, would you?" I fill the pot with water and place it on the stove to boil, then I pull out a pan to cook the chicken and place it on the stove.

"You need a girlfriend." The knife I pull from the drawer slips from my hand and clatters onto the countertop. "A proper, stable, game-attending girlfriend."

"That's insane. No."

"You said whatever I say goes."

"Yeah, well, I take it back. You've officially lost it." I regain my composure and start slicing the chicken breast, still shaking my head in disbelief.

"This could work. You get a girlfriend. You're photographed a few times with her: going for dinner, to the movie theatre, on the field after a game. It's perfect. You keep your nose clean, you show them you can be steady and dependable for someone, you drum up some good press in the meantime, and after you sign, we can release a statement that you two broke up."

"I am not dragging some poor girl into this world, knowing I'm just going to break up with her. She'll get attached. It will get messy," I say down the phone. This is a bad idea. A very, very bad idea.

"Don't worry about that. It'll be a PR relationship. You'll both know what it really is. An even playing field and clear expectations. We do this shit all the time."

"What the actual fuck, Hollie?" I curse down the phone while seasoning the pieces of chicken. She has got to be kidding. Right? People don't actually have fake girlfriends. No way.

Do they?

"Yes," she decides. "We're going with the girlfriend plan. I will sort it out and come back to you with options in a few days. Till then, do not get photographed with any females and, for god's sake, do not get into any more fights."

"Hollie. I am not getting a fake girlfriend," I say with a sigh. Drizzling some oil into the hot pan, I scrape the sliced chicken on top. It sizzles, immediately filling my kitchen with the smell of spice and seasoning.

"Oh yes, you are," she replies, and the tone of her voice warns me not to argue. "We'll talk about it in a few days when I get it organized. Keep your head down."

"Hollie—"

"No, Flynn. You got into a fight, and it got caught on camera. You fucked up. But, luckily for you, I am going to fix it. Focus on winning games and let me do my job," she clips. "Okay?"

I sigh, absentmindedly turning over the pieces of chicken. "Fine."

"Great. Be a good boy. Talk soon." The line goes dead before I get another word out.

Goddamn.

This is not how I imagined this going.

I thought, at best, I would have a few charity visits in my future. A couple of extra appearances at causes the team supports and maybe a few extra dinners with the major sponsors. Those I can get through. A girlfriend, though?

I can't even imagine what that is going to look like. I don't even know where to start.

By the time I sit down on my couch, a bowl of chicken and pasta in my lap, there's only one face in my head. Only one person's opinion on this plan I care to hear.

Will she care if I get a girlfriend? Will she be annoyed?

Do I want her to be?

Fuck, this is *so* not a good idea.

CHAPTER THREE
KATIE

I'M NOT EXACTLY SURE when or how it happened, but sometime between graduating with honours in a degree in education and actually working in a classroom, I fell out of love with teaching. Don't get me wrong, the kids are great, and I learn a lot about the next generation with every new class I teach. Yet, I can't deny that sitting at a desk, in front of a class of twenty-six students staring expectantly back at me, has lost its allure.

My heart isn't in it. My head is elsewhere.

It's at the bar.

It's in my office there, the one I turned into a small studio.

It's in the music that I'm planning to record later when school gets out. It's in the dreams of turning the space into something other than just a sports bar.

I guess I should be sad about the teaching thing. Most people would be. They would be sad about losing the love for something they worked so hard on, for so long. My parents spent thousands sending me to college so I could become a teacher, and it turned out that the moment I stepped into the classroom, I lost the love I once held for it.

Or maybe I never loved it at all. Maybe I chose it and then just decided it was easier to settle for it.

Like Grant.

I chose him. We got four years in, and I guess, somewhere along the way, I decided that I had to settle for him. It was fine. Teaching was fine. Being with Grant was fine ... in the beginning.

But I wanted more. I *still* want more.

What that *more* is, who knows?

I sigh, trying my best not to disturb the room of quietly studying students. There are a few at the back on their phones, but I don't really mind. They're quiet. If they don't get their work done, it's on them.

I'm subbing for a history teacher today. One with a full schedule and a terrible habit of not leaving lesson plans for me. Today, I've mostly been asking kids what they've been learning, determining I don't know enough about the subject, and then letting them use the period as a study session.

It's giving me a lot, and I mean *a lot*, of free time to think about my life choices.

The current one plays over and over on repeat in the form of a video on TMZ's Instagram feed. The short twenty-second video clip has been open on my laptop all day, and I have probably replayed it over a thousand times.

Flynn Reed, punching and then tackling a guy outside my bar a few nights ago. The same guy who creeped me the hell out with the way he looked at me and leered over the bar. The same guy who I had one of the other servers that night gently advise to head elsewhere if he and his friends wanted to be served.

Flynn fucking Reed.

Tight end for the Boston Broncos, my best friend's fiancé's best friend, and my rebound guy.

I didn't mean for it to happen. It just sort of did.

I blame Italy. I blame the sun and the wine and the fact that I spent weeks with Flynn Reed without a shirt on.

God, he is so hot.

My eyes go back to the video as I gently hit play again. My stomach clenches as I watch Flynn rear his fist back and then slam it into the other guy's face. I don't normally condone violence. I hate when fights break out at the bar. I hate that on game weekends, we have to double the security because a patron always takes it too damn far, but I can't lie, watching him throw that punch is possibly the sexiest thing I have seen in a long time.

The more I watch it, the more the little details start to jump out at me.

The vein in his neck pulses just before he lunges forward. He flexes his hand after the first punch, but never takes his eyes off the guy. His instinctual dodge just before he takes the guy to the ground.

It's all very attractive and all very, very annoying.

I didn't mean to fall into bed with Flynn Reed. I really, really didn't.

After Grant, I vowed to stay single for a while. My head was all over the place. It is still all over the place. My contract at school as a substitute was over, and I wasn't sure I even wanted a new one. I was being pulled into two different directions, and then Grant and I ... well, we fell apart.

I got on the plane intending to spend a summer in Italy with my best friend and figure out what I wanted. I did not intend to get on that plane, sit next to my secret football crush, and then spend the summer flirting instead of thinking.

I certainly never intended to *sleep* with him.

A quiet hum of chatter breaks out, and I sigh, close my laptop, and lean my cheek on my hand. Most of the students are no longer paying attention to their own work and have decided to chat amongst themselves. I glance at the clock hanging on the back wall of the classroom. It's ten to three. Ten minutes before today is over, and I can go home, crawl into bed, and likely watch the video another few hundred times.

Maybe I should just go to the bar after work. That will at least buy me more time away from my mother and her questions. I could go to the bar ...

But Flynn Reed will likely be sitting in the booth in the back corner, staring at me all night if I do go. I don't really feel like putting in the extra effort to ignore him and his lingering gaze tonight.

My phone vibrates, rattling against the desk. I turn it over, seeing a text from my mother.

> **Mom:** Can you bring Sammy home? I'm stuck at the salon.

Well, there goes my bar plan.

***

Dinner at the dining room table in this house is rare.

We might have done it more when it was just Mom, Dad, and me. They didn't work as many nights when I was little because there wasn't anyone to look after me, but even then, they normally alternated. Then, my mom got pregnant with Sam, and it got a lot more hectic around the house. The age gap was hard for them. I was turning into a teenager, and Sam was a toddler. We didn't exactly have the same schedule that allowed for family dinners. When I was in high school, my parents both worked full-time at the bar, and I spent most nights babysitting my younger brother. I went away to college, and then I met Grant.

Now, I'm back living at home for the first time since I was seventeen, and apparently, dinner at the dining table is a thing.

"What was the peak of your day, Katie?" my mother asks as she serves herself some vegetables.

I push a few peas around my plate. "Uh, I didn't really have one. It was a boring day." Untrue. This morning, I woke up to half a million subscribers on my YouTube channel.

Secret YouTube channel, that is.

"Oh, come on, pumpkin. Something good must have happened today," Dad says.

"Uh—" Sometimes, I do wish I hadn't chosen to keep the channel a complete secret. But it's my outlet. My safe place. And besides, Mom has a big mouth and too much time on her hands these days. "Okay, well, when I picked up my coffee this morning, I was in one of those pay-it-forward chains. Someone had paid for my coffee, and sadly, but also kind of a peak moment, there was no one behind me. So, free coffee."

My brother scoffs. "Tight ass."

"Hey!" I stab a potato with my fork and point it at him. "Just wait until you have bills and rent you have to pay, then you'll also get excited about free coffee."

"I won't have to worry. NFL money, baby." Sammy dances a little in his seat, and it makes my dad chuckle. I simply shake my head but say nothing. Sammy is a great player. But an NFL-level player? Who knows. He's just turned fourteen and is on the reserve varsity squad. Which he only just made.

"Work hard, son, and you just might make it to the NFL," Dad tells him. Mom moves on, asking Sam what his peak was for the day. He, of course, says something football-related and then dives immediately into a story about some kid called Samson and another called Stacey. I tune him out.

Oh, to be in high school again and free of worries. Sam's lucky. He's only just starting out. I feel like I've run the full marathon and came in last place.

"Katie, have you given any thought to applying for the full-time opening I sent you? The one at the high school for the music teacher?" Mom's question pulls me out of my thoughts.

"Huh?"

"One of the music teachers at the high school is retiring. They're going to advertise for a full-time position there starting after Christmas break." Mom sets her knife and fork down, staring at me. "Did you not read the text I sent you yesterday? Katie, come on now. You're supposed to be looking for a full-time teaching job."

"Mary," Dad warns her in a low tone.

"I never said anything about being a full-time teacher," I correct her. I work hard to keep my voice calm and non-combative. I really, really do not have the energy to have a fight with her tonight. "I like working at the bar. I think, well, I could do that full-time. You know ... manage it properly. Formally, I mean. For you."

My mother's mouth drops open. "The bar? You want to work full-time at the bar?"

"Maybe. I like it there. I enjoy the work. It's different every day, and it's fun. Keeps me on my toes." I sit straighter in my chair. "And I've got heaps of ideas on how we can drum up more business for the summer months—"

"You should apply for the teaching job. You belong in a school," Mom states. I sigh and back down. It's not worth it.

Dad clears his throat. "We were, uh—we were thinking about hiring a full-time bar manager. Someone to be there on a regular basis and manage the day-to-day. Most of the evenings and such."

My cutlery slips from my hands, clattering against my plate. "What?"

"We, your mother and I, just thought it would be a good idea to have someone there when we aren't. We're getting older. We have the means now to get help at the bar." He reaches over and covers my hand with his. I stare at it as he keeps talking, anger beginning to bubble away in my chest.

"*I'm* there most nights. I am the bar manager. You are literally getting someone to replace me," I argue. I suck air through my teeth in an effort not to completely lose it. It feels as if my temper is at the end of its tether these days.

"You aren't there, though. You come and go. Which is fine. I love that you have freedom, but Katie, you need to commit to something." Dad nods and squeezes my hand. "If you decide you want to be there full-time, the job is yours."

"I—"

"You should be teaching. You did all that work, to be teaching," Mom exclaims from the other side of the table, glaring at Dad like he's just said exactly what she asked him not to. He probably did.

"I don't know what I want," I say. "I just ... I need time to figure it out. Please?"

Mom clicks her tongue but doesn't say anything else. Dad squeezes my hand again, drawing my attention to focus solely on him. "When you've made a choice, let me know. Until then, I have to do what I have to do to keep the business running, okay? The sooner you decide, the easier it will be, though."

I can only nod. I fall silent at the table as the conversation turns back to my brother. He's entertaining my parents with another story about his classmates.

I sink back into my chair, wishing I could disappear into my room and put on a record. Something loud and emotional, something to drown out all my confusing thoughts and replace them with those of the artists.

My phone vibrates in my pocket, over and over.

I pull it out from my back pocket and glance down at the screen, my heart jumping to my throat the moment I see whose name is flashing up at me.

Grant.

Chapter Four

Flynn

Hollie is scary over the phone, but it's nothing compared to when she asks—no, demands—that we meet in person. The text came in this morning.

Pat's. 4pm. Do not be late.

Hollie and her fucking periods. When I was a rookie, fresh out of college and the draft, Hollie's periods in her texts and emails sent me through a tailspin. She's younger than me, she's five-foot, and when I met her in the office for the first time, she seemed sweet. Then, I signed with her. The sweetness disappeared, and she's been busting my balls ever since. Every time I get a text from the woman, it is in short, sharp sentences and full of periods. She always sounds mad. She normally is. My teammates once caught the tail end of one of her infamous lectures, and they visibly recoiled as she walked past them.

Mind you, she's gotten me some of the best advertising deals in the business, and I'm one of the highest-paid tight ends in the league, so whatever she does, it works.

Still, a summons text is never good.

At least I know Scott got the same text, and he's done nothing wrong.

"I can't believe I'm getting roped into this shit with you. I haven't done anything wrong." Scott tugs his cap further down his face. "Why is this place so busy for a fucking Monday anyway?"

"Monday night football, idiot," I say.

"We're not even playing," he grumbles back. He glances over his shoulder at the door.

"Sports fans. They'll watch anything." Scott peers over his shoulder again, and I smirk. "You saw her this morning. In fact, you've been with her all weekend, bar the few hours you had to do your job on Sunday afternoon."

"She's going to be my wife. I'm allowed."

"You're obsessed."

"Fine, I'm obsessed." Scott shrugs and takes a sip of the beer in front of him. I've got to give it to Ivy because ever since she came into the picture, Scott has completely relaxed. Football used to be his sole focus. He didn't date, he didn't go out, he barely even liked bonding with the team.

Then Scott met Ivy. She caught his eye, and now he can't take them off her.

Like, ever.

"You going to say hi to Doug?" I ask, my eyes scanning the bar and its patrons. Scott's right, it is busy here today. With the NFL, the NHL, and the NBA seasons in full swing, the bar only gets busier and busier the closer the leagues get to their playoffs.

This bar is only really ever quiet in the summer, and even then, they always have their regulars.

"Nah, but Ivy will likely drag me over later, after she gets here."

I grunt in response, my eyes snagging on the blonde standing by the service window into the kitchen. Katie leans in through the gap, arguing with one of the chefs. Her jeans stretch deliciously over her round ass, and her shirt is coming untucked the further she leans over. Her hair is loose and in curls. There's a small sliver of exposed skin on her lower back, and my mouth goes dry.

Jesus Christ.

You'd think I'd just gotten a glimpse of her fucking tits, the way I'm acting.

Scott makes a sudden movement, jumping up from his side of the booth, and it draws my attention away. He drops his cap to the table, and my eyes follow him as he walks towards the front door of the bar. Ivy is shaking out her coat, a little wet from the light drizzle outside. He takes her bag and leans down, catching her with a kiss hello.

My stomach twists with something foreign, and I tear my gaze away.

Right back to Katie.

She's watching the pair too, with soft features and what I can tell, even from across the room, is a sad expression. I saw the same one on her face many times in Italy. Scott would do anything remotely romantic, and Katie would have this look in her eye as she stared at them. It wasn't jealousy or annoyance. It was longing.

Longing for something she wanted so badly for herself but had never experienced.

I hate her ex for that look.

For a minute there in Italy, I was the one to make that look disappear. For a minute, I thought maybe I could keep that look from ever crossing her face.

But no, I fucked that up too, somehow.

Scott steers Ivy back to the booth and slides in, her hand in his, tugging her to sit down with him.

"Hang on, let me just go say hi to Katie." Ivy pulls her hand out of Scott's, and the gesture makes him scowl. I can't help my laughter.

"Careful, Ivy. He's been on edge all day without his fix of you."

"Shut up, Reed."

Ivy just laughs, kisses her boyfriend, and then skips off to the bar where Katie is now waiting for her. The girls hug, and I watch as Ivy twirls a piece of Katie's long hair around her finger. I scowl, jealousy coursing through me. I want to twirl her hair around my finger.

"What's up with you?" Scott asks, and my attention shifts back to him.

"What?"

"You're staring."

"No idea what you're talking about."

"You ever figure your shit out with Katie? Find out why she hates you?"

"No," I grumble, sinking into my seat. I haven't told Scott just how far Katie and I went. I have no idea how much Katie told Ivy, either. My guess is that they know something went down, but not the full extent. Scott became protective over Katie after the breakup with Grant. Like he took on the big brother role in her life without her asking.

"I think she's still hurting after Grant. Or, at least, that's what Ivy thinks." He takes another sip of his beer, still half full, while my glass is empty. "I guess she probably hates all men at the moment."

I only hum in response, my eyes flickering over to the girls again, sliding the empty pint glass on the table between my fingers. I'm about to get up and head for the bar, order another drink, and see if today is the day Katie may spare me a glance, when the door opens again.

Hollie is here.

"Goddamn, why does she always look angry?" I mumble under my breath as she makes her way over to us.

Scott turns his head and lifts a hand in greeting. "Because she *is* angry. With you."

"Boys." Hollie places her designer bag on the table and slides into the booth next to Scott, across from me. Her brown hair is tinted red, up in a slicked ponytail, and her fingers are covered in rings.

"I'm twenty-nine, Hollie. Stop calling me a boy," I say, annoyed. I can't help the way my gaze flickers to Katie, praying she wasn't in earshot of that.

"When you fuck up the way you fucked up, you're a boy," she snaps. I press my lips together and hold a reply. It doesn't do anyone any good to argue with this woman.

"I just came from a meeting across the road." She pulls out an iPad and unlocks it. Across the screen, I can see a page full of detailed notes. I gulp.

"And?" I ask, glancing at Scott, who just shrugs and takes another sip of his beer.

"Good news first," she says, scrolling down the page. "Scott, they want to make the captaincy official, so I will be doing a series of collaborative posts on your account this week. I need you to do a photoshoot tomorrow—"

"But I have to—"

"Whatever part of your house you're renovating right now can wait. Tomorrow, the stadium, in a gameday suit, ten o'clock. Do not be late, and you will be done within the hour." Hollie looks at Scott and frowns. "I promise. No longer than an hour."

"Fine." He sighs, giving in.

"Good. Now, you." She points the iPad's pencil at me. "They are royally pissed. I managed to convince them it was a one-off and you were having a moment. That the guy antagonized you, and you just snapped. You will apologize to the team at Wednesday's practice and to the coaching staff. Yes?"

"Yes." I nod.

An apology. Thank god. Since we'd spoken last week, I had been stressing over this whole *fake girlfriend* thing that Hollie had gotten into her head was a good idea. It has been on my mind all weekend. It isn't a good idea. Not even in the slightest. I urge myself to stay facing forward and not seek out Katie wherever she is in the bar. An apology is easy and much deserved.

"And, I have five candidates for you to look over for your new girlfriend. I've gone for brunettes. You still prefer those, don't you?"

"Something tells me he's more interested in blondes these days."

"Shut up, Harvey," I hiss. "Hollie, no. I said I'm not doing the girlfriend thing. It's fucking weird, and while you say that these girls know what they're getting themselves into, I don't fucking believe you. They will get attached, and when I break up with them, they'll write a tell-all about it."

"Oh my god," Ivy says as she slides into the seat next to me. Scott looks noticeably upset that he's not closer to her, so to add insult to injury, I stretch my arm across the back of the booth and over Ivy's shoulder. "You sound more dramatic than Scott."

"He *is* being more dramatic. People do this all the time, Flynn." Hollie locks her iPad and places it on the table again. "You would be so surprised how common this is. Justin and Hailey. Tom and Zendaya. Timothée and Kylie, although they are the real deal now, I believe. It's *common*."

"What the hell are you on about? They are all still together," I say.

"Yes, well, their fuck ups were bigger than yours," Hollie responds with a shrug. Her phone buzzes on the table, and she glances at it before sighing and flipping it over.

"I'm not doing it, Hollie."

"Yes, you are, Flynn." She slides the iPad across to me, a headshot of a girl illuminated. She's pretty. Brown hair, brown eyes, cute smile.

"Now, once you pick a girl, I will arrange a meeting with her and her management team, and we can go over a contract. There is normally a non-disclosure put in place, and we set out the terms. How many dates, physical touch guidelines, housing arrangements—"

"Housing arrangements?" Scott asks, curious. I shoot him a glare.

"Normally, they have to be seen staying or at least coming and going at times that make it *look* like they were staying at your place. It's all about public perception, so it's important that we stage the right photographs and send the right message. She doesn't have to move in, but it's best she does."

"You want this stranger to move in with me? Are you insane?"

"Only if they agree to. It's much easier, but we can work it out if she doesn't." Hollie taps the iPad. "Whoever you pick will come to every home game. You will eat meals in public with her, get seen at places like the gym, pump gas into her car. *Boyfriend*-type things."

I look down at the girl again. She really is pretty.

But she's not blonde. Her eyes aren't blue. She doesn't have *her* smile.

Dammit.

I slide the iPad back. "No."

"Well, if you won't take a girl I found, we will have to find you another." Hollie turns her head, scanning the bar like she's going to pick a girl from the crowd.

Scott laughs and smirks over his glass, murmuring, "There might be one here he'd fancy."

"Who?" Hollie's attention snaps to Scott, and he smiles even harder. I can feel my face heating, and I sink lower in the booth. Ivy is giggling behind her hand, and I gently slap her arm.

"Stop it. Be on my side," I whisper to her.

"I actually think this plan is genius. A girlfriend might do you good," she whispers back.

"It's a *fake* girlfriend. How will that help anything?"

"It doesn't have to be fake." She raises her brows before turning back to the table. Hollie is still glancing around the bar.

Before I can get her attention, rebuff her plans, or say no to this plan for the millionth time, Hollie's attention catches on something else.

Someone else.

No. No, no, *no*.

"Who is that?" She points to the bar.

"Oh, that's Katie. My best friend," Ivy says calmly.

"How best is best? Like sorority sisters that just happened to come from the same town and stay in touch after college, or sister from another mister type best friend?" Ivy giggles at Hollie, and I roll my eyes, fighting the urge to glance over at Katie again.

"Best, best. Sisters." Ivy nods.

"She has a key to our house," Scott grumbles under his breath. I watch Hollie's eyes widen and light up.

"No."

"She's perfect," Hollie says at the same time.

***

"I can't ask this of her," I murmur under my breath. Scott and I sit at the back of the team's theatre. Wednesday nights are late ones for us. We practice outside in the mornings, break into teams after lunch for meetings, and then review game tapes of the next team we'll play in the evenings.

"You're sort of friends, aren't you?" he replies, not looking away from the tape in front of us.

"Not really. She can't even look me in the eye." God, do I miss her looking at me.

We fall silent, Coach's voice from the front of the room echoing around us and the rest of the team. Scott takes a deep breath and glances over at me. "What the fuck happened in Italy?"

I cringe. "What do you mean?"

"I mean, one minute you two are practically eye fucking across the dinner table, and the next, she's slapping you and shutting a door in your face. What the fuck happened?"

I take off my cap and run a hand through my hair. So, Katie didn't tell Ivy. Or at least, she did, and Ivy didn't tell Scott. Unlikely, considering the two of them tell each other everything. After the way their relationship started, neither keeps any kind of secret from the other anymore.

"Nothing. Nothing happened."

"Liar." Scott shakes his head. "Fine, don't tell me. Just say you're sorry and then ask her to be your fake girlfriend. Hollie is kind of right. She's the perfect candidate. She won't sell you out to the press after it's over, and the backlash won't be massive on either of you because she's not really in the public eye. They'll likely move right on once you say it's over."

I shake my head. "It's complicated. She won't go for it."

"I don't know what to tell you. You shouldn't have punched the guy, and you definitely shouldn't have gotten caught on camera, but you did. If Hollie says that the way to fix this is to show the team you can be dependable, then we have to trust her. This is what we pay her thousands of dollars a year for. Ask Katie. I bet if you make the point that she can sit in the same box as Ivy at every game, she might just agree."

"I'm so going to get slapped again, aren't I?" I groan.

"Probably." Scott smirks.

"Fuck." I bury my face in my hands and squeeze my eyes shut. Fucking hell. How am I going to convince a woman who can't even look me in the eye to move in and play house with me for a few months?

"You know what? I'll get Ivy to feel her out for you." My head shoots up to stare at Scott.

"You will?"

"Sure, man." The shock must be written all over my face because he shrugs. "You're looking at me like helping you is a foreign concept. Did you forget who argued our way out of the frat house party incident of 2016?"

"I just didn't think you and Ivy would want to be involved in my mess. All that shit with the press and Ivy, after last year ..."

"She's getting the support she needs to deal with the press. Besides, you're my best friend, and I want you to stay on this team. I just got here, and we have a ring to win, remember?"

"Hell yeah, we do." I hold my fist up, waiting for Scott to hit his knuckles against mine.

"God, you're a loser, Reed."

He fist bumps me anyway.

Chapter Five

Katie

IF I HAD KNOWN tonight was going to be an ambush, I would've just stayed home. Or at the bar. Anything would've been better than hearing Ivy go on and on about how Flynn Reed needs my help.

"He's a nice guy," Ivy says for the millionth time tonight. I nod in reply because I have run out of things to say.

After Italy, I never told Ivy what happened between Flynn and me. All she knows is that one day, we were flirting with one another, laughing and smiling at our inside jokes and getting closer by the day, and then the next, I hated him.

I never told her that I know just how nice Flynn really is. That I know how he can make you laugh to the point of running out of breath, or feel at ease with a simple touch. I never mentioned that I knew how he could make a girl smile with a simple few words whispered quietly into their ear, or turn them on with only a look.

Me and every other girl he's ever come across.

I would like to think I'm special. I would like to think the moves he used on me were for me alone, but that would be naïve of me. He's Flynn Reed. Boston Broncos tight end. Infamous for having woman after woman on his arm at events. A big, fat flirt.

We got swept up in the Italian summer of it all.

I got swept up.

"Please, Katie? Please, please, will you help?" Ivy begs. I look up from my place on her couch. She's sitting at the coffee table, her school work spread out in front of her as she sorts a pile of finger paintings into different colored folders.

"Sorry, Ives, I was a million miles away for a moment there. What are you asking me?"

"Flynn needs a fake girlfriend for the season."

The glass in my hand nearly slips through my fingers as my jaw goes slack. "He *what*?"

"Katie, weren't you listening to anything I have been saying?" She sighs and turns to face me. "So, ever since the footage of Flynn hitting that guy outside Pat's got leaked, he's been in huge trouble with the team. Like, Scott said that they told Hollie to start looking elsewhere for him to sign."

"Oh my god, what?" Flynn is one of the better tight ends in the league. I can't believe the Broncos would drop him over a video.

"Apparently, he hasn't been playing all that well lately, and they think he's distracted. Unstable. The video just came out at the wrong time. Poor Flynn." She takes her wine glass from the coffee table and sips it. "Scott says he's having confidence issues."

"Flynn Reed? Confidence issues?"

"Yep." She takes another sip. When she sets the glass down on the table, her mouth opens like she has something else she wants to say, but she shakes her head a little.

"What is it?" I prompt.

"Huh? Nothing," she replies, her head still shaking from side to side. "It's nothing."

"Ivy." I sigh. "Just say it. You know you want to."

Ivy glances toward the hallway that leads to the stairs. Scott is redoing their guest bathroom at the moment, and every so often, we hear a thud or groan coming from the floor above.

"Should he be renovating during the season? What if he hurts himself?" I ask, amused a little as a string of curse words filters down to us from upstairs.

"He won't listen to me. Insists on doing the demo himself." Ivy shakes her head. She gets off the ground, grabs her glass, and takes a seat on the couch next to me. "So, Scott was telling me that Flynn has been having doubts about whether he wants to even stay in the league."

"Jesus. And he told Scott this?"

"Well, no. Scott overheard him talking to his mother. Who, apparently, has never been all that supportive of his career choice. She even tried to talk him out of entering the draft."

"Really?" I lean forward. Flynn never mentioned this to me. All the talks we had, all the late-night chats, and not once did he mention anything about his parents being unsupportive.

"He denies it, I think, and Scott says she's nice, but she make comments about him not being as good as other players. Little digs that he shouldn't be in the NFL." Ivy shakes her head. "Which is crazy because Flynn is one of the best damn tight ends I've ever seen. Scott thinks so, too. When his head's in the game."

"And his head hasn't been in the game lately?"

"I think he's been distracted. Uncle Jeff is even getting frustrated with him not playing to his full potential."

"So because he's been distracted, he needs a fake girlfriend?"

"*No*. He needs a fake girlfriend to help show the team he can be dependable again. To show he's in a stable relationship and therefore stable in his home life. He's in a contract year. If he doesn't prove it to them, they're going to release him." Ivy nods like I should have known all this, and it should make sense to me. "That's where you come in. You'd be his fake girlfriend, help him show the team he's fine, and then at the end of the season, after he signs his contract, you guys can break up."

"That's insane."

Ivy giggles. "That's what Flynn said."

"Seriously, though, a fake girlfriend? That kind of stuff is romance novel worthy. It doesn't happen in real life," I say.

"Apparently, it does. Justin and Hailey. Tom and Zendaya. Kylie and Tim—"

"No way. Absolutely not. There is no way that Kylie and Timothée are faking it." I cuddle my wine close to my chest and shake my head furiously. "Their chemistry is unmatched."

"Well, apparently it's how they started, but now they're the real thing." Ivy nods. "I agree. I love them together."

"He's so cute. And she deserves a guy like him. The love loudly kind." I sigh, ignoring the dull stabbing pain in my chest.

"Agreed." She holds up her glass, and I clink mine against it. She takes a sip and eyes me over the rim. "Please. Will you please agree to help Flynn?"

I close my eyes and lean back into the couch cushions. Agree to help him? What does that even mean? I don't want a front row seat to his flirting with other women. I've had one and I hated it. And, I don't want to get sucked back into his web of charm, that sexual pull.

"I can't, Ives. It's too ... it's just not a good idea."

"Okay," Ivy says, taking a deep breath. She leans over to set her wine glass on the coffee table before taking mine from my hands and placing it down next to hers. She sits up on her knees and takes my hands in hers. "I know whatever happened between the two of you in Italy rattled you—"

Railed me, more like.

"—but I am begging you to consider it. You can get out of your parents' house while also still saving money. You will be around the corner from me, and we can hang out, like, *all the time*, and you can come to all the games with me. Even the ones I was going to travel to this year. Plus, Flynn is like a brother to Scott. I know he doesn't show his emotions all the time, but he would be devastated if Flynn got released."

"Your boyfriend is a giant, soft teddy bear. I hope you know that." I sigh and look at Ivy. She's using her best puppy dog eyes and practically begging me with her expression.

"Urgh, fine," I groan. "I will talk to him. Only talk. I am not agreeing to anything—"

"Thank you, thank you, *thank you*," Ivy squeals, falling forward and onto me for a hug. I laugh and wrap my arms around her.

"You have to promise me that next time we go away, I can sit next to you on the flight."

She grins. "Deal."

"Really? That's going to fly with the big guy?"

"I'll bribe him with airplane sex. Easy."

I scrunch up my nose, laughing. "Gross."

***

The front of Flynn's brownstone is so clean. Where Ivy's house is covered in vines and weathered bricks, Flynn's is so ... new. There's no greenery climbing the walls or big trees casting shadows across the brick. The garden is bare, and the stony path beneath my feet is too white.

I clutch the strap of my bag as I make my way to the front door and once again, try to convince myself this is the right thing to do. Ivy made some good points. I do need to get out of my parents' house if I am going to have a chance at figuring out what the hell I want to do with my life. And, yes, it would be nice to be closer to her rather than across town. And, obviously, the box seats to every home game would also be a bonus.

For the briefest of moments, I imagine the look on Grant's face if he found out I was sitting in a box for the season. If he saw me at the games, on the field before and after, mingling with the players. Would he be jealous? Would he be mad?

I suck in a sharp breath and stop myself from taking another step. I shake my head and squeeze my eyes shut, saying the same mantra over and over in my head that I have been for months.

He didn't care then, and he won't care now. I want nothing to do with him, even if he's changed his mind.

I say it once, twice, and a third time for good measure before allowing myself to continue on. My point was, I could see this as a chance to get myself back on my feet. If I'm not at home with the constant questions on what I'm doing or if I've decided, then maybe I just might have enough room to figure out whatever it is I *do* want.

And, I could save some proper money. I don't regret walking away from my relationship with Grant. It was for the best. But in doing so, I walked away with nothing, and there was no way I was planning to grovel back, asking for my share of anything in that house.

I never wanted to set foot inside the place ever again. In fact, never might be too soon.

I shake my head again. I need to focus on the task at hand.

The terms. The rules.

I lift my fist to knock, but the door opens before I get a chance, and I'm left standing there, my arm suspended in mid air.

"Why does it take you a lifetime to walk up a path?"

I narrow my gaze. "Were you watching me?"

"Yes."

"So honest."

"Always am."

I scoff. "Liar."

Something in Flynn's gaze softens, and it makes my stomach twist. "Katie—"

"Nope. No way. I am not here for that. I am here for—actually, you know what?" I raise my eyes to the sky and suck in another breath. "I can't do this. Forget it. This was a bad idea." I turn on my heel, about to make my way down the steps and back to my car so that I can drive away as fast as I can, when I feel a warm, calloused hand wrap around my wrist.

"Wait." His voice is quiet and soft, pleading. "Come inside."

I look over my shoulder and, for the first time in months, for the first time since that afternoon in Italy when I watched him flirt with a girl right in front of me after our night together, I look into his eyes.

Flynn Reed is gorgeous. Six foot four. Blond hair. Green eyes. Made of muscle.

Yet it's the dimple in his cheek when he smiles, and the lines that appear beside his eyes when he laughs, and the way his presence makes you feel comfortable and at ease, that makes him something like a god.

He has charm, yes, but when he speaks to you, he gives you his full attention. Like you're the most interesting person in the world and he only ever wants to hear you, and you alone, speak for the rest of time. He asks questions and is curious, and when you ask him something, he answers with sincerity.

Well, most of the time.

He's not the person the media makes him out to be. Not the playful boy that the team portrays him as on their social media every time he's highlighted. He's deeper than that. I saw the depth of him all those nights we stayed out by the pool, staring at the Italian sky, exchanging secrets, and believe me, I've experienced just how deep he can go. It's not a night I will ever forget. And unlike my relationship with Grant, I don't think I ever want to.

He's a *man*, yet he's still treated like a boy by everyone in his life. If Ivy's right, even his mother still doesn't see him like she should. Grown, accomplished, talented.

"Come on, Katie. Just come inside and we can talk." He lets go of my wrist, and my arm falls limp at my side. He opens the door wider and stands aside. "*Just* talk. I promise."

I stare at him, trying to find something I don't like, don't trust, in his expression. I sigh when I can only see sincerity and step past him into the house.

His scent completely engulfs me. The walls are painted in dark colors, and the stairs are a walnut wood. It's moody and emotive. Yet, it's inviting. I imagine on a sunny day, the light would stream through his front windows and turn it into a bright walkway.

Lining the walls are a few framed records. The Beatles. Queen. Frank Sinatra. Huh. That's interesting. There's a mix of different musicians hanging in his hallway. From rock to jazz, and even pop. I reach the end of the hall and smirk at the last record hanging.

"Taylor Swift? Really?"

"She's a genius. You cannot deny that." Flynn's voice is quiet, deep and sensual, and oh so close as he follows me down the hall. I repress a shiver.

"I guess not." I move into the open living and dining area. It's fully furnished, decorated immaculately down to the fresh flowers in the vase on his dining room table. Across the back of the house on the first floor, with wide open windows looking out into the large back garden, his kitchen matches the dark and moody vibe of the rest of the house. Yet, the countertop is probably one of the most gorgeous pieces of butcher block I've ever seen.

"This is gorgeous," I say, placing my bag gently down and running a hand on the smooth surface.

"One of a kind. Had it made specially for this kitchen." He's still so close, and when I glance back at him, he's staring at my face like he's studying one of his playbooks.

"It's wonderful. The oak was a great choice."

"You know your woods, Murphy. That surprises me."

I shrug. "Ivy watches *Real Housewives*, I watch renovation shows."

There's a beat of silence, and like I can feel him before he moves, I look down just in time to see Flynn lift his hand, his fingers inches from brushing along my arm. I suck in a sharp breath between my teeth and step away from him.

"Ivy told me you're in trouble with the team."

If he's shocked, or surprised, or put off by my sudden movement and change of subject, he doesn't show it. Flynn simply turns his body, facing me even as I move around him and into the center of the room, and leans against the countertop.

"I am."

"Because you punched someone outside my bar?"

"Yes."

"Are you going to tell me why you punched someone outside my bar?"

"No."

I narrow my gaze. "You won't tell me why, but you're asking for my help?"

"You came to me, Rockstar. I haven't asked you a thing." My heart skips a beat at the nickname and, to avoid looking directly at him, I spin on my heel and take in the room's décor a bit more. Oh, how I hate the smug tone he uses and the smug look on his face and the smugness he probably feels just knowing exactly what the nickname does to me.

A giant, C-shaped couch. A fireplace with a TV mounted on the wall above it. An eight-seater dining set. Artwork on the walls with lighting fixtures illuminating each one. There's a plant in the corner, and a buffet set along one wall that houses a stack of what I can only guess are playbooks from Flynn's years playing football. It's all so ... *him,* but in the most unexpected way.

"I hope you realize that a fake girlfriend is a terrible idea and only works in romance novels. There is a high chance they won't believe us for a single minute," I say gently when I feel strong enough to turn and face him again.

"I told Hollie this, but she's insisting." He runs a hand through his hair, green eyes flashing down my body for a moment. "Does this mean you're considering it?"

"Ivy told me. Begged me to help you. For the record, I think it's a terrible idea."

"I do, too. But Hollie knows her stuff. I trust her enough to try."

"Flynn," I say, crossing my arms over my chest. His eyes track every single one of my movements. "What do you want?"

I can see the misunderstanding of my question fall over his eyes the second I ask it. He's searching my face, and his hands dive into his pockets. This man—this football god—stumbles to find the right words. "I, well, we—I mean, after Italy, I didn't think you—"

"No." I shake my head, stopping his stuttering. "I mean, what do you want from this plan? What do I need to do? If I agree to be your *fake girlfriend,*" I say, lifting my hands to quote around the fake girlfriend part. It makes me cringe.

This really, really isn't a good idea. I knew it when Ivy told me about it. I knew it when she begged me to help. I knew it when I was tossing and turning last night before I slipped my finger down the front of my sleep shorts and got myself off to the memories of Flynn Reed.

Fucking hell.

"Hollie said the games, a couple of dinners, some organized paparazzi shots of you coming and going from the house. Maybe a few of us, you know, being a couple ..." He trails off.

"Being a couple?" I ask.

"You know, kissing and stuff."

"*Kissing and stuff?* What are you, twelve?" I laugh, and for some reason, the sound feels like it's the pin that bursts the tension bubble we're stuck in.

"Okay, smartass. Listen, we just need to look like a couple. You can move in here, and—" I raise an eyebrow at him. "Or not. Whatever you want."

It only takes me a moment before I break. Moving to the couch, I round the edge and take a seat on the end. Flynn follows me and sits across from me. "Listen, I need to get out of my parents' house. After Grant—well, I just need some space to figure out what I want. Being at home with my Irish father and my Italian mother, it's hard to do that. I have zero privacy."

"Sounds like a loud household." He smirks, leaning down to rest his elbows on his knees.

"Louder than it should be with just four of us." I shake my head.

"Four? I thought you were an only child?"

"I have a younger brother. He's still in high school."

"You never mentioned a brother." He cocks his head to the side, brows furrowing together.

"I never mentioned a lot of things." The silence engulfs us once again. "Moving in here would help. With getting some space, I mean."

"Okay. Good. Great, yeah, of course you can," Flynn mumbles, fingers burying themselves in his hair again.

"We need rules," I say quickly.

"Rules?"

"Yes."

"You hate following rules."

"Not these ones."

"Okay, I'll bite. What rules do we need?"

I take a deep breath and count them out on my fingers. "No seeing other people." He nods, leaning forward with his attention solely on me. "No acting like it's real. Even when we have to kiss for a camera, no tongue and no roaming hands." I hold up a second finger. "No sex." Flynn's eyes roll at that one. "And no catching feelings. Ever."

"Catching feelings?"

"You cannot fall in love with me. It will only make a mess of everything," I say, like it's the most obvious thing in the world.

"And what if you fall in love with me?" He raises one brow.

"I won't."

He considers me for a moment, holding my gaze and not wavering. After a beat, I break away as he speaks. "I will do my best to stick to your rules."

"Do your best?" I ask.

"I promise to do my very, very best. But, you and I both know, neither of us are very good with rules, are we?"

Snippets of conversations play in my head. Laughter and games played under the Italian sun. Games with made-up rules that we broke every single time. Friends. We can't touch one another. We can't go any further than a kiss. Only once.

All broken.

Every single one.

"Fine," I agree.

"Katie." He follows me as I stand from the couch and head for my bag. It's time to get the hell out of here. I can text him for the rest of the details I need. Or, I can go through Ivy. Yes, good plan. She wanted me to help so badly that she volunteered to ask me for him. I will put her right back in the middle and have her play messenger.

"Katie," Flynn says again, catching my wrist as I'm halfway down the hall. A current runs from the place he makes contact, all the way through my nervous system to my heart. I still, looking down at his fingers curled around my wrist. "I want to be friends. Whatever I did in Italy to make you hate me after we—after that night, I want to fix it."

Raising my eyes to meet his, I study him for a moment. Dammit. There's that unwavering sincerity again. I slowly pull my arm out of his hold and head for the front door, closing it gently behind me without giving Flynn an answer.

Chapter Six

Flynn

Sweat drips from my forehead, and I focus on counting my breaths.

In for ten, out for ten.

My legs turn slowly on the exercise bike, warming my body down. I flex the fingers on my injured hand, and the sting sends a hiss through my teeth. I should definitely be unwrapping my hand and cleaning the healing skin underneath. A few weeks after the bar fight, I'm still feeling the effects. I know I've likely fractured a finger or deeply bruised the bones in my hand, but if I say anything to the trainers, they'll pull me off the field. It will also serve as a clear reminder that I fucked up so royally.

So, no. I will just douse the hand in antibacterial wash, wrap it again tonight, and I will hold out for the bye week. It's only a few games away, and that will give my hand some proper time to rest. After that, I will continue to strap it, and it will heal. Eventually.

I scroll through my phone while sitting on the warm-down bike. Social media doesn't hold much interest for me these days. I used to enjoy reading comments from fans and watching the content the team posted. I even used to like posting a bit of my own content, but since Italy, I search for one particular handle to like, comment, or even simply view my posts. When she doesn't, it just makes me feel like shit.

Now, even just scrolling through my feed can't hold my interest for long.

I search Katie's handle and click on her profile. There's a new photo from tonight. A packed-out bar, arms in the air, a sea of glasses being held aloft. Everyone faces the wall of TVs that all show tonight's Broncos game.

Her caption: *That's a touchdown.*

In a moment of weakness, I pinch the screen of my phone and zoom in. It's much too blurry for me to make out the time or the quarter on one of the screens in the picture. I frown at my phone. Selfishly, I hope it's one of mine.

I haven't heard from Katie since she walked out of my place after I told her I wanted to fix whatever I did and that I wanted to be friends. Hell, she's agreed to be my fake girlfriend—I think—surely, we can figure out how to be friends.

Like I summoned her with a single thought, my phone vibrates in my hand.

> **Katie:** I'm moving in on Tuesday. Ivy and Scott are coming as well. We're going to use his car for the boxes. Can you be home?

I ignore the skipped beat from my traitorous heart and stare down at my phone.

Why did a part of me believe she wouldn't really move in?

Me: I can help too.

Katie: It's fine. We can manage.

Me: Don't be stubborn, Rockstar. Let me help. I have a truck anyway. Way better for moving things in.

Katie: Everyone knows you're compensating for something by driving that thing.

I smirk, and then, out of nowhere, a laugh crawls up my throat and bursts out of my mouth. This girl. She's going to be the death of me.

***

"Christ, Reed, how many bedrooms do you need for one person?"

"They came with the house," I murmur, my eyes traveling down her long legs. She's wearing those tight, black jeans again. The ones that hug her ass and make me drool a little. She leans further into one of the empty guest bedrooms, and the hoodie she's wearing rides up, the smooth skin of her lower back exposed.

"You've styled all four of them as guest bedrooms. Couldn't think of anything else to use them for?"

I run a hand through my hair. There is no way I'm telling her the real reason I bought a house with so many bedrooms, so I simply shrug. "Somewhere for the guys to sleep when they crash here."

Katie looks back over her shoulder at me and hums, unconvinced. I hold her gaze, not wanting to let her win. The door she's knocking on isn't one I want to be opening to her, or to anyone, any time soon. It would be far too revealing, would make me far too vulnerable.

"This one." Katie nods in approval as she stands straight, her hand on the door frame. My gaze zeros in on her nails. Her blood red, painted nails. I suppress a groan at the thought of those nails wrapped around my—

"I'll take this bedroom. There's a bathroom attached, and it gets nice morning light."

I clear my throat. "Okay. My—uh, my room is down the hall."

"Oh?" She spins on her heel and looks past my shoulder, toward the only other door on this floor. "Neighbours then."

"Friends."

"Roommates," she challenges.

"Friends," I say, holding firm. I was serious when I told her I wanted to be friends and to figure out whatever I did to make her go from screaming my name in pleasure to not giving me the time of day in less than twenty-four hours.

"Remember the rules, Reed." I roll my eyes as she pushes past me for the stairs. "Stay in your lane. This is a business deal."

"A business deal? I thought you were helping out a friend? Me being the friend," I reply as I follow her down the stairs. I've done that a lot since she got here this afternoon. Follow her around. It's as if I'm drawn to her, like there's a rope attached to me and she's holding the other end, tugging me along at her pleasure.

"I am offering you my fake girlfriend services for a free place to live. It's an exchange of goods. A business deal." She hops off the last step and looks up at me, her bright blue eyes sparkling with sarcasm and playfulness. God, how I missed those eyes over the last few months.

If nothing else, I am grateful that she's finally looking me in the eye again.

Katie thinks she's a closed book. She hides behind this wall of stubbornness and sarcastic comments. When I met her over a year ago, she was loud and boisterous. She was Ivy's loud friend whose laugh sounded like something musical, yet her happiness never quite reached her eyes. I don't think Ivy really saw it.

Or, maybe it's only because I started becoming more and more of a regular at the bar after practice just so I could stare and study her. You see, Katie Murphy was a mystery I was determined to crack the moment I met her.

She had a job, friends, and what Ivy described as a boring yet loving boyfriend at the time, but as someone who masks their own feelings about things, I am a master at recognizing when someone is faking their way through their day. I watched the way her gaze would linger a little too long on couples who sat close enough to be in each other's laps whenever they came into the bar. I saw the small cringe whenever that asshole would come in, kissing her on the cheek as a hello and then ignoring her for the rest of the night while he drank with his buddies and she worked, serving them all. I saw the way she looked at Ivy and Scott, like she was seeing right before her very eyes what she had settled without.

She confirmed it to me herself that night in Italy. She spilled those secrets and made me promise not to tell anyone. She took off the mask.

Katie Murphy is loud, stubborn, and hilarious. She's a good friend and a dutiful daughter.

But she's also a big, fat fucking liar.

I see her.

I see the way she struggles with control over her own life and the way she thinks she's failing. I see the way she declares she's independent with a hint of regret in her tone because, deep down, she would just like someone to lessen the load sometimes. I know she knows all of this, that her internal struggle is constant because she knows the difference between settling for less and knowing she deserves better.

She's just way too damn stubborn to see that *better* could be me.

I think.

"Where do you want this one?" Scott says, walking through the open front door with a box in his arms and clothes, still on their hangers, piled on top.

"Second floor, bedroom at the front of the house." Katie points to the ceiling, dazzling Scott with a smile he returns with a scowl.

He passes me on the stairs. "Second floor guest bedroom. The one across the hall from you?"

"She chose it herself." I shrug, giving him one of my cheeky grins. He narrows his eyes and sets off up the stairs.

"That's the last one," Ivy says, also coming through the door and patting the pile of boxes just inside the entryway.

"What is all this stuff?" I ask.

"Clothes. Shoes. Handbags," Katie rattles off, and it makes me frown. Katie wears black. Black jeans, black hoodies, black shoes. I haven't seen her in anything other than dark clothing in months. Who thought she'd have so many different options for black?

"I'll bring up the rest. You guys can head off if you want." I nod at Ivy.

"Good," Scott says as he comes back down the stairs.

"No!" Katie says at the same time, her voice pitching as she grabs a hold of Ivy's arm. "We should order takeout. First dinner in the house and all."

"I have a bathroom to finish tearing the tiles off in. No dinner."

"Don't be a grump," Ivy says, untangling her arm from Katie's and taking a few steps up the stairs so she can kiss her fiancé. "The bathroom can wait. Let's order dinner. I'm starving."

"You're always hungry."

"And you always feed me. Let's stay." It takes only a couple of seconds for Scott to cave. He and I take the rest of the boxes up to Katie's new room before joining the girls in the living room. They've made themselves at home, both tucked into the couch with a glass of wine and a packet of chips between them.

"What do you feel like?" I ask them.

Katie looks up, her blue eyes gleaming as they find mine. There's a challenge in those eyes. Like she's planning all the ways she's going to make these next few months the hardest of my life. "Italian."

Oh yeah, this is going to be fun.

***

Darkness settles around me again as I lie flat on my back, my legs going still as I force myself to stop moving. I've been tossing and turning since I turned out the light over an hour ago. My thoughts are stuck on the woman down the hall—if she's comfortable, if she needs anything. I turn my head, staring through the darkness in the direction of my closed door. I hate sleeping with a closed door. It makes me feel ... claustrophobic.

I got drafted straight out of college and moved to Boston. With my signing bonus, I bought my own apartment, and I lived alone. For the first time in my life, when I came home every day, there was silence. Not the echo of my parents fighting, not the echo of Scott's moody grumbling under his breath as he studied in our dorm. Just me and the silence.

It was nice. I liked the quiet. Still do, whenever I'm in the safety of my own home.

But it was almost too quiet at night. With the door shut, boxing me into my bedroom even though the apartment beyond it was completely empty, I felt too closed in. So one night, I opened the door and I haven't looked back.

I wonder if that's weird. Do other people sleep with their bedroom doors open?

I groan, turning over in bed again and burying my face deep into the pillow. I squeeze my eyes shut and slow down my breathing. I count the seconds for every inhale and exhale, trying to force my heart rate to settle.

It doesn't work.

Sighing, I shove the covers off my legs and swing them over the side of the bed. I don't bother with my sweats, simply readjusting the black briefs I wear to bed and tugging my door open.

Fuck it.

Katie or no Katie, I cannot sleep with my damn door shut.

I glance toward the end of the corridor at the other bedroom door on this floor. It's firmly shut, and there is no light coming from underneath it.

She's asleep.

I run a hand over my face, my body wired for some unknown reason. Well, sort of unknown. I am almost certain it is due to the woman living under my roof who knows exactly how to get under my skin. Taking the stairs, I decide a glass of water will be best to cool down.

There's a faint light coming from the entryway, from a lamp that I also have on. It's a vintage find, gold brass with fabric covers. It even has one of the dangling strings that you pull to switch it off and on. My mom is always eyeing it off and telling me how gorgeous it is whenever my parents come to stay.

I wonder if Katie likes it?

Maybe, if she doesn't, I should just give it to Mom then?

I halt, staring at the lamp and shaking my head furiously to myself. What the actual fuck. *I wonder if Katie likes it?*

I shouldn't care if she does.

I should not give one fuck what she thinks of my décor or my house, or the way I've styled the four guest bedrooms.

Still shaking my head, I head down the corridor. I expect to find the space empty, but I'm greeted by the outline of a woman sitting on my countertop, silhouetted by the light pouring out from the open fridge.

Her hair is messy now, the normally tame and perfectly curled waves all over the place as they fall down her back. It's long too, almost at her waist. A flash of those same blonde strands wrapped tightly around my fist, me kneeling behind her, and her eyes flashing at me as she looks over her shoulder, flashes in my mind, and it makes my cock jolt awake.

I ignore the feeling and clear my throat, making my presence known as I cross the open room toward her.

"Fucking hell." Katie jumps, cursing as her head whips around to stare at me, her eyes wide.

"Sorry," I say as I round the corner. I don't stop to look over at her, going straight to one of the cupboards for a glass.

"You scared me," she mutters, and I can feel her eyes boring into my back.

"Again, sorry."

A beat of silence, and then, "It's your house. You don't have to be sorry."

Something in her voice makes me glance over at her. The faucet keeps running, and as I take her in, I feel the water spill over onto my hand. Now that I've looked, I can't seem to take my eyes off her, so I shut it off, place the over-filled glass down in the sink, and feel around for the teatowel hanging over the cupboard door.

"What are you doing?" I ask, wiping my hands dry.

She holds up the items in her hands. "What does it look like?"

"It looks like you're sitting on my benchtop with the fridge door wide open and eating directly from an ice cream container."

"Correct."

"Why?"

She simply shrugs. "Couldn't sleep."

"Is the bed uncomfortable?"

"No. No way. That bed is like a cloud and, to be honest, I think I want it in the breakup."

I try not to cringe at the word *breakup*. I also try not to think about why that bothers me so much, or why my first gut reaction is to tell her that there will never be a breakup. I force myself to smirk. "You can have it if you call me your friend."

"Fine," she says, eyes lifting to mine as she scoops another bit of ice cream out of the container with her spoon. It hovers in front of her lips as she says, "I'll buy my own cloud-like mattress."

Then, she places her lips around the spoon before slowly drawing the ice cream into her mouth.

If my cock wasn't awake before, it fucking is now.

Jesus fucking Christ.

I look down at my abandoned, over-filled glass and take a deep breath in. I tip some of the water out and lift it to my lips, returning my gaze to Katie, only to find her licking the last remnants of her scoop off her spoon. I gulp down the water.

"Do you always walk around the house in nothing but your underwear?" Her eyes track down my body, and I don't miss the way they catch on my abs. I fight the urge to run my fingers over the hard ridges, to emphasize the defined lines and solid muscle.

Instead, I keep my mask firmly in place. She wants to play games, then I can play, too. "Yes. Do you always sit on the kitchen bench at home wearing nothing but an oversized T-shirt?"

She looks down at her outfit—a faded blue T-shirt that drowns her. The hem is worn and creeps up her thighs with every single movement. Her smooth legs fall over the edge of the countertop, the bare skin taunting me. She smiles knowingly and crosses her legs before carving out another scoop.

I drain the rest of my glass and place it back into the sink. Then, I move to stand next to the fridge, opposite her. From here, the light illuminates her completely, and I can see every single one of her emotions. All of the ones she gathers up during the day and locks away, thinking no one would care to hear about them. But here, in my kitchen, she's laying them all out. I wonder silently if she knows that she bears them all to me, or if she's completely unaware of how far she's let her guard down.

It could be the wine. Or, it could be the fact that she's never had to hide from me. Not before, when I was simply her football crush that she accidentally flirted with across a bar, not in Italy with the stars above us and secrets between us, and certainly not that night.

Not when I thought we were starting something I'd almost given up on finding completely.

"Earth to Flynn." Katie waves the spoon in front of my face, drawing my attention back to her.

"Do you?"

"Do I what?" She drags the spoon over her lower lip.

"Wear that to bed?" I gesture to her outfit once again. Up close, I can tell it's a man's shirt.

Irrational jealousy surges through me.

Is that her fucking ex's shirt?

"This is my favorite shirt. My comfort shirt, if you will," she explains, like that's supposed to mean anything to me.

"You mean comfortable?"

"No, I mean comfort." She stabs the spoon into the remaining ice cream, ensuring it holds itself up in the container, and places it down on the bench. Then, she smooths her hands over the fabric of the shirt, causing it to mold to her body.

My eyes go straight to her hard, pointed nipples, prominent through the fabric. Holy fuck, do I miss seeing those. Her boobs are ... well, they're perfection. No other word for it.

"I've had it for years." Please don't be her ex-boyfriend's. Please, please. Anyone other than him. "It was my dad's. I stole it after college when I moved into our—I mean, *my* own place."

Thank fuck.

I take a step, and then another. My stomach is mere inches from her knee. My fingers flex by my sides, itching to touch her, before they finally settle beside her instead. I press my palms into the countertop to stop myself from losing all control and sliding them up her thighs and under that fucking shirt.

I lean in. "Let's be friends, Katie."

She stares at me, mouth parted slightly and breathing shallow. "No.

"That word coming from your mouth is starting to turn me on." My thumb slides further from my palm, reaching out to brush her thigh. "Come on. You're living here. We're going to be playing pretend lovers. The least we can do is be friends." I glance down at her lips. "Please."

There is a moment, in the quiet of the kitchen, the dim light illuminating the two of us, where I swear to fucking god, Katie leans in. She shifts in her spot, her eyes tracing over the features of my face and down toward my mouth. I stare, wrapped in her expression as she studies me. Then she does it again, she leans in.

She brings the spoon back to her mouth. The scoop of ice cream on top passes between her pink lips, disappearing as she closes her mouth around the spoon. In slow motion, she draws it from her mouth, clean of the ice cream. Her tongue licks her lower lip, and she smiles.

It's the same, satisfied smile she gave me after I made her come.

"I love it when you beg," she whispers. Then, she hops off the counter, her chest brushing against mine as she replaces the lid on the container, then the ice cream into the freezer.

She doesn't say another word, simply shuts the fridge door and disappears down the corridor toward the stairs.

She leaves me there, standing frozen in the wake of her words and the image of her lips wrapped around the spoon, my cock as hard as a rock.

Chapter Seven

Katie

"You can't wear that," Ivy says, staring at me with a wild look in her eye as she pulls on her jacket.

I look down at my outfit. Black jeans, black boots, and my favorite oversized hoodie. "Why not? It's cold out."

"You have to wear something with Flynn's number on it, obviously." Ivy tuts and pulls out her phone. "You aren't even trying to look like his girlfriend."

"You're not wearing Scott's number," I mutter under my breath. Ivy simply looks up at me and smiles. She turns, showing me the back of her jacket where a giant navy blue and white eighteen is stitched into the back.

"And I have this." She holds up her left hand, flashing the engagement ring sitting delicately on her finger. Then she puts all but her middle finger down.

I laugh. "Someone's sassy today." I tug uncomfortably at the sleeves of my hoodie.

"I'm so excited to have you at the game," Ivy says, bouncing on her toes around me. "I hate going alone."

"You've been doing well." I take her hand in mine and squeeze. "Pops would be really proud of you, Ives."

Ivy goes quiet, sinking back onto her feet, and I see her take a deep breath. Her eyes well with tears, but she blinks them away before they can fall. "I hope so."

Silence falls around us as we stand in the entryway of Flynn's brownstone. The dark walls are illuminated by the lights lining the hall, showcasing the records he has displayed. Over the past two weeks, the house has grown more and more familiar. Whoever decorated for Flynn did an incredible job. It's warm and cozy, and feels like a home. Even with too many bedrooms for just one person. It's very *him*.

Flynn Reed is different at home.

He's comfortable. Grounded.

A few nights ago, he came home just as I was coming down the stairs after a shower. The plan had been to curl up on the couch and watch the newest episode of *Love It Or List It*. Instead, I stopped in my tracks when a key in the lock turned and the front door pushed open. I watched him cross over the threshold, and his whole body relaxed. Like he was a different person between these walls. It fascinated and annoyed me, both at the same time.

"The driver is waiting, but if you want to change, he can wait," Ivy says gently.

I glance at myself in the hallway mirror. Damn it. Ivy is right. I look like I'm going to work. I always look like this these days.

Before Grant, I used to love fashion. Clothes, hats, handbags. I was obsessed with putting together the perfect outfit. I was a color enthusiast and never, ever afraid of a pattern. I collected items from thrift stores, loving their one-of-a-kind pieces. In my eight a.m. classes in college, other students would turn up in their pajamas while I looked as if I was about to walk a runway. It was my thing.

Where did that girl go?

"You don't have to change," Ivy says, touching my arm. "You look great in whatever you wear."

I give her a small smile and shake my head. "I'm going to change. Give me five minutes."

***

Standing at the sidelines before a game is nothing like I have ever experienced before. Ivy and I are situated behind a velvet rope on the edge of the field, watching the team warm up. Players and coaches are scattered across the field, the media running amongst them as they try to catch someone to talk to.

Ivy bounces on her feet next to me, her jacket hanging off one shoulder, and she furiously waves her arm in the air. She doesn't need to. Scott hasn't focused on his warm-up since the moment we walked out onto the field tonight.

"He sees you, Ives." I laugh, shoving my hands into the pockets of the leather jacket I changed into. After staring at myself in the mirror of my bedroom for a solid minute and a half, I switched my black skinny jeans for a pair of blue denim straight legs, a white tee, and a leather jacket. I'm not in the team colors, and I'm not wearing Flynn's number, but at least I don't look like I just got off a shift at the bar anymore. Still, even though I'm wearing what feels like my old armor again, discomfort crawls up the back of my neck and makes my hands sweaty.

I know it's because of Grant. He's a football fan. A big one. We used to come to almost every home game he could get tickets for. He was too cheap to buy season tickets, but would get them on discount if any were going at the last minute. Scott offered us his family friend's tickets most of last year, even if Ivy wasn't coming to the game, and Grant jumped at the chance. Barely said thank you. We had a huge fight over it. I got annoyed that he was using Scott for free tickets and tying us to him, especially because Ivy was struggling with the whole *Scott's an NFL player* and her grief.

Grant didn't give a shit. It was a red flag that I chose to ignore.

I glance into the stands, wondering whether he's in there somewhere. It makes my stomach turn over. Inside the safety of my jacket pocket, I clench my fist and dig my nails into the palm of my hand. I force myself to laugh at Ivy, still waving at her boyfriend … sorry, *fiancé* … across the field. Dirty blond hair flickers in the periphery of my eyeline, and my gaze catches on a man walking toward Scott.

With his pads and uniform on, with the helmet hanging by his side from his fingers while his other hand racks through sweaty hair, Flynn Reed is a god.

On a football field, he's otherworldly.

He smiles. He plays around with his teammates. He laughs loudly, and his movements are big. He doesn't have to ask for anyone's attention because he knows it's already on him. He's a character out here.

One very different from the man who wears super-hero-branded T-shirts at home after he showers and watches renovation shows with me.

I wonder what's real. The player or the homebody?

Like snow blanketing the ground in the wintertime, silence falls when he looks at me. The stadium seems as if it goes completely quiet. His eyes travel down, and then up my body. Fingers grip the helmet by his side, and when the other drops from his hair, it flexes before he lifts it and waves.

I'm stuck on him. His gaze traps me and, for a moment, I'm taken right back to Italy. That night, with him, I felt … *alive*.

Getting caught in his gaze when he's in his element feels the same. It sets my skin on fire, and my heart starts pounding in my chest. It gets hard to breathe, and I feel as if I could run a marathon. In which direction, who knows?

A hand wraps around my elbow, and the sound of the stadium comes crashing back in. The noise is deafening as Flynn pulls his gaze away from me, and the hand on my arm tugs me around.

"You're here," the small woman holding onto me says. She's got long reddish-brown hair and a Louis Vuitton Alma BB hanging from her wrist. She's a little shorter than I am, but when I look down, I see the five-inch heels she's balancing on. This must be Hollie, Flynn's publicist. Or is it manager? Agent? Maybe it's all three.

"Hi, Hollie," Ivy says, finally looking away from Scott.

"Good to see you, Ivy." She barely spares Ivy a glance before focusing back on me. "You'll do. We need to get you a jersey, but this is fine for today. I'll send over a bit more of a brief for the next game."

"Uh?" I cross my arms over my chest, feeling a little defensive. A brief? The brief I got from Flynn was that I just needed to show up to games. Maybe kiss him on the cheek and clap when he gets a touchdown. Is there more to the brief?

"Don't worry, I'll provide the team gear. You won't have to pay for anything." She must mistake my confused look for worry. Hollie pulls out her phone and starts typing furiously. "I've organized a photographer from the *Boston Daily* to get a picture of you and Flynn kissing. It'll run on the front page of their gossip section tomorrow morning. Working title, *Flynn Reed finally wifes up*." She waves a hand in front of her face as if she's visualizing the headline in lights on Broadway. I cringe a little.

"Wifes up?" Ivy giggles behind her hand.

"I know, it's a little much, but if Flynn hadn't decided to punch someone in front of a camera, then we wouldn't be having this problem, would we?" She looks up from her phone and out to the field of players. "Where is he?"

"Over there." I point before I can stop myself.

"Reed!" Hollie yells out. For a tiny woman, her voice carries right across the field to where the guys are standing. Flynn's head whips back around, his eyes momentarily connecting with mine again before sliding over to Hollie. She waves him over, and he begins to shake his head. Then, I see the moment he realizes why she is here and what that means. His shoulders sag a little, and his hand shoots to the back of his neck, tugging at the strands of hair as Scott says something to him.

With a clap on the shoulder from Scott, the two of them walk toward us.

I didn't see Flynn before he left for the field this morning. Over the last week, we've met in the kitchen at dinner time, decided on what to order to eat, and then sat on opposite ends of the couch until Flynn decided he needed to head to bed. I always follow not long after because once he's gone, my interest in the show completely vanishes. We discuss whichever show we're watching, we argue about which Thai place on the delivery app is better, but we never talk about the situation we've found ourselves in. I realize as he walks toward me now that perhaps we should have.

Scott makes a beeline for Ivy, sweeping her up in his arms easily and keeping her close. Flynn slows down as he approaches, taking slow and calculated steps toward me.

Hollie has disappeared, but I can hear her directing someone quietly behind me. I don't turn to look, and I don't try to listen to whatever she's saying any harder because that would mean I would have to take my attention off of Flynn.

And, as we have already established, doing such a thing is almost impossible for me.

"Hey," he says when he's close enough to not have the words drowned out by the growing crowd filtering into the stadium around us.

"Hi," I whisper, staring up into his face. His hair is still dry, one small curl falling across his forehead. I refrain from lifting my hand to wipe it away.

"You look nice." He glances down my body, and I feel my skin begin to heat again.

"Thank you. I'm trying something different."

"Wasn't feeling the all-black look today, then?"

"I don't always wear all black."

He hums, a smile creeping across his lips. "Mm. Yes, yes you do."

"It's just what I wear at the bar. Easier when I am there all the time." I shrug, trying not to let my nerves show through.

Flynn leans down, his breath hot against my ear as he whispers, "You ready, Rockstar?"

"Ready? For what—" My next words are cut off as Flynn slowly bends, gently dropping his helmet to the ground. He stands to his full height, his hands finding my cheeks. His thumb gently swipes across my bottom lip, and he smirks as my eyes flicker between his gaze and his mouth.

Then, he drops his head and kisses me.

If I thought the stadium went quiet when he looked at me before, it is nothing like the feeling I get when his lips meet mine.

I am thrown into the memories of our first kiss under the stars, by the pool that night in Italy. How we had been laughing and drinking wine, sharing secrets.

How he'd looked at me like I was a breath of fresh air, and he was dying to breathe me in.

His lips move gently, slowly against my own. His fingers stroke my cheek, his hands keeping me firmly in place. I feel myself step into him, my hands sliding across the fabric of his jersey at his waist and clutching it in my grip.

I lose time when I kiss him.

He pulls back, not removing his hands from my face, and he rests his forehead against mine. I work to control my breathing, to slow my heart rate down. It's going to be a long few months if I can't keep my emotions in check.

When I look up and into the mix of blue and green swirling in his eyes, I force myself to remember the sinking feeling in my stomach and the stabbing pain in my chest that I felt the night after we slept together. I force myself to relive the memory of watching him flirt with a girl across the bar, right in front of me, and how it felt to hear in the bathroom later on that he actually gave his number to her. I overheard the girl bragging to her friends about it.

So even though he kisses me like he's trying to tie me to him forever, I cannot get attached to Flynn Reed.

***

My heart is pounding, and my hand hurts. Ivy is holding onto me so tightly that I feel like she is definitely going to break a few bones before the final whistle goes. The atmosphere is electric. The Broncos took an early lead, but it's been a close game. New York are unofficial rivals. The game is always a little messy, but it feels different to me this year.

I can't tell if it's because I'm mirroring Ivy's anxiety over watching her fiancé get sacked over and over, or if it's because I'm feeling my own every time one of the New York defensive line catches Flynn and takes him to the ground.

The same defensive line breaks through the pocket again, and Scott falls to the ground, the ball still in his hand. I groan, the Broncos fans below us echoing my sentiment.

"Ives, I love you, and I know you're anxious, but you're going to break my hand."

"Shit. Sorry." She lets go and gives me an apologetic look.

"It's a close game."

"Scott is going to blame himself if they don't win. He's always so grumpy if he gets sacked in the pocket during one play, let alone a few."

"You'll cheer him up," I say, bumping my hip against hers. "Just give him a blowjob when you get home and he'll forget all about it."

"Gross," she murmurs, but her face immediately heats up and her cheeks turn a furious shade of red.

"Oh my god, you were already going to, weren't you?" I laugh, taking a seat as the teams switch over on the field below us.

"I love home games." Ivy sighs and sits next to me. Her eyes find Scott on the sidelines, and I follow her gaze. Flynn sits next to him on the bench, his head bowed as Scott speaks to him. "Scott's always got so much adrenaline after a game. It's some of the best sex I've ever had."

I snort, lifting the beer I'd left on the empty seat next to me to my lips. "Good for you, Ives."

"So," she says, turning my body and eyeing me carefully. "You and Flynn."

"What about us?"

"That kiss looked cozy," she says. "You looked pretty comfortable."

"So? It was a kiss."

"You just ... I don't know ... moved together. Made it look easy."

"Is kissing not easy for you?"

"It is. It always has been with Scott. But, before him, it was always a little awkward the first time with someone new."

"What's your point, Booker?" My fingers press into my palms.

"Just saying that you looked comfortable. Like you'd done it before."

I stay very still, my eyes blurring a little, and the grass of the field below going out of focus. "It was just a kiss."

"Do you like him?"

"No," I whisper. Not even I believe me, so I don't expect Ivy to. I look over at her. She's staring at me, her hands on her lap as she fiddles with her engagement ring.

"You know," she starts. "It's okay if you do. You have been broken up with Grant for months, and it's okay if you want to move on."

"I know."

"And, well, I noticed that you and Flynn seemed to … get along. In Italy, I mean."

"We did?"

"Yeah, I mean, I haven't seen you laugh that much in ages. You were different this summer." She reaches over and pats my hand. "Happier."

"Nothing happened," I say, answering the question I know she is begging to ask. I hate myself for lying through my teeth to her.

"You sure?"

"Yep." I take another sip of my beer. The liquid tastes sour, and it burns my throat. God, I'm a shit friend. I don't know why I don't want to tell her.

Well, I do.

The whole scenario left me embarrassed. Falling for his charm and his nice guy act only to have it thrown back in my face the next day? It's embarrassing.

"Okay, well, for the record"—Ivy sits back on her seat, lifting her drink to her mouth and smiling. She glances back at me—"I think the two of you make a very cute couple."

"What can I say? I'm very cute. I would bring anyone's cute status up." I smile, forcing it to reach my eyes. "It's fake, though, Ives. We're just using one another to get through the next few months."

"Uh-huh." Ivy nods, taking another sip of her drink. "Whatever you say, Murphy."

Chapter Eight

Flynn

Playing on or close to Halloween is always fun. The fans come out in costume, and the atmosphere gets wild. It's electric. The moment I step onto the field, I feel it seeping into my bones. It shoots through my nervous system like bolts of lightning, sending waves of energy rippling through me. The stadium is packed, the seats full of fans. Nothing is better than playing against New York on Halloween.

Except maybe knowing that tonight, in one of the corporate boxes, is a woman who drives me absolutely mental. Katie has been to games before. Scott gave her and her douchebag ex-boyfriend season tickets last year when he thought Ivy would come to more games if they came with her. This isn't the first time that she's seen me play in the flesh.

It is, however, the first time she's watching me play with my last name across her back.

After our kiss, caught in 4K thanks to Hollie, I watched both Katie and Ivy be ushered from the field as they closed it off for the game. Hollie followed them, and when they reached the tunnel, her assistant met them in the opening, handing Hollie a brand new jersey. I watched as Hollie ripped open the plastic and gave it to Katie.

They must have argued back and forth because I swear I saw Katie stamp her foot before she finally surrendered, took off her jacket, and pulled the jersey over her head.

I caught a glimpse of my name across her back between her long strands of blonde hair as she made her way down the tunnel. I won't lie, the sight almost made me hard.

But Katie's been doing that a lot lately.

Being around her has become increasingly difficult. I mean, I'm not going to stop, but it's not been easy. I have her routine memorized and her schedule pinned in my phone. Every night, I make sure I'm downstairs by six-thirty. I pretend to be indecisive enough about dinner until she finally caves and just orders whatever she feels like, then I let her put whatever stupid renovation show she wants on and we watch it until I have to head to bed. It was something close to satisfaction when I realized she now goes to bed straight after me.

She's here tonight watching, cheering for me.

Well, cheering for the team. I'm not naïve enough to think that she would be cheering just for me. Not yet. Soon, though. I hope.

I am still figuring out how best to befriend her again. To try and get her laughter back. God, do I miss her real laugh. Not the fake one she gives me now, but the real, whole-body laugh she had when we were in Italy. I would give anything to know what

I did to have it taken away from me and what I could do to get it back.

I have a plan, though. Half a plan. Okay, the start of a plan.

It's getting there.

"Reed, head out of your ass and catch the ball." Coach slaps my shoulder as he passes me. He crouches in front of Scott and me, sitting on the bench and waiting for the play to turn over again.

"My head is firmly out of my ass, Coach," I murmur, earning myself a hard look.

"Harvey, what's with you?" I glance at Scott when he doesn't answer right away. He and Coach have grown closer over the off-season. After Ivy's grandfather passed away earlier this year, Coach Brady is the closest thing to family Ivy has left. He used to coach her dad in college. Ivy even calls him *Uncle Jeff.*

"I'm good," Scott says, but I notice that he glances up, his eyes searching. I follow his gaze and squint. I can tell where he's looking, who he is trying to see. I've been throwing glances toward the same corporate box all game.

"Get your head on this field and in the game." Coach smacks Scott's shoulder gently. "Get Reed the fucking ball and get a fucking touchdown."

"Yes, Coach," Scott and I both echo.

When the play turns over and we run back out onto the field, I feel a new sense of adrenaline running through my veins. I flex my fingers and crouch in position, bouncing a little on my toes before I go completely still, waiting for the snap.

I feel, more than see, our center move, snapping the ball back to Scott, and I take off. Power pumps through my thighs, taking me along the exact route of the play Scott called. I ignore the crowd's noise and the shouts from my teammates. The world quiets. I turn my head, my legs still pumping underneath me, catching sight of the ball soaring through the air. My feet pound into the ground, and when I outstretch my gloved hand, the ball lands easily into the center of it. I grip it, tuck it into my body, and keep running.

A New York defensive back is right on my heels, so I push harder.

When I cross the line, throwing the ball down in the end zone, the noise crashes back in. I point to the box I know Ivy and Katie are sitting in and pound on my chest. Turning, I find the nearest camera and as my teammates close in around me to celebrate an excellent play and touchdown, I throw it a wink.

***

I've never brought girlfriends to a game.

Sometimes, in the past, I would ask them to meet me after, either in a bar or at my place. I've never walked into the family area after a game and had someone I wanted to beeline to almost immediately.

Her blonde hair falls down her back, messier and more tangled than when I saw her before the game. It looks as if she has been running her fingers through it all night. Was she stressed watching me play? Or was she bored?

God, I want to ask her and find out. Even if it's the latter, I want to know what she's feeling. I want to know why she feels it.

I just want to know.

Her bright blue eyes are focused on Ivy, and she nods easily at whatever her friend is telling her. When her lips quirk up in a small smile, anticipation claws at my chest.

Go on, Katie. Smile.

I want to see her smile.

Fucking hell.

Scott ruffles my hair as he passes me, making his way toward Ivy and wrapping an arm around her waist.

"Stop doing that," I say as I follow him over to where the girls are standing and fix my hair. "It makes me feel like your younger brother, and I'm older than you."

"You are?" Katie asks. When I look down at her, she looks surprised and a little confused, like she hadn't meant to say the words aloud.

"Sure am, Rockstar." I slip my arm around Katie's shoulders. She tenses but doesn't throw me off. A win in my book. "He's the baby out of the two of us."

"Fuck off," Scott murmurs.

I laugh, tucking Katie further into my side. On instinct, I turn my face toward hers and lean down, burying my nose into her hair. Fuck, she smells good.

A little like cinnamon and whiskey.

A deadly combination.

"I'm exhausted," Ivy says, burying her head in Scott's chest to stifle a yawn.

"Let's get out of here," he says, nodding at me to start heading for the exit.

"I—uh …" Katie hesitates. "I caught a ride with Ives."

"You want me to take you home?" I wriggle my brows at her, loving the way a red tinge seeps into her cheeks.

"I would like to get a lift with you," she answers, pushing gently on my chest. It's not hard enough to make me want to let go, so I keep my arm resting around her shoulders. "You know, to the place we both live. As roommates."

"I hate that word." I scrunch up my face. "I would, Murphy, but you know, I only give my *friends* a lift home."

Katie rolls her eyes. "Don't be an ass."

"Just call me your friend." I lean closer, whispering against her ear, "Call me your friend and I'll take you home."

My hand slips off her shoulder and down her back. My fingers glide through the silky strands of her hair, untangling the loose knots that appeared throughout the game. I turn toward her, our bodies so close there are mere inches between my chest and hers. I twist a blonde lock around my finger and gently tug. Katie barely reacts, but her bright blue eyes flare with warning as she allows me to change the angle of her head.

If looks could kill, I'd let this woman slaughter me over and over again, just knowing her eyes were on me, and me alone.

"Let that hand drop any lower, Reed, and I'll kill you in your sleep," she warns, her words a quiet threat.

"That's very unfriendly." I pout.

"My bite is bigger than my bark." Her eyes flash again, and I feel my cock stiffen. God, she's hot. I think I want her to bite me. "Don't push me."

I lower my lips to her ear, not removing my hand from her lower back but also not letting it drop any lower. "Call me your friend and I'll stop."

Katie makes a low noise and I laugh, my breath skittering across the back of her neck and raising goosebumps on her soft skin.

"Fine." I place a gentle kiss just below her ear. She shivers against me. Another win.

"Let's go," Scott says, cutting through our moment. I shoot him a glare but step back from Katie. Her chest heaves a little, the only sign that she's affected by me at all.

Scott leads the way out of the waiting area and through the arena toward our cars. I picked Scott up this afternoon and drove us both over, knowing he'd be heading home with Ivy, and Katie would come with me.

As we approach my truck, I step in front of Katie and open the passenger side door for her. She glares at me before hopping in, but it only makes me smile wider. Katie stays silent on the way home. The music she puts on fills the cab of the truck, but she doesn't strike up a conversation.

No, she's too busy rubbing her thighs together and avoiding my gaze.

I got under her skin, and I plan to stay there.

The smirk stays plastered on my face for the entire ride home, fixed in place until we step over the threshold.

"Are you hungry?" I ask, striding into the kitchen and opening the fridge. I didn't eat enough after the game, and now I feel like my stomach is trying to eat itself. I pull out some leftover pasta and a bowl.

"No," Katie says, placing her bag on the kitchen island. When I have the pasta heating in the microwave, I turn to face her, leaning against the counter. It's the same counter that I leaned on nights ago, before I almost kissed her.

When she told me she liked to hear me beg.

When she left me hard as a rock in the kitchen and I had to count to a hundred before following her because I was so fucking hot, I was scared that if I had to watch her walk up the stairs, I would've snapped.

I stare at her, watching as she nervously plays with the hem of the jersey she wears. A jersey with my name on it.

If it wasn't a kink of mine before, it is now.

"We need to—"

"You look good in—" we both say at the same time. I watch as a gentle blush makes its way onto her cheeks as she realizes what I was about to say. I smile and finish my sentence. "You look good in my jersey."

"A jersey," she murmurs.

"Pardon?" I say.

"It's a jersey." She tucks her fingers into the hemline and scrunches the fabric in her fist. "Not yours. It was new."

"It has my number on it." I take a step toward her. She responds and steps back, but hits the edge of the counter. "It has my name on it. I think it's mine."

"You don't own it," she snaps. Katie glances up at me through her lashes as I take another step, right into her space.

"Hollie definitely used the black card of mine she has to buy it." I reach out and tug the fabric of the shirt out of her clenched fists. "So, I do, actually."

Silence fills the space between us. Nothing but a quiet house and our uneven breathing. I stare down at her, my gaze landing on her lips.

I could just—

"We need ground rules," she whispers. I can tell she meant to say it differently because she looks shocked at herself. Annoyed, even. Knowing Katie, she probably wanted to say it with her whole chest.

I make her nervous.

Good.

"Ground rules?" I ask.

"We are dat—fake dating," she quickly corrects herself. I hum in agreement, slipping the fabric through my fingers. Back and forth, along the hemline. I could step back. I could make this easier for her.

But, I really don't want to.

"We don't have to be one of those touchy-feely, PDA couples. We don't have to be so *handsy* in public." She crosses her arms over her chest. The movement only makes her boobs more pronounced, and I feel like pulling her against me. I want to feel her against me, the way her toned curves match my hard muscles in every way.

It's been so long, and I never want to forget what she feels like.

"We could be." I tug at the fabric I'm holding, trying to pull her to me. For a moment, I think she might take a step and give in. But Katie remains leaning against the bench, close but not close enough.

"We're not a couple. In public, where we have to pretend, we are not the kind of couple that likes public displays." The microwave beeps, and I glance over my shoulder. She uses the distraction to slip away from me. "Keep your hands to yourself, Reed."

I sigh and watch her ass sway as she gives me her back.

"I'll do my best, Murphy." I'm lying. Obviously. Like hell I will.

She rounds the corner, and I listen for her muffled footsteps heading up the stairs moments later. I take the pasta out of the microwave and sit at the counter silently as I shovel in bites.

If I think about the events in Italy, I can't pick where things went wrong. Everything seemed fine until it wasn't, and Katie slammed a door in my face. Looking back on it, I should've pushed a little harder, asked more questions. I thought she just needed a moment because it was likely the first time she fucked anyone after her breakup. So I gave her space.

In hindsight, I wish I had smothered the fuck out of her until she'd told me what I did wrong.

Nothing has changed. I want her. Having her here, in my house, only cements that. A fake relationship was a fucking terrible idea until it was Katie that was the one I would be in the relationship with.

I sigh, putting my empty bowl in the dishwasher and wiping down the benches before heading upstairs. Katie's door is open and she's sitting on the edge of her bed, scrolling through something on the TV with the remote. Slowing my steps, I peek inside the room.

To my surprise, she hasn't changed the décor all that much. The clean white bedspread is rumpled, and the green decorative pillows I picked because I thought they would add color to the room are scattered across the floor.

I feel a smile curl on my lips as I realize Katie's messy.

Her things are all over the place. Clothes spill out of the closet, and there are at least three different pairs of jeans on the floor in front of her mirror. A pair of shoes that I recognize as the ones she wears to work are just outside the door and would stop it from closing if she tried. I can't help myself, so I bend down and place them neatly just inside the door. When I glance up, she's staring at me, eyebrow raised in a question.

I just shrug and look around the room again. My gaze snags on a guitar sitting in its stand in the corner. I nod toward it.

"Do you play?" I ask.

"Sometimes." Something new crosses her face. Something between excitement and disappointment. She doesn't elaborate, but she looks over at the guitar with longing.

"You'll have to play something for me sometime." It takes everything in me not to beg her to pick up the guitar right now. I wonder if she can sing. I wonder what her voice will sound like. Fuck, I wish I could hear it.

"Mm. No, I don't think so." She shakes her head and stands, coming to stand in front of me with a hand on the open door.

"I'm hurt. Why not?"

"I only play for my friends." Her phone is in her hand, face up and brightly lit, as she points it at me. "And we aren't friends."

Her tone is light and joking. She's teasing me. I chuckle, leaning forward. "We can change that. Anytime you like."

Her mouth curls into a playful smile, and that same anticipation from earlier this evening crawls up my throat. Come on, Katie. Laugh. Play. Be bright with me again.

Before she can say anything further, the phone in her hand buzzes. Katie goes still as we both look down at the name on the screen.

Grant.

I open my mouth, about to ask her why the hell her ex-boyfriend is calling her, but with a flick of her wrist, the door shuts in my face.

What the actual fuck?

Chapter Nine
Katie

November is all pumpkin spice lattes and orange leaves. It's a picture-perfect month for fall. The orange, the reds and browns. It makes you feel warm and cozy even though winter is right around the corner. The weather is cool, but we still have blue sky days. When I was in college, I used to sit in the middle of the quad, my shoes off and my guitar in my hand. I would play for an hour or so before heading to my next class. Students would make requests, and I would let my voice carry over the small crowd that gathered, off in the wind.

Back then, music, whether it was in public while playing in the quad or in private while I sang gently to myself on my bed and strummed along with my guitar, was my release. My hobby. It was something I loved, for myself and to share.

Now, it's my secret. My safe space.

I stare at the guitar in the corner of the room. It's the same one from college, but it's not one that I use anymore. My other is at the bar, tucked away in my office, along with all my other equipment. I haven't played the one on display in years.

Grant didn't think I was any good, and he wasn't shy about saying it aloud. To be fair, I am self-taught. A few extra classes in college, and I know enough, but I haven't studied music. He thought I was wasting my time when I sat in front of a YouTube video and tried to teach myself about keys, reading music, or a new instrument. Whenever I hummed along with a song, he'd tell me to be quiet or *just listen to the artist sing it.*

Grant is a dick. I know that now, and I never should have let him manipulate me into thinking music was only for people with extreme talent. He just couldn't understand why I didn't bother trying to take it more seriously or take lessons.

Truth is, I don't want a record deal. I don't want to be a famous musician.

I simply like playing.

Eventually, I stopped playing when Grant was around. Then, when other people were around. Now, I just hide it away and retreat to the makeshift studio at the bar. My new, away-from-the-world safe space.

I lean forward, focusing while carefully threading the gold hoops through my ears. I glance down at my outfit. Loose jeans, a T-shirt tucked in, and a belt tying them together. I'll take a jacket, but Flynn told me that wherever he is taking me is indoors, so I don't have to worry too much about the elements. It's a rare weekend night off. He flies out for Colorado tomorrow for a Monday night game, and normally, it being a Saturday, I would have to work, but he requested I make myself free. After the week I've had, I didn't have the fight in me to refuse him.

I sit on the edge of my bed to pull my white sneakers on just as a gentle knock sounds at my door.

"Come in," I call out, focusing on the laces of my shoes more than a normal person probably would. Halloween was two weeks ago, and I haven't been able to get the way that kiss felt out of my head. The way his hands trailed over my body, or the way I loved the sensation of his hot breath against my ear as he demanded I call him a friend.

Flynn Reed is getting under my skin, and I am not even sure I mind all that much.

Although, as I have reminded myself for the last few weeks, I should mind. We went there. We did the thing. He's a flirt and a playboy.

I don't want a flirt and a playboy.

I don't want Flynn Reed. My brain knows this, logic knows this.

My body, however, needs time to catch up.

"You look good," he says. I suppress a blush as the words practically fall down my spine, warm and inviting.

"Thank you." I stand, grab my handbag from the bed, and turn to face him. My eyes glance over at him; jeans, T-shirt, button-up flannel thrown over the top, kept open. His sleeves are rolled to his elbows, and his hair sits effortlessly touseled and perfect on his head. Goddammit.

"And me?" He smiles, waving a hand down his own body and turning around as if showing off his outfit.

I roll my eyes. "You look good, too. I guess."

"The *I guess* was unnecessary."

"Someone needs to keep your ego in check. I am happy to take one for the team on that one." I throw a hand over my heart and nod seriously.

"Good. Scott's been holding down that job for far too long," he says, moving to the side to let me pass as I step out of my room. I smile gently and make my way downstairs. "He's gotten very slack ever since he became obsessed with Ivy."

"So he's the one who allowed you to become so over-inflated with confidence?" I turn to look at him, following me down the stairs over my shoulder. There is something I don't recognize in his features, but when his eyes meet mine, it disappears. I shake it off. "So, where are we going?"

"Hollie told me we have to be photographed more in public," he grumbles, sitting on the bench by the door to slip on his shoes.

"I figured this would be a *fake dating* thing." I nod, crossing my arms over my chest.

"Doesn't mean we can't have a little fun."

I raise a brow. "That doesn't answer my question."

"You'll see, Rockstar," Flynn says as he swipes his keys from the bowl by the door and ushers me out.

Something I'm learning about Flynn is that he's been raised a gentleman. He may be a flirt and a playboy, but he's the kind that will open a woman's door for them. And, he has. Every damn time.

Since I started living with him, if I'm with him and there is a door to be opened, or a jar that I can't pop without struggling just the slightest bit, or an item too high up in a cupboard to reach, his first reaction is to always step in.

It's not in an obnoxious way or in a way that would attract attention. It's calm and subtle. He will take the jar from my hands gently, opening it up, and then he places it right back in my hand. He will lean over me, his chest pressed against my back for a moment, reaching for the item I'm trying to get before he delivers it into my outstretched hand.

And he will step in front of me, quickening his pace just a little so that by the time we reach the truck parked in the driveway, he is already there, gripping the door handle, poised to open it up for me. Like right now. I make my way down the front steps, leaving him to lock the front door and follow me, but before I can get more than halfway to the truck, he's already in front of me. It makes my chest tighten, and I say a quiet, "Thank you."

Flynn Reed is a lot of things, and a gentleman is one of them.

The drive is quiet. Since I have no idea where we are going, I scroll through a playlist on my phone. I have the terrible habit of playing a song, then changing it halfway through. I don't want to miss out on playing a good chorus or a catchy hook just because we are only on the road for fifteen minutes.

'Better' by Khalid fills the cab, and I hum along quietly to the lyrics. When I realize that my humming has turned into gentle words, singing along with the artist, I cringe and force myself to stop.

I feel Flynn's eyes on me, boring into the side of my head before he stares back at the road, but he doesn't say anything. I go back to humming as the chorus plays again, but I suppress the urge to sing the words. I look down at my phone and add the song to the playlist I keep called *Recordings.*

I'm about to skip to the next song when Flynn turns into a parking lot in front of a bowling alley.

"Really?" I laugh, looking out my window up at the giant pins and bowling ball boards that make up the sign. "This is your big date idea?"

"Yep." He parks the truck, hopping out and rounding the hood before I can even unplug my phone from the car. He opens my door and holds out his hand. I slide my palm against his. "I'm going to kick your ass, Murphy."

When was the last time I went on a date?

Before Grant? Maybe. Definitely not during Grant. He wasn't really a date kind of guy. He was comfortable with me. He didn't put in the extra effort of date nights or flowers. I got used to it. I got comfortable with it.

Staring up at the bowling alley's brightly lit sign, my stomach does a little flip, and my heart skips a beat. I'm ... excited.

Flynn closes the car door as soon as I'm out of the truck and sticks out his arm. I hesitate, looking around for people. There isn't another soul in this parking lot with us. No one is milling around outside the entrance or walking along the sidewalk.

Do I still need to take his arm if there is no one watching us? Do I want to?

Yes. I do want to.

I reach out and slide my hand into the crook of his elbow. He tugs me closer to him, and I laugh when he starts to pull me toward the entrance like an excitable child. Whenever he's out and about, Flynn operates like he hasn't got a care in the world. He laughs and smiles, and he acts like a kid sometimes. Then, when he's at home, he's calm and collected. He always does his washing on Tuesday unless we have a sunny day. Then he'll break the schedule, so he can hang the laundry on his clothes line that he said he installed himself. He doesn't like cooking, but when he does, he cleans up immediately after he's done.

He holds open the door to the bowling alley for me, and we walk inside. The place is bustling, almost all the lanes are full, and the music that plays overhead is so loud I can barely hear myself think.

"I haven't been to a bowling alley in so long," Flynn says, leaning down to say it right next to my ear so I can hear him. There's such joy, such excitement in his voice. I have to smile and laugh along with him.

I'm starting to realize there are two sides to Flynn Reed. There's his public persona, and then there is *him*.

One at work, and one at home.

I wonder how many people get to see both? Probably not too many. Maybe Scott, maybe Ivy. Possibly his parents, too. But as I watch him lean on the counter, talking to the young, star-struck teenager behind it, I suddenly feel lucky to be included in the few.

***

"How are you doing that?" Flynn whines as I take another bow.

I laugh and shake my head at his disbelieving look. I just bowled my third strike in a row. A total and utter fluke, obviously. Was I going to let on to Flynn that my performance tonight was likely just beginner's luck? Absolutely not.

"It's raw talent." I shrug, smirking at him.

"You're cheating." He shakes his head, looking up at the scoreboard where I am a good thirty points ahead of him. "You have to be."

"How can I be cheating? I don't think cheating is even possible in a public bowling alley." I laugh, patting Flynn gently on the shoulder and walking toward the small table in the middle of the seating area. Another young teenager is placing two large pizzas onto the table. I pick up the soda that was brought earlier and take a sip, my stomach growling as I eye the pizzas. Flynn comes up behind me, slipping a hand around my waist and pulling my back to his chest.

"Thanks," he says, nodding to the teenager. I glance up at Flynn only to see that he's staring right back at me. Suddenly, my chest tightens, and I let my gaze drop, only for a moment, to his lips. My mouth feels dry, and I suck in a breath. I feel Flynn's fingers tighten against my waist before he lets me go.

He steps away, and I silently mourn the loss of his warmth. Damn it.

I am the one who said we shouldn't be so touchy-feely in public. I am the one who wants the ground rules. Yet, here I am, thinking about whether his mouth still tastes like spice and red wine, or if that was just in Italy. If it was, I really want to find out what he tastes like now that we're home.

Flynn takes a seat on the small plastic chairs, and I sit next to him. Our thighs squish together.

Why am I torturing myself?

"I cannot believe you are one of those pineapple on pizza people," he murmurs, shaking his head. I stare at him, then I look at the pizzas. This time, more closely. Sure enough, the one closest to me is covered in cheese and sauce, with peppers and mushrooms, ham and sausage, and ... pineapple.

"You remembered," I mutter.

"Well, yeah." He takes a piece of the other pizza, which looks as though it has just about every type of meat there is on it. "Hard to forget when you committed a food crime every time you asked if they did pineapple while we were there."

I laugh, picking up a piece and taking a bite. The cheese bubbles in my mouth, and I groan. "This is good."

Flynn just shakes his head at me before taking a bite of his slice. We eat in silence, letting the atmosphere infiltrate the bubble we seem to have created over the last hour or so of gameplay. The sounds of bowling balls rolling down the laneway, the crash of the pins, the cheers of the victorious as they celebrate their points are accompanied by a generous range of music playing above us in the speakers. It's a Saturday night, so the lanes are lit up and there are strobe lights of all different colors lighting up the area. It's kind of a vibe.

When I hear Whitney Houston's 'I Wanna Dance With Somebody' come over the speakers, I squeal and start bobbing my head to the music.

"I love this song," I tell Flynn between bites. I take another sip of my soda and move in my seat. "Whitney is my mom's favorite singer. We used to dance around the kitchen, blasting her music while we cooked."

"You're into music, huh?" Flynn turns to me, his pizza half gone now. He stretches his arms over the back of the small plastic seats. I am hyper aware of how close his hand is to my arm, and when I feel his fingers lightly brush over my skin, I have to suppress a shiver.

"I love music." I sigh, nodding. "It just ... it helps define my mood."

"The guitar in your bedroom," he states, now drawing gentle patterns with his fingers against my arm. I don't think he even knows he's doing it.

I raise a brow. "What about it?"

"Do you ever use it? I've never heard you play."

"I—uh," I say, cringing a little. "I used to. Not as much anymore."

"Why not?"

For a moment, I think about confiding in Flynn about Grant. I think about how freeing it might feel to tell someone what actually went down with him and how my eyes were opened to all the things Grant forced me to change about myself. I think about how therapeutic it might be to confess the real reason we broke up that very last time.

I stop myself, though.

I got his number. Flynn Reed's actual number. I'm so going to fuck him.

The words sound distant and far away, but it's a clear memory, no matter how quiet. Flynn Reed is a playboy. I can't forget, even when he makes me feel like I should. Even when he opens car doors and makes me laugh, and looks like he will devour me if I give in and let him kiss me again for real.

"I just … stopped." I shrug and take another bite of my pizza.

"Why?" he asks again.

"I don't know. I just did."

"Well, you should consider taking it back up." Flynn takes one of the napkins sitting next to the pizza plates and wipes his hands. "You're probably just as good at playing guitar as you are at ten pin bowling."

I laugh and shake my head, cleaning off my own hands and standing again. "This is a fluke. The last time I came to one of these places, I was probably still in high school, and I remember sucking so bad, my friends asked me to just skip my turn."

"That's fucked up." Flynn shakes his head, a smirk toying at his lips.

"I'm glad I've made a comeback," I say as I pick up one of the balls and get ready to hurl it down the lane. I glance over my shoulder, giving Flynn my best smile. "Just in time to kick your ass."

***

I'm in the *Boston Times* gossip column.

Me. Katie Murphy. Local Boston girl who grew up stealing the column from my dad's newspaper every other week, *in* the damn column.

I am almost positive that the spread is completely thanks to Hollie, but that didn't stop me from squealing and running out to buy a copy when Ivy texted me a picture of it. Pictures of Flynn and me covered the column. A small write-up accompanied it, but it was just speculation about who I was and where we met. Hollie fed them a story, and they ran it, and now I'm in the fucking *Boston Times*.

I stand behind the bar, waiting for the last of the locals to filter out so we can lock up. The paper is open to the gossip column in front of me. The pictures are mostly from the game. There are a few of Flynn and Scott on the field before the game, warming up, a few of Ivy and me celebrating the touchdowns in the box, and, of course, there is a giant one of when Flynn kissed me. To my surprise, though, there's an addition from Saturday night. The picture is grainy. It's dark, and the only thing lighting our figures are the strobe lights, but it's undeniably Flynn and me. We're standing so close together, smiling and staring at one another. I'm laughing, and Flynn has his hand up, obviously in the middle of tucking a piece of my hair behind my ear.

In the moment, I forgot about all the cameras and the people that were likely watching us because Flynn is so famous. It felt like I was hanging out with a friend.

No.

It felt like I was on a date.

A scraping sound pulls me from my thoughts. Justin is pulling the chairs from under the tables and stacking them on top. My chefs closed up the kitchen over an hour ago. Monday's aren't all that busy, but I gave myself a shift tonight knowing that Flynn would be out of town. The house is a little too empty without him there. It feels weird.

The game was on here anyway. Flynn scored three touchdowns, and I watched every single one.

I look back down at the picture of us in the bowling alley. It makes me feel …

I don't know. Or at least, I can't name it.

It's not butterflies or anxiety. It's not nervousness. It's almost as if it's comfortable. I'm relaxed and happy, and laughing in the picture, so I feel all of those things looking back at it. But then I remember what happened the last time I let him in, and I can't seem to correlate the two feelings.

It's confusing.

"Whoa." Justin leans over the bar and looks at the photos. "I cannot believe you're dating Flynn Reed. That's so awesome."

"Uh-huh," I murmur, not really paying any attention.

"Are you just staring at pictures of the two of you making out?" Justin laughs when my gaze shoots up, and I scowl at him.

"No." I close the paper and tuck it away in my bag under the bar. "There's a picture of Ivy and me that I really like and want to keep."

Justin just laughs as he collects his things. I walk him to the front door. "Drive safe," I tell him as I wave him off. It's just past eleven p.m., and as I lock the front door to the bar and start my rounds of all the windows to check their locks, my fingers start to feel like they're buzzing.

When I'm confident I'm safely locked inside of Pat's, I turn out the lights to the main bar area and make my way down the hall to my office. Two years ago, when I started doing more of the management stuff for Mom and Dad, I decided to convert the office into a secret studio. I never sat in here doing any actual work, so it was hardly used, and Mom has her own down the hall, so it's all mine.

I turn on my computer, get the recording program up, and then set the camera to the right angle. It isn't a very fancy setup. I don't have the same production value as some videos I see across the site, but considering this is my secret channel, I don't think anyone cares.

Years ago, when I gave up playing music and singing in the quad, I started to feel like I had lost my connection to music and how happy it made me when I was playing it. Grant obviously hated me playing at home, so when I started to work more here at the bar, I just switched.

I started staying late and extending my hours. I started adjusting my schedule so I would close the bar down because once I did, I retreated into the office and I played.

Then, one day, I posted a video of myself playing and singing an acoustic version of a reworked Adele song onto an anonymous YouTube channel. It blew up.

So I posted another. And another.

Never showing my face. Never saying anything other than when I sang the lyrics to the songs I chose. I didn't have any fancy editing or production. I record directly onto the site, and then I just press upload. No caption, nothing.

Just me and my music.

I take a deep breath, getting up the sheet music and the lyrics for 'Better Man' by Taylor Swift on the screen in front of me. When I press record, and I strum the first few bars of the music on the guitar in my hands, everything fades away. Grant. Flynn. Fake relationships. Real feelings.

While I'm playing, while I'm singing, I'm free.

Chapter Ten

Katie

Wedding magazines take over the dining table. There is a large piece of cardboard with circles drawn on it and other smaller pieces of paper stuck around the corners. Of course, Ivy would make her own seating chart. Any excuse for arts and crafts.

"Katie, look," Flynn whispers from his seat beside me. I glance up from the magazine I'm looking at. He's got a grin on his face as he holds up the little pieces of paper with our names on them. "It's us in seating chart form."

I shake my head, suppressing a laugh as he turns the two little pieces of paper into one another and touches them together, like he's a child playing with dolls. Flynn and I are sitting next to each other with Ivy and Scott on the other side. This morning, I got a panicked call from Ivy, freaking out that she'd been engaged for almost six months and hadn't planned a single thing. She begged me to come spend my Sunday with her to get the ball rolling.

I was almost out the door when Flynn caught me, made me tell him where I was going, and then decided to come along. "I'll drive," he'd said, and then he just ushered me to his truck.

It was probably a good thing that he did come along in the end. Ivy's been a mess all day, and Flynn knows how to make her smile. He even cut the little name tags out for the seating chart for her.

"Do you think we should be inviting more than a hundred people?" Ivy says, waving for Flynn to put the two tags back down on the chart.

"No," Scott grumbles from beside her, fist wrapping around the beer Flynn put in front of him just before. "We should invite less."

Ivy slaps his shoulder gently. "This is the bare minimum list. You have a lot of teammates."

"They don't have to come."

"That's rude." Ivy narrows her eyes. "Stop being a grump about this."

"Sorry. It's just ... I would marry you right now, right here, just with these two as witnesses. We don't need all those people." He leans over and gently kisses her hair, tucking a piece behind her ear. "But, if you want to invite them all, then I'm happy. As long as you are."

I ignore the stabbing pain in my chest at the image of the two of them. It's been happening more and more with these guys lately. Watching them be happy and in love, it kind of hurts.

I feel a foot tap against mine from under the table, and I glance at Flynn. He's staring at me, waiting for me to look his way. When I meet his gaze, his eyes flicker toward the couple across the table, then he pretends to gag.

I laugh.

Out loud.

Oh my god. I clamp down on the smile so fast, but it's too late. Flynn is out of his chair, his arms above his head. "I did it. I made her laugh."

"You're an idiot." I roll my eyes, but my smile breaks through, and I can't be bothered to taper it down again.

He comes around the table, placing one hand on the back of my chair and another on the table in front of me as he leans down, his face inches from mine. "You laughed. This means we're friends."

Then he kisses me on the cheek and heads for the kitchen, one fist firmly in the air like he's just won a game or something.

"You're blushing," Ivy states across the table. Scott has gotten out of his seat too, following Flynn.

"I'm not." I am. I press the back of my hand to my cheek. It's warm. I'm definitely blushing. Damn it.

"You guys are cute together. He's the kind of Golden Retriever energy you need in a man." She nods to herself as she flicks through the magazine in front of her.

"Golden Retriever? We're comparing men to dogs now?"

"Uh-huh. It's the newest thing on the internet."

"And what would Scott be?"

Ivy pauses, glancing over her shoulder at her fiancé. "German Shepherd."

"So," I say, looking to change the subject from whatever complicated and confusing feelings I'm having for Flynn onto something else. "Have you guys picked a date yet?"

Thankfully, she accepts it. "No. It will have to be in the off-season next year. I can't go through trying to plan a whole wedding while he's always away for games. It's too hard."

"I'm here to help with whatever you need." I reach a hand out, offering it to her. She smiles and takes it.

"I ... I want to go dress shopping soon. Will you come with me?" My heart squeezes when I see the tears flood her eyes. Unlike last year, when she was just starting therapy and still working through the grief for her parents, Ivy blinks back the tears instead of letting them fall. I know she's likely thinking about her mom and how she wishes she could be here.

"Of course I will, Ives." I shake her hand a little. "You know what we should do? We should have a girls' night with wine and ice cream and watch your mom and dad's wedding video. I bet she was a gorgeous bride. You could get some ideas of the things she chose for herself and your dad if you wanted to incorporate something she might like."

"Yeah." Ivy blinks a few times and lifts her hand to run her thumb under her eye. "That's actually a nice idea. I haven't watched that video in ages."

I smile gently as Scott joins us again, leaning down to place a gentle kiss on Ivy's throat. "We're going to put the football on. Do you want to order some food?"

"Sure. What do you feel like?"

"Whatever you want, baby." He kisses her and walks toward the lounge, taking a seat on the couch with Flynn. For a moment, I catch Flynn's gaze and my cheeks heat again.

It's so easy being here with him. Our friends. His and mine. That right there is another reason he and I would be a bad idea. If we blew up again, if it didn't work out, we would forever be tied together by the friends we share.

He winks at me, throwing me a cheeky smile before turning to the television that now plays the pre-game interviews. The boys are on a bye week, so it's a rare weekend off. A lot of the team went to Mexico for the week to blow off some steam. I expected Flynn to join them, but when I asked, he merely shrugged and told me, "There's nothing in Mexico for me."

"Maybe a February date? Do you think it will be too cold?" Ivy draws my attention back to her.

"Do you plan on getting married in the snow?"

"No?"

"Then you'll be fine if you want to do it in February."

"I just ... to be honest, I wish we had just eloped in Italy when Scott asked me to."

"He what?" I look up at her with shock.

"Yeah. On the second last night there, he said, 'We should just get married here.' I freaked out."

"Of course you did." I laugh. "Ives, why didn't you just elope?"

"I don't know." She shakes her head a little. "I had it in my head that I wanted to get married here. Where my family is. Even if they can't be at the wedding."

My heart clenches, and I nod. "I get that. So why do you wish you had now? Is it the stress of planning?"

"No." She glances over her shoulder at Scott. "I just want to be his wife. Like, right now. Waiting for the season to be over feels like torture."

"You two are disgusting, you know that?"

"Disgustingly in love." Ivy nods solemnly, agreeing with me.

I laugh, getting up from the table. "Do you have wine?" I ask her.

She follows me into the kitchen and pulls an unopened bottle of rosé from the fridge. I grab two glasses from the cupboard and place them in front of her.

"So, February then? After the season is over?" I ask as she pours out two glasses.

"Yep. February."

"So ... when can we do the bachelorette party? I'm thinking New York?" I take a sip of my wine as Ivy laughs and shakes her head.

"Absolutely not. No New York. I already know what you're thinking, and you're not allowed to get me strippers."

I pout. "Why?! What is the point of my best friend getting married if I can't enjoy getting her strippers for her bachelorette?"

"No strippers." My voice must have traveled because when I look up, Scott is glaring at me from across the room.

"You're a buzzkill, Harvey." I hide my smirk behind my glass of wine.

"Wait," Flynn pipes up from beside Scott. "I can still get *you* a stripper for your bachelor party, right?" We all laugh because Flynn looks so stressed, faced with the idea that he might also miss out on getting strippers if Scott vetoes them. I ignore the same pang of jealousy that flourishes in my stomach, and we join the boys on the couch to watch football.

***

"Why did you convince me that walking home was a good idea?"

"Because we've both had too much to drink to drive my truck home."

"You ever heard of Uber?" I grumble, shivering against the chilly evening air.

"It's a beautiful night."

"It's freezing."

"Yes, but look at the sky. No cloud cover. If we were in the country, we'd be able to see stars on a night like tonight."

I look up. He's right. There are no clouds tonight. The moon shines so brightly, and it mixes with the street lamps and the lights pouring out of people's windows. Flynn doesn't live far from Ivy and Scott's place. A few streets, a fifteen-minute walk.

We ended up staying there for dinner and watching another game of football. I still can't quite understand why they want to play it, train for it, live football day in and day out, and then even on a break, they're still obsessed with watching it. But, they do. Even Ivy was getting into the Sunday night game that we watched between Texas and California, Scott's former team. Unlike him, Flynn was drafted to Boston. He's never played anywhere else, if you don't count college.

Because we stayed, I drank more than I should have. Ivy just kept filling my glass, and she kept supplying beer to Flynn. By the end of the night, we both had too much to drive. So here we are, walking.

Flynn's brownstone comes into view when we round a corner and turn into his street.

"Oh, thank god." I pick up my pace, leaving Flynn behind. I reach the front door and turn to wait for him. He smirks at me as he climbs the front steps.

"You didn't bring your keys?"

"I forgot. You whisked me out the door, and I just ... I don't know, turned my brain off."

He hums in response and leans around me to unlock the door, pushing it open for me to walk through first.

I sit on the bench and toe off my shoes, throwing them onto the pile that sits by the door. Most are Flynn's, but mine are slowly starting to join them. I'm starting to pick up his habit of taking my shoes off as soon as I come through the door.

I hear him tut as I walk down the hallway, and I glance over my shoulder. Flynn is bent down, neatly lining up the shoes I just took off next to the other pairs. I smile and head for the kitchen.

"Do you want another drink?" I call out to him.

"Are you having another?"

"Yeah." I pull out two beers, but only crack one of them open. "I got called in for a sub day tomorrow, but why the hell not?"

Flynn makes it down the hall, hand ruffling through his hair. "Why not? I'm already halfway drunk, may as well finish off the job."

"That's the spirit," I say, popping the lid on the beer and holding it up to him. He leans over the kitchen island and takes it from my hand. Bringing it to his lips. I'm mesmerized by the way his throat works as he takes a sip. I take a sip of my own, trying to use the alcohol to soothe the newly ignited flames in my veins.

It could be the alcohol talking, but staring at him drinking a beer, completely relaxed in his own home, is probably the hottest thing I've seen him do. He's removed the flannel he wore today, and the T-shirt underneath stretches tightly over his muscles. When he slowly lowers the bottle, catching my eye, I feel myself go bright red. Damn it.

I head for the couch, planning to bury myself in the corner of it and wait for the embarrassment of being caught staring at him so intensely to fade. But, of course, Flynn follows me.

"So, what did Ivy decide?"

"About?"

"The date. For the wedding." He takes the seat across from me, in the other corner of the large C-sectional lounge.

"Oh. February. After the season is over."

He nods, taking another swig of his beer. "Good for them."

Silence fills the air, and I feel like I can taste my nerves. The last time I was drunk and in Flynn Reed's presence, I ended up in his bed. It was the best night of my life, but I suppress the memories. I only ever let myself think about that night if I'm desperate and need a release. Otherwise, they are on lockdown. I don't want to see him that way.

He's my roommate. My friend's friend. My fake boyfriend.

Our relationship is practically a business deal, an exchange of goods. If I think about that night, especially when I'm drunk and have the loosest lips on earth, I will say something stupid.

"Do you ever want to get married?" Yep. Stupid things like that. I resist the urge to smack a hand against my mouth. I need to work on my drunk filter. Badly.

"Yeah. One day," he replies. He eyes me closely, and I can feel his gaze on me. It heats up my skin.

"You'll do the big, white wedding? With all the guests and the planning, and the strippers at bachelor parties?" I try to joke.

"I guess it depends on who my wife will be. But, yeah, if it were up to me, I think I would." He rests the bottle on his thigh, twirling it between his fingers. "I like the idea of standing up in front of all of my closest friends and extended family to declare my love for a person. I'd want them to know. I'd be proud of it."

I hum, thinking about Grant again. My phone has been oddly silent since the night after the Halloween game a few weeks ago. He called me non-stop until about two in the morning, but I've heard nothing since. When we were together, he never talked about our future. Not until the very end, when he threw it in my face like it was nothing.

"My parents had a big wedding. My mom still talks about it." I smile fondly. "Even though she had me and my brother, I think it was the best day of her life."

"I keep forgetting you have a sibling."

"He's a lot younger than me. He … he actually wants to be a football player." I glance up at Flynn, momentarily meeting his gaze before looking back at my lap.

"What does your family think about our relationship? Or, do they know it's fake?"

"I haven't really … told them yet." I cringe.

"You haven't? They wouldn't see it on social media and think it's weird you've not said anything?"

"My mom and I, while I love her, we don't always see eye to eye. She thinks I can't make a decision and that I'm wasting my life by working at the bar instead of being a full-time teacher. My dad just stays silent to avoid the argument. They ... they focus on Sammy. It's easier."

"That sucks."

I look up and see him watching me again. God, this man. It's like he never looks away. "Why?"

"Because your parents should care what you're up to. No matter how old you are."

"Do yours? Care about what you're up to, I mean?"

"Yes, and no." He takes another swig from the almost empty beer bottle, but he never takes his eyes off my face. "My dad is my biggest fan. He loves that I play pro-ball and he calls me all the time after a game to discuss it play by play. He wasn't very athletic, so I think he enjoys being able to live through me a little. He's a good man. A little selfish, and I recognize that he probably pushed me into football for the wrong reasons, but I love him."

"And your mom?"

"She's ... harder."

"Are they still together?"

"Yes." His words are clipped short. Harsh. "They shouldn't be."

"What do you mean?"

"They should get a divorce. They should have gotten one years ago. God knows why they stay together, but they hate each other. I think ... I think my mom knows that I have a better relationship with my dad and she thinks, in some twisted way, that if they split up, I'll take his side."

"Would you?"

Flynn hesitates, his fingers tapping against the bottle. "I don't know."

Silence fills the air between us, and it becomes thick and hard to breathe. I shift in my seat, edging out of the corner and closer to Flynn, just a little. I don't say anything else. I can tell that he hasn't finished. I'm patient enough to wait.

"She's cheated on him. A bunch of times."

My heart sinks. Fuck.

"I caught her when I was eighteen. I was about to leave for college, and I dropped by her work. I was going to take her to lunch as a final goodbye. School was only two hours away, but something in me told me that I wasn't really ever going to come back." He leans over and places the now empty bottle on the coffee table. I do the same. When I sit back into the couch cushions, I'm even closer to him as he talks. "She's a personal assistant for some hotshot CEO. I walked into their office, expecting to find her at her desk. Instead, she's on top of it and her boss is fucking her."

"Shit."

"She freaked out. Begged me not to tell my dad." He runs a hand through his hair, tugging a little on the strands. I want to lean over and take it in mine. I have the overwhelming urge to crawl into his lap and wrap my arms around him. But I don't.

"Did you?" I ask in a quiet voice.

"No. Never." He shakes his head. "I think he knows. He has to. The affair didn't end."

"I don't get it. If he knows, why not leave her?"

"No idea. It's toxic as fuck."

"Yeah."

"I'm terrified I'll turn out like her," he says. I look up, my eyes widening. How can he even think that?

"Have you ... have you ever cheated?" I think back to the girl in the bathroom, bragging about getting his number. Did he fuck her, too? It wouldn't be cheating. We weren't together. It would've been gross on his part, but it wouldn't have been cheating.

"No. Never." His words are strong, definitive. Believable.

"Well then, there you go. You aren't your mom." I pat his leg gently and smile. "You can't be anyway. You're far too much of a Golden Retriever for cheating."

"Golden Retriever?"

"Yeah. Like you have Golden Retriever energy." I nod like I am making perfect sense.

"What does that even mean?" He laughs, leaning forward.

"It means you have this hyper energetic, lovable, loyal vibe going on. Ivy said it's what all the guys on the internet want to be."

"Guys want to be compared to Golden Retrievers?"

"It's the newest trend." He is closer now, but he's also smiling. Thank god. My heart couldn't take the serious, upset expression for too much longer.

"Kids are weird."

"Tell me about it." I turn to him, and somehow we've gotten even closer. We're inches apart now. We've crept so close to one another, and I didn't even notice. "Do you think you'll have kids one day?"

His eyes shine with something close to excitement. "I hope so. I would love to have kids."

"Even though they're weird?"

"Yeah, even then." He edges closer, and I don't pull back. "I think I'd be a cool dad. I'm fun."

I nod gently, agreeing. "You are."

"What about you?" he asks. His warm hand slides over my knee, and I glance at it. His fingers are spread over my thigh. It's so large, it takes up half it.

Fuck. Fuck. *Fuck.*

"What about me?" I whisper.

"Do you want to have kids?"

"I don't even know what I want for breakfast tomorrow." This makes Flynn laugh. I sigh. "Maybe. One day."

"One day?"

"Yeah. If I'm with the right person." Flynn looks deep in thought, but he never takes his eyes off me.

"Who's the right person?" he asks. I shake my head a little and shrug. "Katie ..."

My breath hitches. My eyes move down to his lips, and I swallow hard.

"I think …" I lick my lips, trying to think clearly. "I think we should go to bed."

"Is that what you want?" he asks in a quiet voice.

I don't answer. I can't answer. I'm torn in half. Part of me knows this is a bad idea, that I set ground rules, and I should keep them. But the other half, the one that's horny and remembers what it feels like to have Flynn Reed's mouth on mine in great detail, begs me to just lean forward.

I shake my head, the tiniest bit, and he takes it as an invitation. His lips meet mine, and I sink into him. He tastes just as good as he did months ago.

Chapter Eleven

Katie

Grant.

His name flashes across my screen for the fifth time today. I ignore it. I've been ignoring a lot of things lately. Grant's calls. My mother's calls. Flynn. After our kiss in the living room over a week ago, I have been avoiding him like my life depends on it. On Monday, I snuck out of the house and hid at the bar. Then he went back to training after their bye week, and I swapped my day shifts at the bar for nights. I've posted four new videos this week on the channel simply because I didn't want to go home.

Kissing him was ... unexpected.

The alcohol helped, but I wanted him, too. The moment he started talking about his parents and his mom's affair, I had the overwhelming urge to hold him, to comfort him. I moved closer. I put myself right next to him. I wanted him to kiss me, and I let him do it.

It was the after that was the problem. I broke the rules. I told myself we could never go there again. I made a promise to myself when I moved into his house and agreed to be his fake girlfriend that I was just using the opportunity to get some space from my family and my past, and figure things out. I was supposed to be using him just like he was using me to get a contract, to re-sign and help his reputation.

Except, I'm not even sure that's his reason anymore. Maybe they weren't his at all to begin with. He wants to be friends. He takes me bowling for a laugh and lets me choose the takeout we eat each night. He even watches my stupid renovation shows.

But, he's also a playboy. A flirt.

It's confusing and I hate it.

How am I supposed to figure out what I want with my life when I can't even figure out an open book like Flynn Reed?

Not to mention, my son of a bitch ex-boyfriend won't stop blowing up my phone. I should just block his number. But, if I do that, I'm scared he'll turn up on my doorstep. Or worse, he'll turn up on Flynn's.

I wish that when he'd gone radio silent after the game where Flynn and I hard-launched, he would've stayed there. Grant is making this so complicated. My finger hovers over the decline button, but there's no need to press it. It stops ringing, and I let out a breath.

Maybe I should tell someone about what actually happened between Grant and I. Every time my phone rings, it's like he's coming back to haunt me, reminding me that I haven't dealt with him, that I haven't really closed that chapter in my life. I preached therapy and healing to Ivy for so long, yet I can't take my own advice.

Why can't I just take my own advice?

My phone vibrates against the bartop, and I glance down at it, dread filling my stomach. Grant was never one to text me before. He preferred a phone call, even for the little things. It was annoying as fuck. He would get so pissed off when I didn't pick up.

My heart skips when I see the name on my screen.

Flynn: Are you going to come home tonight, or are you still hiding out at the bar?

Instinctively, I look up and around the bar like I'm expecting him to be sitting in a booth in the corner, watching me. He's not. Am I disappointed? Maybe.

Me: I have a shift.

Flynn: Yeah, yeah. You're avoiding me. I get it.

Me: I'm working. Not everything is about you, Reed.

I groan and drop my head on the bar. I'm a liar. I'm such a liar.

Flynn: We're playing in Texas Sunday, so I'll be flying out tomorrow and will be back on Monday.

Flynn: You can safely return home as I won't be there.

Me: I'm not avoiding you.

Flynn: You're making yourself a liar. You good with that?

A smile tweaks at my lips, and I hate that I want to laugh. I hate that without even trying, he's starting to understand me and read my moods. I don't even know when I let him in, but he's in, and he's not leaving.

Me: It's football season. The bar is busy.

I tap my fingers on the bartop before replying to him again.

Me: Have a safe flight, and good luck with the game.

Flynn: I know you'll be watching, being the manager of a sports bar and all. I'll make sure to give you a shout-out when I score.

I laugh, closing the text chain. The man is ridiculous.

I rest my cheek against my palm and look over the patrons in the bar. It's a quiet night, a hockey game is on the TV screens, but it's not a Boston team, so they're barely watching. Before we started this fake dating charade, Flynn would be in here most nights. He'd order a burger and a beer. He'd sit in a booth with his phone propped up, watching game tapes. He'd also watch me.

I always felt his eyes on me, and now that they're gone, I'm finding that I miss them. He's only come back to the bar after the fight. I'm not sure if it's because of Hollie and her directive, or if he simply doesn't want to. Or, maybe it's because he sees me at home.

Who knows.

I miss him, though. I didn't realize how ... special it made me feel, wanted even, when he was here each night. I ignored him, I avoided eye contact, and I threw him nasty glares, but he kept coming back. He kept coming up with ways to talk to me. He kept staring at me. In the four months between Italy and the bar fight, Flynn became a constant in my life, and I didn't even realize it.

I open the text thread with him, my fingers hovering over the screen as I think about what to say. What is there to say?

I miss you, but I hate that I miss you.

I want you to kiss me again, but I think I'll have a meltdown if you do.

I swipe up and out of it, going for the YouTube app on my phone. When it loads, it almost crashes while loading all of the notifications. I swipe through some of them. My cover of 'Better Man' has blown up. Just over a million views and still counting. My other, older videos are creeping up as well. I smile a little and refresh the screen. More subscribe notifications pop up.

This channel started as my release for when I needed to play music. It is a safe space that is mine, and mine alone. Now, according to the comments, it's others' safe space too, and I think I'm okay with that.

***

Flynn: Did you see my celebration of the touchdown in the 4th quarter?

Me: You mean the incredibly cheesy wink and the kiss you blew toward the camera?

Flynn: That was all for you.

Me: And everyone else who was watching the game.

Flynn: But you watched, and that celebration was for you.

Me: *eye roll emoji*

Flynn: Are you home?

Me: No, at the bar working, why?

I watch the three dots appear and disappear twice before Flynn goes silent. I tap my nails against the bar and stare at my phone. Nothing.

Damn it.

Ever since he messaged and called me a liar on Friday night, we've been texting. One long, non-stop conversation. Sometimes, when I don't know what to say and leave him on read for too long, he'll just text me something random, like *What's your favorite pasta?* and change the subject. It's been the longest conversation I've probably ever had over text, and I've been smiling at my damn phone all weekend. Every time I see his name on my phone, I jump for it.

On Sunday, I leaned on the bar for the entirety of the Broncos game against Texas. Ivy came by to watch it with me, both of us glued to the game. I caught the wink. I caught the kiss blown. Knowing it was for me like he'd said, my face turned the same color as a tomato, and I had to go sit in the walk-in fridge in the kitchen until it went down.

It is becoming very inconvenient because I'm always checking my phone and waiting for his reply. After Grant, I promised myself never again. After Italy, I promised myself never again with Flynn. He was a rebound. I was supposed to look back on my one-night stand with him with fondness, but I was supposed to be realistic.

Smiling at my phone and waiting for his text is so far from realistic.

I frown at my screen, quiet with no reply, and shake my head.

"Get a grip," I whisper to myself, and I throw it underneath the bar and into my bag.

"Are you talking to yourself now? You know they say it's one of the first signs of madness," a deep voice says, amusement laced in his words.

I look up. Flynn Reed, with his bright eyes and bulging muscles, stands in front of me. He is so devastatingly handsome, it hurts. Blond hair, a greeny-blue mix swirling in his eyes. I would never admit it to him, but I could stare at him all day.

I suck in a breath and try to control the smile that is threatening to break out. "Hi."

"Hey." He lifts a hand in an awkward wave as he comes over to the bar. He shrugs off his coat and leans down, resting his forearms on the bartop. My gaze follows the deep lines his veins create along the muscle, and I swallow.

"What are you doing here?" I ask. I knew he was flying home today, but I expected to see him at home. Or tomorrow, depending on whether I stay late to play music tonight.

He shrugs. "We ended up leaving later than we thought, and I was getting a ride with Scott. When you said you were working, I thought I'd come keep you company."

"Oh, I ..." I look around for his game bag. "Where's your stuff if you came straight from the airport?"

"Okay, so I went home first."

"Uh-huh?"

"I wanted to see you. Sue me." I roll my eyes, but my stomach is doing somersaults, and my heart is skipping every other beat. Since when did I start losing my cool around this man?

Since he kissed me, probably.

"You've seen me. I'm working, like I told you I was. You can go now."

He just smiles and takes a seat at the bar. "No. We need to talk."

"I'm busy," I say, gesturing around me.

Flynn raises a brow. "There isn't anyone here. You're dead quiet."

"I have lots of paperwork to do before tonight. There's a game on, and we're doing a two-for-one on steak. It's going to be busy."

"So talk to me now. While you're not busy."

"I—" I try to think of some other excuse to give him, but I fail.

"Please, Katie? I think we really need to talk."

My heart sinks at his expression. He looks like a lost puppy, and it pulls at my emotions more than I'd like it to. "Fine, we can talk," I agree. "Do you want a drink at least?"

"Nah. You're good." He shakes his head.

I settle in front of him, my hands clasped together on the bartop, inches from his. He leans further forward. "I'm sorry for kissing you last week."

My face immediately heats up at the memory. The kiss.

Kissing Flynn had felt like getting rain after months and months of drought. Like I had remembered what it had been like, but my mind had dampened the reality over time. His lips were soft, urgent, molding to mine so perfectly, I thought I might kiss him forever. Yet I could tell he held back.

I look up at him through my lashes. "Oh?"

"Judging by the way you ignored and avoided me all week, you didn't want me to."

"No, I—" I take a deep breath and raise my chin. "It's not that. I just ... I just don't think us getting involved is a good idea."

He stares at me, his eyes flickering over my face. When his gaze settles back on mine, and we spend a minute just staring at each other, he finally lets out a breath. "Do you regret it?"

"I don't know." It's the most honest answer I can give him right now.

"Do you want to kiss me again?" he asks.

My body lights up at the thought, but my brain screams at me to say no. "I don't know."

Flynn simply nods. "Okay."

"Okay?"

"Yeah, okay. You don't know what you want right now, and that's fine. I can give you time to figure it out. I won't kiss you again until you ask me to." He looks up, his next words sharp, and there is no way for them to be misinterpreted. "To be clear, I would very much like to kiss you again. But I'll wait."

I'm not sure what to say to that, so I stay silent, gently nodding my head and dropping my gaze. I study my nails. Jesus, they're looking neglected.

"But I want to be friends."

My head snaps up. "Friends?"

"Like proper laugh and talk and have a fun time together friends. No more avoiding, no more lying about you working because I know you switched your shifts last week to avoid seeing me."

I narrow my gaze, challenging him. "I really was working, though. My regular night bartender wanted to do a week of days."

"Ivy told Scott, who told me." He smirks smugly.

Goddammit. I am never telling Ivy anything ever again.

Okay, that's a lie, but she's definitely going to hear about this from me.

"Please?"

I lean back, studying his face. He looks genuine, and I suppose it would make spending time with him in public a lot easier. The heat on his drunken bar fight has died right down now, and there probably isn't much point continuing the charade, but as Hollie told me last week when I called to ask her how much longer this would have to go on, the team still hasn't committed to re-signing Flynn.

So, we're in it for as long as it takes.

"Fine." I hold out my hand to him. "Friends."

His big hand envelopes mine, swallowing it as he takes hold and grins at me.

I'm so screwed.

CHAPTER TWELVE
FLYNN

Friends. She's agreed to be friends.

Even though I can't stop thinking about the kiss from the other week, I'll take the agreement to be friends with open arms. It's something. It's definitely more than what she's given me over the last few months.

I can work with friends.

Katie and I have fallen into a comfortable routine. From the inside, we're friendly and good roommates. We eat together and hang out at night. We catch each other in the morning at times, and if I'm making coffee, I'll always make her a cup. If I'm heading to a late afternoon gym session, I'll ask if she wants to join. If I'm finishing late at the stadium and I know she's working, I'll walk over to Pat's, sit at the bar, and order a burger to keep her company.

From the outside, we look and act like a fucking couple.

Scott pointed it out one Saturday afternoon when the girls roped us in to following them around the mall while they shopped. Every time Katie made a purchase, I immediately put my hand out for the bag. I would've paid too, but the first time

I tried, she looked like she was going to rip my balls off and keep them in a jar just for suggesting it.

I prefer to keep my balls exactly where they are, thank you very much.

As I carried every single bag without complaint, laughed and joked with my friend, Scott was watching. The next day, as we were warming up on the field for our home game, he bluntly said it.

"You don't look at her like a friend."

"What?" I replied, too busy trying to find where the girls were sitting. They'd opted for seats on the barrier rather than the box, even though it was freezing.

"You and Katie. You don't look at her like a friend. You don't act like her friend either." I didn't have an answer for him, so I shrugged, and he dropped the subject.

He is right, though.

I don't look at her like a friend because every time I look at her, I'm thinking about kissing her. About having her in my bed again. Every time she's close, I come up with an excuse to touch her. I tease her. I want to get under her skin like she's under mine.

My thoughts and my actions are definitely not *friendly,* but I'm getting really good at pretending.

"Something smells amazing," Katie says as she appears in my open living and kitchen area. The fire is going, and I decided to forgo the takeout this evening, opting to cook her my infamous vodka pasta that I learned from a TikTok video last year. What? I enjoy a doom scroll as much as the next guy.

"I'm making pasta for dinner if you're keen for some." I fold the cooked pasta through the sauce, generously covering it. I take the chicken breasts from the oven and place them in a bowl, using forks to gently pull them apart.

"Where did you learn to cook? I thought your culinary skills began and ended with ordering takeout every night for dinner." She leans over the kitchen counter as she watches me.

I laugh, tapping the fork against the edge of the bowl before turning around to the stove so I can pour the chicken into the sauce and pasta. I stir it all together and turn off the heat. "I learned in college. Scott and I moved out of the dorms after freshman year and lived in an apartment on campus. If we didn't learn how to cook, we didn't eat."

"Your college team didn't have chefs?" she asks as I dish up the food.

I nod. "But not living on campus meant that we didn't always stay at the stadium for meals or go early enough to grab break-fast before training. I don't know if you've noticed, but Scott's a bit of a loner. He was the exact same in college."

"And you aren't the same?"

"I like to think that I've grown up."

She hums, pulling the bowl toward her. "Bet you were a party boy," she says, smiling at me like she has me pinned.

"I had my fun in college, but I was a division one athlete. I couldn't have too much fun. I was there to play football, so that's what I did."

"So, you and Scott played for the same college?"

I nod, watching her face melt as she takes a bite of the pasta gathered on her fork. "I was actually a QB in high school. But when I got to college and was in training camp, competing against Scott, it was obvious he was the better man for it. So I shifted. I wanted to be on the field, and it turns out I'm not half bad at catching a ball."

"Mm." She nods, her mouth full. I smile as I watch her swallow and her eyes roll into the back of her head. "Fuck, that's really good."

My chest almost explodes at her praise, and I lock down my smug smile. I tuck into my bowl of pasta, sneaking glances at her every now and then. Katie scrolls on her phone while she eats, looking through playlist after playlist as she adds songs she finds to another playlist. I want to lean over for a better look at her screen, but I don't. That would be a breach of her privacy, and I'm trying to get on her good side. Besides, I would never do that to her, even if she has me curious.

Something vibrates against the benchtop, and I glance up, my gaze zeroing in on Katie's phone. My stomach drops, and all the joy I felt only moments ago, watching her devour something I made her, completely fades.

Grant.

Fucking Grant.

Ex-boyfriend Grant.

I hold in a groan as I watch her eye the phone. She doesn't stop it; she doesn't send him immediately to voicemail. She just lets it ring out.

"You don't need to take that?" I say, my words coming out with more bite than I intend.

Katie glances up at me. "No."

"You sure?" The phone vibrates again, and we both stare at it.

Even though she doesn't make a move to pick up the call, or even text the guy after it goes to voicemail, red-hot jealousy surges through me. Why the fuck is he calling her? Twice in a row, too. How often does he call? Does she ever actually pick up? Or is she just not picking up because I'm sitting right across from her and she doesn't want to take it in front of me? Does she want to talk to the douchebag?

Fuck. I want to ask her to answer all of my questions. I want to demand to know what's going on, but I resist. I'm trying to be a gentleman, to be respectful, so I can't demand to know these things when it isn't my place.

The brutal reminder that our relationship is fake slams into me.

I take a deep breath and push my chair out. "Do you ... I mean, I can give you some space if you want to talk to him?"

"I don't." She stabs another piece of pasta with her fork.

"Are you sure?"

"Yep," she replies, popping the *p*.

I continue to stare at her, tracing the lines of her face and her features. I can't tell if she's angry or sad. That's the thing about Katie—sometimes she's an open book and others, it's like she's hidden herself behind these hundred-feet-high and ten feet thick walls. No one gets past them unless she lets them.

When her walls are down and we're laughing and having fun together, I see the girl I started falling for in Italy. The one that I was so sure was falling for me, too. When they're up, it's like the lights have gone out and I'm walking around blind.

We finish dinner in silence. Katie stops scrolling on her phone and starts absentmindedly playing with one of the curls that's fallen over her shoulder as she stabs at the pasta. When she finishes, she looks lost in thought and a million miles away, just twirling the fork in her hand.

"I'll take this," I say gently, not wanting to startle her out of her thoughts. I reach over and slide her empty bowl toward me, then I take the fork from her hand.

"Thanks for dinner," she replies quietly. "You should cook more often. You're good at it."

"I can make that and grill a good steak. That's about it."

"I'm an okay cook. I suppose I could teach you? Purely to ensure that your football millions aren't being wasted on food delivery." She smiles a little as she pushes back from the kitchen bench. Hesitating, she grabs her phone and heads for the hallway.

I stare at her, hair swaying down her back as she walks away from me, and my heart clenches. I don't want her to go. Whatever mood those phone calls have put her in has pissed me off. She was smiling before, laughing and teasing. Now, she's gone into her shell. I hate it.

And I hate fucking Grant for doing it.

"Want to watch a movie?" I blurt out. It's not too late, but it's definitely not early enough to be starting a movie and hoping to still get to bed on time. I will pay for being tired at training in the morning, and will likely fall asleep in the meetings by the afternoon, but it's worth it.

"Don't you have a strict bedtime?"

"*Wicked* just dropped on Netflix. Sue me, but I'm an Ariana fan from way back."

Katie giggles, and it feels like a victory. "Of course you are. First, you have a Taylor Swift record mounted in your hallway, and now you're admitting to being an Ariana fan."

"I'm a pop music fan." I step around the kitchen bench and toward her. When I stand close enough in front of her, I wrap a finger around the curl she was playing with before. "Are you judging me for my music taste?"

"No." She laughs. "No, of course not. I'm just saying, it's predictable."

I smile and tug on her hand. "Come on, I'm dying to see it." I take a few steps back, toward the couch, pulling her gently with me.

"It goes for three hours or something. Are you sure?"

"Yeah, why the hell not? I'm an adult. Bedtime, shmedtime."

"As long as you don't blame me if you're tired and grumpy when you wake up tomorrow, fine. I have a day off, so I can sleep in."

Another victory.

I pull her over to the couch and sink into the cushions. Katie moves over into the corner of the couch. This is her favorite place to sit, tucked into the corner and being swallowed by the cushions. I swipe the remote and turn on the TV.

"So is it just Taylor and Ariana, or are you a fan of Olivia, too? Katy Perry? Adele?"

"Adele is a lyrical genius." I nod. The movie starts to play on the screen. I toss the remote onto the seat between us and settle back. "Shh. It's starting."

"You're worse than a teenage girl," she says, laughing

I smile, my chest tightening at the thought that I think I actually succeeded in bringing up her mood. I throw her a look of feigned annoyance. "Shh."

***

When I wake up the next morning, I'm sprawled across the couch. One leg dangles over the edge, my foot resting on the floor.

A weight presses into my side, my arm numb, and that side of my body warm. I am desperate to stretch out, to wriggle my fingers and toes and get the feeling back into my body, but something in me warns me to go slow, to be careful.

I crack an eyelid open, and then the other. Blinking in the low light, the room comes into focus. I inhale cinnamon and whiskey. *Katie.*

I look down. Her body is wedged between me and the back of the couch, her legs tangled with mine. Her face is pressed into my chest, eyelashes fluttering as she sleeps. Her hair is thrown over my arm, covering some of the back of the couch. One of my arms, the numb one, is curled around her, holding her to me. The other is thrown up and behind my head. As I wake up properly, I realize that there's something warm pressed against my crotch. It could be a pillow; the throw from the couch could be bundled right on top of it. I stare at the roof and take a deep breath. When I look down, a grin spreads across my face.

Katie's hand is on my dick.

Her hand, so warm and relaxed, is down my shorts, her fingers splayed over my cock. Her hands are warm and relaxed. And, in case you missed it, resting against my cock.

Jesus fucking Christ.

We fell asleep watching *Wicked*, and at some point, we tangled together. What a way to wake up. I close my eyes and will myself to go back to sleep, to savor this moment. My feelings for Katie have only grown since having her in my space. I want to unlock her secrets and get into her head just like she has mine. I'm starting with friends, and I'll respect it if she puts her foot down and says that's all we are, but until that day, I'm going to keep trying.

Fake relationship or not, there's nothing fake about what happened in Italy.

That felt—that was—all real.

I stare at the ceiling for what feels like another hour. The sun is fully risen, and the room is bathed in light. I haven't been able to fall back asleep, but I close my eyes and just lie here, breathing her in. Gently, so as not to wake her, I stroke my fingers through her long hair.

It's soft and silky to the touch. I wrap one of the loose curls around my finger, twisting the strands before letting them fall loose again.

I can pinpoint the moment Katie wakes. Her breathing changes, her body freezes. She goes impossibly still against me. My eyes are still closed, and I force myself to relax. I do not want to embarrass her, or let on to the fact that I knew her hand was on my dick and I did nothing about it. I feel her move, her hand twitching against me. I start counting backwards from a hundred to keep myself in check.

Her hand moves again, her fingers flexing, and I have to hold in a groan.

Ninety-seven ... ninety-six ... ninety-five ...

Don't get hard. Don't get hard. *Don't get hard.*

Her hand starts to slide away and over my hip, and I feel the breath I was holding in my chest release. Once her hand is clear, I feign a stretch and open my eyes.

Bright blue stares up at me through long lashes. Her cheeks are flushed, rosy pink, and her bottom lip is pulled between her teeth. It's so cute, I want to tug her lip free and devour her mouth.

But I won't.

She's not there yet.

"Morning," I say, my throat dry and my voice deep. I feel her shiver against me, still staring.

"Hi," she whispers. "We fell asleep."

"You may have been right about the three-hour movie."

"I'm always right," she says, a smile forming on her lips.

I smile down at her, and the hand I still have wrapped around her gently traces a path down her arm. She shivers again and then pushes a palm into my chest and sits up. "Oh my god, what time is it?"

I look around for my phone. "No idea."

Katie finds hers first, gasps, and then turns the screen toward me. Eight oh one.

Shit.

"Fuck, I'm going to be late." Untangling our legs, I rush off the couch, throwing cushions on the ground in search of my phone. I find it buried under a few in the corner at our feet. Thankfully, no missed calls or texts. I shoot off a text to my offensive coach and tell him I might be late. I'll get fined, but if I rush, I might just make it to walk out.

I make my way to the hallway, wanting to rush upstairs to splash some water on my face and change before I jump in the car, but I stop, my socks sliding against the wood flooring as I grab hold of the door frame. I turn on my heel and head back to the couch, where Katie still sits, yawning and blinking to wake herself up properly.

"Thank you for watching with me. Even if we fell asleep halfway through." I bend down and kiss her on the cheek. Her blush deepens.

"Oh," she replies, her voice a little breathless. "That's okay. It was nice. Watching a movie."

"Agreed. We should do it again." She opens her mouth, probably to disagree, but I just wink and jog out of the room. Yes, I jog. I don't want to give her any time to push back on me and put those walls up.

The drive to the stadium is easy since I don't live far. I make it to the locker room to change into my practice gear and run out onto the field just as the last of the boys are walking out. My phone dings in my pocket, so I fish it out.

Hollie: You will be attending the Annual Boston Thanksgiving Charity Ball next weekend. Black tie. Get Katie a dress. You will be photographed. No ifs, buts, or whys. You're going. I will drop the tickets off this week.

Chapter Thirteen

Katie

I should never have agreed to this.

Never.

Not in a million years.

Here I thought it was going to be a few dates, maybe even a double with Ivy and Scott, and some appearances at the games. A kiss here and there for the paps. I thought I would get some space from my parents, my past, my future choices, and only have to play pretend at home games. If I knew when I agreed that a ball—a proper, long gown and black tie ball—was going to be involved, I never would've said yes.

"Oh my god." I tug at the fabric around my stomach again, cursing at the way it hugs my figure. The dress I chose was on a whim. Ivy and I went to the mall last weekend, after Flynn dropped the whole 'we have to go to a charity ball' on me. He was incredibly generous and handed me his credit card as I walked out the door. I took it, only because I knew nothing I could afford would likely measure up to the kind of gowns the women who go to these things would be wearing.

We went to every store. I must have tried on over fifty dresses. I hated them all.

This one, I hated less.

Today, I hate it.

"Urgh." I groan again, trying to pull the dress up. It's a baby blue, strapless satin gown. It hugs my chest and makes my boobs look incredible, but it also hugs my waist and my hips. I have lived in my work clothes for the last few months, and now I am expected to step out in a dress that hugs every single curve I've been trying to hide?

I know I did this to myself, but still.

I stare at myself in the mirror, touching my hair and wriggling my toes. The shoes are five inches—at least—peep-toe strappy heels. I put on fake tan for the first time in years two days ago, and my skin is subtly glowing. There's a slit in the skirt, showing off my long legs. I am loving my hair, though. The hairdresser styled my natural wavy hair into some Hollywood curls. They fall freely down my back, the blonde bright against the blue of the dress and the tan on my skin.

Maybe if I hadn't spent four years with a man who never complimented my appearance, I wouldn't be having such a hard time right now. I adjust my boobs once more and turn back to my bed. I borrowed a small gold clutch from Ivy that isn't even big enough to fit my phone.

I place my lipstick, a powder brush, and a small, travel-size perfume into it. Holding that in one hand and my phone in the other, I stare at it for a moment.

I'll just ask Flynn to hold my phone. Men have pockets in suits; it'll make him useful.

I take one last glance at my appearance in the mirror, send up one last wish that when I get downstairs, he'll tell me it's been canceled and we can spend the evening at home ... maybe on the couch, watching a movie again.

I pause on the top step, the memories of waking up just over a week ago in his arms, on the couch, flooding me. Our legs were so tangled, my face was warm from being pressed against his chest, and my hand, well, it was doing just fine copping a feel of the infamous Flynn Reed's dick. Thank god I woke up first and managed to slip it out of his shorts before he noticed.

The thing is, I don't know if I have ever slept better. Maybe the night in Italy, where, again, I slept in his arms.

Once is a fluke. Twice is a pattern. I think?

I shake my head. I can't think about that now. I promised myself that day that I would be better at drawing the line with him. I imagine us on a beach, standing across from one another. Then, I imagine taking a giant stick and drawing a long, deep line in the sand.

Friends. We're friends.

The line is drawn.

I just need to be stronger at sticking to it.

Flynn is playful and cheeky. He's a flirt. I just can't let myself get confused over what's real and what's not. He's my friend, so we laugh and have a good time, but we aren't together, and we shouldn't be.

Right?

I groan again, but this time the noise echoes down the staircase. I hear a deep chuckle carry back up to me before Flynn appears.

I have to grab a hold of the railing because, goddamn.

He wears a black tuxedo with a crisp white button-down and a black bow tie. His hair, which is getting longer now, is styled to perfection. It looks as if it's had just the right amount of fingers run through, and there is one curl that falls over his forehead.

I take the stairs one step at a time, careful to hold on to the railing because the last thing I need is to fall down, embarrass myself in front of this man, and ruin the very expensive gown I purchased with his money. When I get to the last few steps, Flynn holds out his hand, and I let go of the railing, taking it instead.

His hands are rough from playing football, calloused and uneven. But, they're also warm. So warm, I get the urge to have him run them all over my body just to warm me up.

No.

No, Katie. I cannot think like this. I need to be strong.

Friends. We're friends.

"Thanks," I say, allowing him to guide me down the last steps. In heels, my five-foot-seven is more of a six-foot-something, making me closer to him. He normally towers over me, but now I could just lift up on my toes and press a kiss to his lips.

I won't.

But I could.

"You look ..." He trails off. "Gorgeous. You look really, really gorgeous."

I watch as his eyes roam over my body, and I heat under his gaze. I flex my fingers over my phone and mentally shake myself out of it. I cannot let myself get distracted by the way this man looks at me.

"Thank you." I do a small courtesy on a whim, and I feel my face go bright red. "You don't scrub up half bad yourself."

Flynn grins at me, taking my cue and bowing a little. Instantly, his actions put me at ease, and I relax. I even feel a smile tugging at my lips. "I knew I'd have the prettiest girl on my arm tonight, so I needed to make an effort."

"You're flattering me." I roll my eyes. "You're trying to get me to forgive you for inviting me to this charade."

"Is it working?"

"A little," I admit.

Flynn laughs and holds out his arm. "Shall we?"

I take his arm. There is a town car waiting outside. Hollie must have organized it for us because inside, there is a bottle of champagne and a note that says not to forget to smile and look like we're having a good time.

Flynn just shakes his head and pops the cork on the champagne, pouring it into two glasses. No Uber I've ever ordered had this kind of service.

"A girl could get used to this," I say as I raise the glass to my lips. Flynn just smiles and sips at his champagne. "So, have you been to this before?"

He nods. "A few years back, the team bought a table, but many of the boys couldn't show during the holiday. They all spend it with their families if we aren't playing a game on the day, and if we are, then they definitely don't want to spend the rest of the weekend at a ball in the city. So, I volunteer. My parents barely ever make it out this way."

I ignore the comment about his parents. I don't want to bring his mood down, and after what he shared, I feel like talking about his mom is a sore spot for him. "What's it like?"

"Boring. So, so boring." He takes a sip of his champagne. "A lot of small talk and then they dance for a while before some socialite eventually gets too drunk, makes a scene with whatever boy she managed to come with, and then everyone starts to leave. There is never really an end time; you just know when it's time to go."

"How strange." I pause, holding the burning question on my tongue before I can't any longer. "Were you the one who took the drunk socialite a few years ago?"

Flynn winks at me and grins. "Yes, but I only took her because I knew she would cause some sort of scene, and Hollie would be furious, then she would never make me go again. I've had three years off because of Heather Myer. Bless her."

"Heather Myer? As in the influencer who went on *Love Island*?"

"The very same."

"Hm." I take another sip of my glass. Heather is ... very pretty. She just isn't someone I imagined Flynn would go for. She's got short brown hair, is stick thin, and her social media presence is dubious at best. She's been canceled for things she's said on Instagram many times now.

"I know what you're thinking," he says, interrupting my thoughts.

I glance up at him over my glass. "Oh yeah? What's that?"

"That she isn't my type." I mash my lips together, staying silent, annoyed that he knows me well enough to guess right. "You're an open book."

He lifts a hand and tucks a stray curl behind my ear. "I am?"

"Tonight, you are."

"I'm not always?" I ask quietly.

"Not all the time. Sometimes you can be really hard to read, and there isn't a chance in hell that I'd know what you were thinking. But, tonight ..." Flynn runs a gentle finger down my bare arm, and I suppress a shiver. "Tonight, you're giving me everything."

His tone is deep. The words come out in a husky rasp, leaning closer to me as he says them. The shiver I tried to suppress rolls through me anyway, and I feel myself leaning in too.

It feels as if we stare at each other for an eternity. The air thickens, the silence engulfing us. I forget that we're in a car. I forget that we are headed for a charity event with a few hundred other people. I forget it all as I stare at Flynn Reed, the man who said he can read me.

You're so closed off. I never know what you want. You're emotionless unless it's a sarcastic comment.

Grant's words swirl around my head, over and over.

Whenever I asked him to do something, whenever I tried to communicate what I needed from him to feel better in our relationship, Grant would reply that he wasn't a mind reader. That he didn't ever know what I truly wanted because I'm so closed off. So emotionless. His exact words, in fact. I could only ever be happy and laughing around him; anything else, and he would switch off. He would ignore me until I was back to my 'normal self,' as he called it.

It was exhausting.

But this man, the one sitting with me in a town car, wearing a bowtie, just told me I'm an open book to him. *An open book.*

The car suddenly stops, and the driver's voice filters through the speakers in the back of the car. "We're here, Mr. and Mrs. Reed."

My gaze snaps to the window. Sure enough, the car has stopped outside the Boston Museum of Fine Arts. There are hordes of press waiting for the attendees, camera lights flashing nonstop. The partition's up, so I can't correct the driver on our status—not married, definitely not married—but I narrow my gaze and look back at Flynn.

He's smiling, shaking his head with a playful grin. "Relax, it's Hollie's idea of a joke. She's stirring the pot." My shoulders relax a little. Flynn holds out his hand to me. "Ready?"

I bite my bottom lip but nod. I slide my palm against his, and his grip tightens, holding my hand firmly as he opens the door and steps out. I put the glass back in the ice bucket on the floor of the car and slide across the seat to the open door. Flynn stands directly in front of me, helping me out of the car and shielding me from the cameras while I adjust my dress.

"You good?"

"Yeah, yes," I say, doing a last check of myself. "Oh, wait, my phone. It doesn't fit in my bag—"

Without me asking, Flynn takes my phone from the hand not holding his and slips it into his pocket. I smile gently. "Thank you."

"You're welcome." He tugs on my hand and closes the car door behind us. A small man with a headset on asks for our names, and when Flynn tells him, he lets us know that we are scheduled to walk the carpet for the event, and then we can go inside.

The entire event is nothing like I have ever experienced before. People calling Flynn's name, people calling *my* name. Reporters asking who I'm wearing and which of the many charities we will donate to tonight. Flynn makes a few comments, talking about charities for men's mental health and domestic violence survivors that he'll donate to.

He's switched on. His persona, the cheeky, charming number forty-nine, is out in full force. I wonder if the Broncos know just how much the press loves him. Just how well he represents the team when at events like this. I hope so, because seeing him right now, in his other element and playing to the public's whim, even I can tell that he's not just good at throwing and catching a ball.

I follow him along the carpet, staying silent as he answers questions and smiling as we take pictures. His warm hand doesn't leave my hip the entire time, and it burns my skin through the satin fabric of the dress.

When we finally make it through the front doors and find our seats, I'm falling into my chair just to get off my feet. Flynn sits down, frowning. I look around, wondering what could have possibly upset him, but then he leans forward and drags my chair closer to his.

Our thighs are pressed against one another, and it's causing my body to have all sorts of reactions. My stomach is turning, my heart is pounding, but most of all, I start to feel a gentle yet insistent throb between my legs.

Friends. We're friends.

No matter how many swoony things he does tonight.

Line, drawn, sand.

Remember?

"Do you want a drink?" Flynn murmurs in my ear, his hot breath sliding over my skin and setting me on fire.

"Uh," I stutter. "Sure. Yes, yes, please."

I watch him lift a hand and call over a waiter. He takes two glasses of champagne off the tray and passes one to me. I eagerly take a sip, but all the bubbly liquid does is fog up my head a little more. I'm getting overwhelmed. The sounds of the crowd chattering, the feel of his thigh against mine, and his hand on me, now resting on my knee as he sips his own drink. He's sitting so close that I can smell his spicy scent. It's not helping the brain fog.

"You okay?" he asks. I just stare at him.

You're an open book.

"I—yeah." I take another sip, the glass shaking in my hand as I bring it to my lips, and I feel his eyes on me, watching me so closely, it's as if I'm his favorite subject to study.

Judging by what he said in the car, I am.

"Why do you think I'm an open book?" I ask him, turning as much as I can in my chair to face him.

He looks confused at first, but he shakes it off quickly. "You just are. I can read you. Your body language, your facial expressions, the tone of your voice when you say things." He shrugs like what he's saying is the most normal thing in the world. "You just are."

"How long have you thought this about me?"

"What do you mean?"

"How long have you thought I'm an open book? Just while I've been living with you?" I press, urgency dripping from my tone.

"I—" He removes the hand resting on my knee to rub the back of his neck before setting it down on my leg again. I ignore the flare of heat that shoots through my veins from where he touches me. "Always, I suppose. Since I first saw you at Pat's, when I came in with Scott. It's more noticeable to me now because I'm around you, but I remember thinking that day that you looked like a girl who wears her emotions all over her face. The way you were glaring at Scott when he asked you to pass on his number."

"For so long?" I ask in a whisper. My breath catches in my throat, and I'm finding it difficult to get any air into my lungs.

"Katie? What's wrong? Should I not have said it? I'm sorry, I—"

Before he can finish, the emotions bubble, and I feel the familiar sting of tears behind my eyes. No way will I be crying in public, knowing there are about a million cameras pointed at us tonight. That is not a photo I want spread across gossip pages and on Instagram feeds. I push my chair back and stand. His hand slips from my leg with the movement.

I look around the room and spot the bathrooms, weaving my way through the tables and chairs toward the hallway that leads to them. I stumble on my heels just as I reach the entrance to the corridor, but a strong arm catches me around the waist and pulls me against their chest.

Strong spice, fresh grass, and vanilla surround me.

"Whoa," he murmurs, his voice low and strong against my ear.

Of course, he followed me.

"I'm fine. I just need a minute."

"You don't look fine."

"I am. I just need a minute, I promise."

"Tell me what just happened there." He pulls me deeper into the deserted corridor.

"I'm fine," I repeat.

Flynn lets out a low noise, something sounding close to a growl, and crowds me. I take a step back, and my back hits the wall. He leans a hand against the wall, just above my head, and leans over me. From the main room, where all the guests are, you wouldn't be able to tell we were down here, yet when I look down the corridor, I have a good view of anyone coming our way.

Flynn lifts a hand, his fingers grabbing my chin, and gently brings my attention back to him. "I hate that word. *Fine*. You're not fine. What just happened?"

"Grant never—" I swallow, blinking back the tears that start to form. "Grant always told me he couldn't read me. Four years we spent together, and he couldn't ever pick up on the little things. Yet you, who I've only known for a year or so, can read me like an open book, apparently."

"Not all the time," he says gently, releasing my chin to tuck a piece of hair behind my ear.

"But not never? You can sometimes."

"Most of the time, yes. I feel like I can figure out what you're thinking."

"It makes me mad that he could never do that. That he never tried. And then, I just get sad because I wasted four years with the asshole, just waiting for him to get it." I sniff and close my eyes.

I feel Flynn's fingers trace down my cheek, brushing along the lines of my facial features, waiting patiently for me to open my eyes. When I do, I'm met with swirling green-blue storms.

"Sorry," I whisper, dropping his intense gaze. "You must think I'm insane."

"No. No, I don't. It's a valid feeling." He smiles a little. "To be honest, makes me pretty fucking happy knowing I can do something that douchebag never could."

I laugh. It comes out watery and breathless, but my shoulders relax and I sag into the wall.

"You okay now?" he asks, tapping under my chin, prompting me to lift my eyes back to him. We both stare, our bodies going still. I swear, I can hear his heartbeat in the silence that's fallen around us. It's in sync with mine.

I lean forward, closing the gap and gently pressing my lips to his. I barely touch them, barely kiss him, before I pull back, meeting his eyes again. I'm trying to read him like he reads me, but I can't figure out what he's thinking. He said he wouldn't kiss me again, but I've kissed him.

There's a beat, and then another. And then, his hands sink into my hair, and he pulls me forward, his mouth covering mine.

Chapter Fourteen

Katie

His tongue slides over my bottom lip before his teeth sink down, biting me. His hands are tangled in my hair, and he tugs on the strands, keeping my head angled up and toward him. Our mouths move furiously against one another, fighting for dominance. He wins.

He sucks on my bottom lip, one of his hands dropping from my hand to press into my back. I arch into him, trying to get closer than I am. The satin fabric of my dress sticks to my curves, the slit down the leg falling open as my knee hitches up and against his waist. I feel his hand on my back slide over my waist, down the curve of my hip, and under my ass. His grip tightens, and he tugs, pulling me closer. I curl my ankle around his thigh.

I roll my hips against him, and I can feel the impressive bulge tightening under his suit pants. Fuck, but I missed his cock. Flynn is blessed. All the memories that I put away in a box and locked up from that night in Italy come crashing back in.

His lips move down my neck, using the grip he still has on my hair to angle my head so he has access. He sucks on the sensitive spot at the base of my neck, and I moan. The noise echoes into the empty corridor, and we both pause.

Flynn removes his lips from the spot, gently pressing kisses as he draws a path to my ear. He grazes his teeth across it, and his hot breath sends a shiver down my spine.

"Do you want me to stop?" he asks, sounding as breathless as I feel.

"I will kill you if you do." My eyes close and my head rolls back, falling against the wall. Flynn's hand softens the blow, still tangled in my hair. I feel his smile pressing against my skin as kisses along my jaw line, pressing one last peck against the corner of my mouth before he pulls back again.

He stares at me, his hand leaving my thigh and letting the leg that was curled around his body and hitched at his hip slowly drop to the ground. When he pulls the other hand from my hair, he takes a minute to smooth it out. I watch the green flecks swirl in his eyes as he studies my features. His hand cups my cheek, a thumb running over my bottom lip.

He steps back from me, glancing down the corridor. I follow his gaze, my head lolling against the wall. A few hundred people sit in the room just down the hall, drinking champagne in fancy dress and pushing food around their plates while they pretend not to judge each other. But not us.

No, we're hidden from view unless someone were to walk down the corridor directly toward us. The prospect of getting caught, of someone seeing me being crowded against a wall by

Flynn Reed, sends my head spinning and my stomach clench-
ing.

Do I want to get caught?

Maybe?

He smiles at me again, dropping his lips to mine, kissing me.
It's not urgent, more like he's taking his time. He's exploring,
allowing his tongue to feast on mine.

"You're gorgeous," he murmurs against my lips. "Stunning.
I've been fighting an erection since you came down the stairs."

I huff out a laugh, and he silences me with another kiss.

"You know, I never considered myself a jealous man." He
kisses down my throat again, his lips wet and hot on my skin.
"I'm not sure if it's because I never cared all that much for my
partners because they were temporary, or whether it's because
they weren't you. You, though. You make me a jealous man."

He runs his tongue along my exposed collarbone, pressing his
lips into the bare skin on my shoulder. "I make you jealous?"

"Mm. I wanted to rip every single man's eyes out while walking you through this ballroom tonight, just for staring at you.
For daring to look at the woman I came here with."

"That's ridiculous," I say, completely breathless as he starts
running his hands down my waist and over my hips. His fingers
curl into the fabric of the skirt. I arch into him again when I feel
his fingers brush against my inner thigh. My breath catches, and
I close my eyes again.

"Watch me, Katie," he says in a deep voice. "I'm going to
devour you, and I want you to watch."

Every single logical thought completely disappears as I open my eyes and watch Flynn sink to his knees. His hand curls around my ankle, starting a slow ascent up my leg. It traces up the curve of my calf, flicking the fabric out of the way when he reaches my knee. He leans in, pressing a kiss on my inner thigh.

Dear god.

Fake, who?

Nothing about the way he touches me feels fake. It never has. This right here is why I need to keep a safe distance from him. I knew he felt this good. I knew the moment he touched me, I would melt, right there on the spot. And here I am, watching as he single-handedly turns me into a puddle.

His lips continue their path up my inner thigh, and I hiss when he presses a gentle kiss against my barely-there panties. Damn it. He really is going to devour me.

I watch as he pulls back, his fingers replacing his lips as he strokes me. His eyes dart up to meet mine. There are so many emotions in his fiery gaze, and I have no trouble reading a single one. Desire spreads through me, all starting from the spot where he gently tugs at my panties. He hooks his finger in the band, and they fall down my legs. I carefully step out of them, and he snatches them from the ground. I expect him to hold onto them or hand them to me, so that after this is over, I can put them back on, but he doesn't. He shoves them in his pocket, his hands finding themselves back on my thighs and pushing my dress up to my hips.

Then, he leans forward again, disappearing under the skirt of my dress, his face buried between my legs. I lean back against the wall, trying desperately to balance as his tongue licks the length of me. Pleasure zips through me, and I feel myself getting wetter and wetter.

"Oh my god," I whisper, but the words feel louder as they echo. I take a hand and cover my mouth, muffling the moan I let out when I feel Flynn's tongue flick across my clit.

Fuck.

His fingers dig into my thighs, his lips sucking eagerly on my clit. He's devouring me, just like he promised. I roll my hips and try to move against his mouth, but his hands tighten on my thighs to keep me in place. I'm shaking, unsteady on my feet.

I feel one of his hands loosen and then slide down to my knee before he lifts my leg over his shoulder and presses himself further into me. I moan again, the sound muffling against my palm.

Oh my god. Oh my god.

I reach down, running my fingers through his hair, grabbing hold of his blond strands as he starts moving faster. He's sucking me, his tongue diving into me like it's searching for lost treasure. I gasp, grinding against him, searching for more friction.

A laugh echoes down the hall, and we still. Well, I go still. Flynn continues to eat away at me like I'm his favorite meal. I watch as two women stop at the entrance of the corridor. If they start making their way down here, toward us, there is no way they won't catch us.

Fuck, we're going to get caught.

I feel Flynn squeeze my thigh again, his fingers creeping further and further up. Then, I feel him bury them inside me. I gasp, my back arching as he pumps two fingers in and out of me. His lips wrap around my clit as he goes faster and faster.

He's trying to make me come.

There's someone right there, and he's trying to make me fall apart. He knows we could get caught, that someone could see us, and he doesn't care.

Do I care?

No.

No, I definitely don't.

I lean my head back on the wall, dropping my hand from my mouth and sinking both into his hair. "Please," I murmur, my words a whine of pleasure. "Please, Flynn."

He doesn't let up, he doesn't slow down.

I shatter against his mouth, his tongue, on his fingers. My pussy clenches, and I feel my orgasm surge through me, dripping onto the fingers he still has inside of me and my thighs. He stays where he is and rides out the waves of my orgasm until it completely subsides, and I'm trying to catch my breath. A moment later, he pulls back, adjusting my dress before he stands up.

I feel smaller now, even though I'm still closer to his height with my heels on. Flynn leans over me, his lips glistening with my arousal and curving into a satisfied smile. I smile back, my eyes feeling heavy and tired after coming so hard.

He lifts his fingers, still soaked with *me*, to my mouth. "Suck," he says, the words low and demanding.

I don't hesitate.

I wrap my lips around his fingers and suck them clean.

***

He doesn't give me back my underwear.

After Flynn makes me come in the corridor, he pulls me into the empty women's bathroom and locks the door. He takes a hand towel from the small pile and wets it with warm water from the faucet. Then he drops to his knees and cleans me up, pressing another soft kiss to my upper thigh when he's done.

And I let him. I let him clean me up, not one sarcastic comment or witty quip.

Have I ever been so silent after an orgasm? No.

Have I ever been eaten out like that in a public place before? Also no.

Does a part of me hope he might push me against the counter in the women's bathroom and fuck me instead of cleaning me up? Definitely, yes.

It's probably a good thing we didn't go any further. My spiral tomorrow morning when I finally reflect on what we've just done will be bad enough.

I cross a leg over my knee, and my foot bounces under the table. I keep throwing glances at Flynn's pocket, where my underwear is tucked in. I feel so exposed. The last time I would've sat through an event with no underwear on would have to have been in college. I tried rushing a sorority in my freshman year, but I was too opinionated, too loud for them. I shift in my seat, angling my knees toward Flynn as I lean an elbow on the table.

Dinner was delicious. At least, I think it was. I was too busy replaying the last hour's events to notice the meat I was eating or the taste. I'm completely distracted. I want to go again, even though logic screams at me not to even entertain the idea.

A warm hand slides down my calf, wrapping tightly around my ankle and stilling my movements. I look up at Flynn and, surprise, surprise, he's staring right back at me.

"Why are you anxious?" he asks softly, leaning toward me so he can speak quietly in my ear. I shake my head, a lump crawling up my throat. "You are. Your foot is bouncing like crazy, and you haven't been able to look me in the eye since we sat down."

"I'm fine."

His thumb presses into my ankle, finding a pressure point and circling it. My shoulders relax and I sit back in my chair. "Did I go too far? Did you not want me to touch you?"

"No," I say quickly. I take a deep breath and close my eyes. "I don't know. It was a lot. We had rules."

"Fuck the rules."

"They were there for a reason." I fidget with a fold in my dress, my fingers slipping over the satin. "We ... This was supposed to be just business. Remember?"

"I thought I said I wanted to be friends?"

"Friends don't do what you did to me in a corridor, at a public event," I whisper, avoiding his gaze again. Flynn hums, dropping his grip on my ankle and standing. He holds a hand out to me, and I hesitate.

"Friends dance though, right?" Even without looking up at him, my eyes still trained on his outstretched hand, I know he's smirking as he watches me struggle with indecision.

I slip my hand into his and roll my eyes as I get to my feet. Flynn leads me to the dance floor, my thighs rub together, and it's another embarrassing reminder that I'm completely bare under my dress.

When we reach the middle of the small crowd of people dancing, he wraps an arm around my waist and pulls me tighter to him. I am pressed right up against his chest, and my cheeks heat as I feel my nipples harden at the friction it creates.

Fuck, one round of oral has turned me into a horny bitch.

Large fingers close around my own, and he pulls our hands to his chest, swaying us on the spot easily to the music the band plays. I take a careful look around us, but no one seems to be paying us much attention. They're all too busy having their own conversations.

"You could at least give me my underwear back," I murmur.

He smiles victoriously and shakes his head. "No way. They're mine now."

"You can't keep them." He could. In fact, if he does, it'll probably be the hottest thing a guy's ever done after a hook-up.

Is it weird that I want him to refuse me? Say no and then absolutely keep them? I don't know. Flynn confuses me.

"They're mine." He bends down slightly, pressing his lips to my neck as he murmurs words against my skin. "Besides, it's making me hard knowing you're walking around tonight with nothing on. I could slip my hand down"—the hand he has on my back begins to lower, fingers brushing against the top of my ass—"and just feel you. Bare. Wanting."

My breath hitches, and I bite down on my lip as his hand curves over my ass. His fingers dig into the fabric of my dress, squeezing. I lean forward, trying to bury my face into his shoulder as I suppress a moan.

Fuck.

"Stop it." My voice is breathless, weightless, even though I mean the command to come out strong.

"Are you turned on?" I can hear the smile in his voice. His hand slides back up and rests on the small of my back again, creating enough warmth that I feel as though he might singe a hole in the dress.

"Whatever you're doing, it's not funny," I hiss as I pull back from him. His smile falls just a little, and his brows start to pull together.

"Katie," he begins, bringing his face so close to mine, I can't do anything but stare directly into his eyes. "I'm not sure I want to be your friend."

My heart stops beating in my chest. My mouth goes dry, and I feel my stomach twist. Instead of asking him what he means or why, or trying to have the proper, adult conversation about why I won't get into anything more with him, I divert and distract. "You want to be enemies instead?"

"No—"

"Because we can be enemies, but I think the fighting and the snarky comments and the hatred give the opposite message to what Hollie has been trying to achieve. And, I would win all the arguments. Obviously."

It works, and Flynn rears back. "Why do you get to win?"

"Because I'm always right."

"That's so not true."

I shrug. "These are my terms. If you're serious and you want to be—"

Flynn cuts me off by kissing me.

Well.

That is one way to shut me up, yes.

His lips move against mine, and I sink into him. The hands that I'd hesitantly placed on his shoulders relax and start creeping toward his hair. My arms encircle his neck, and I pull him in, erasing any space between our bodies, his touching mine everywhere.

God, I love the way he kisses me.

My eyes flutter and I see, in my periphery, a flash go off. A camera flash. I jerk backward, and my head spins, trying to find the culprit. Flynn frowns, finding the guy at the same time as I do. He gives us a nod and a thumbs up, then walks off. I cringe. It was a setup.

I step back, out of Flynn's arms.

"I think I'm ready to go." I look around. There are still people everywhere. Dancing, sitting at tables talking, crowding the bar. I don't even know what time it is because Flynn has my phone. "Can we go?"

"We can. If you want," he says gently, stepping back into my space and circling me with his arms again. "But I want to finish this conversation first."

"Why did you kiss me?" I ask.

"Because I wanted to."

"Not because you knew there was going to be a camera and Hollie had told you that you had to?"

"Fuck no." He lifts a hand, brushing his thumb against my lip, and then tucks a loose piece of hair behind my ear.

"I can't be ... I don't want to be in a relationship." I lie through my teeth. What I should have said is that I don't want to be in another relationship like the one I was in. One where I had to fight for attention, and went to sleep each night alone, worrying where my partner was. Where I forgave unforgivable things because I truly believed that's all I deserved. Where, after four years, I completely lost who I was, and now I'm drowning just trying to figure it out.

Flynn isn't Grant. Deep down, I know that.

But I can't take the risk. Maybe Italy was nothing. Maybe it was just harmless flirting. Maybe he would be different in a relationship.

I don't want *maybe*, though.

I want ... no, I need more.

"I—" I can see him searching my face, trying to figure out what I'm thinking, but the mask is on now. I am playing pretend again.

"But I also really liked you making me come," I say, my voice low. My face is certainly blushing a deep red, but I hold my ground. "We can do that again, friend."

"Like ... you want to be friends with benefits?" He sounds confused, eyes still flickering over my features, but I just smile up at him. After a beat, he seems to come to a decision, and his features relax. The set line of his lips curls into a smile, and his eyes shine as he asks, "What are your rules?"

Chapter Fifteen

Flynn

My job comes with a natural high.

The stadium's full of people. The yelling, the chanting. The high after a win, after a play that shouldn't have worked but pays off. Adrenaline rushes through my veins. It makes me bounce on my toes and warms my body. Every time I work out, train on the field, or play, I feel the high that is professional football.

In the early days of my career, I didn't think anything else could feel this good.

Until Katie.

Fucking her. Laughing with her. Getting to be in her orbit.

It's like nothing I've ever experienced.

I crave her. I want to be around her constantly. I want to touch her whenever she's in the same room, to kiss her whenever she'll let me. In a matter of weeks, my life oriented itself around Katie Murphy. Even now, I feel her presence before I see her. I look over to the seats just behind the team's bench on the fifty-yard line, and there she is. She's wearing a white knitted beanie and probably the largest puffer jacket I've ever seen. Her curls fall over her shoulder, and the ends lift with the wind. She and Ivy stand with the rest of the crowd, taking part in whatever celebration is going on as the offense walks off the field and changes over. As we get closer, the red on the tip of her nose becomes clear, and I get the urge to run over to the barrier and kiss her.

She's just so damn adorable.

I won't. Coach would kill me. Hell, Scott would kill me, but only after reminding me how whipped I am by my girl. I grin, running a hand through my hair as I take off my helmet and shake the strands loose. One of the assistant coaches passes me a team beanie, and I shove it on and over my ears.

Since Thanksgiving, Katie and I have practically been playing house. She calls us friends with benefits, but I've decided to ignore that part. She sleeps in my bed. She lets me cook for her, lets me distract her at work, and lets me kiss her whenever I like.

I'm not sure what it is, but it's definitely not fucking friends with benefits.

She laid out new rules. Don't get too handsy in front of her family if they're at the bar, don't get attached, and don't fall in love. I waved them all off and grinned like an idiot. Just as I had been dragging her out of the charity ball, bailing early so I could take her home and give her a few more orgasms, she'd said the one thing that could make my heart stop.

Don't forget the end date. You get re-signed, I make a decision about the future, and we end after the season is over. Go our separate ways.

That's the only rule I'm not sure I can brush off.

I don't want to let her go now that I've got her. I don't think I can.

We're in the fourth quarter, and with less than a minute on the clock, my knee starts to bounce. Not because it's a relatively close game—we're smashing them—but because I know as soon as the whistle goes, I get to have her back in my arms. She's become the adrenaline I chase more so than football, the better natural high.

Kissing her, being with her, is better than anything, and I could probably be happy spending the rest of my days trying to convince her that she should want that with me, too.

So she's put an end date on this *fun*—her words, not mine—that we're having. And yes, she's stubborn and opinionated and does whatever the hell she wants, so I have no doubt that if, at the end of this season, she wants to walk away, she'll do it.

But I don't want that.

I want her to stay.

The whistle goes, the game ends, and I clap my teammates on the back, celebrating a hard-earned win. Another game that cements our position at the top of the leaderboards and will likely help us clinch an early playoffs spot. Something I wanted before, but am desperate for now, because if Katie only wants to give me until the end of the season, then I'm going to make this season the longest one I possibly can.

***

I can hear the music the moment I step out of my car.

Wednesdays are annoyingly long, especially the closer we get to the playoffs. We have morning practice, lunch, meetings, strength training, tape, and more meetings. Game tape sessions can go on forever, knowing who else is likely to get through. I practically ran from the stadium, sped home, just so I could make sure I was in time to cook Katie dinner.

Apart from when I've had to travel for away games this month, I've cooked her a meal every night. I used to hate cooking; it seemed pointless when it was only me. It was a waste because I never felt like eating all the leftovers. But it feels easier now. Last weekend, as we flew home from Atlanta, I spent the entire time on a recipe website, saving all the meals I thought she might like.

I like knowing that I'm the one who gets to feed her, that I'm the only one who gets to see the way her face lights up and her eyes roll back when she really likes something.

So when I pull up to the house and hear the music, my first thought is that she's invited Ivy over and she's having a girls' night. The second is that she's decided to get drunk.

I never expected to find this. I lean on the hallway frame that opens up into the kitchen and living room. Music blasts through the speakers connected throughout the house—Whitney Houston's 'I Wanna Dance With Somebody'.

There's flour all over the kitchen countertop. Eggs, cracked and discarded off to the side. A few mixing bowls are piled in the sink. A bag of icing sugar lies on its side, and a box of sprinkles leans on a plate, the contents spread across it. I take a deep inhale. Cake. Or maybe, cupcakes. Definitely something chocolate.

Katie's back is to me, her ponytail swaying from side to side as she dances around the kitchen. Her hips shake, and when she turns, I can see the chocolate-covered spoon in her hand. She actually sings aloud, matching the music perfectly before taking a break to stick her tongue out and lick the spoon.

I can't help my laugh, and the sound carries across the music, loud enough that she spins, eyeing me. She smiles, chocolate stuck to the corner of her mouth, and I think a little on her cheek.

She sings about needing a man and a love that burns hot enough to last, the spoon held to her mouth as a microphone. She smiles at me, curling her finger and beckoning me into the kitchen. I drop the bag from my shoulder and cross the distance, meeting her just as the chorus hits, which she belts at the top of her voice. My arms encircle her waist, and I spin her. She laughs, holding her spoon microphone in the air as I lift her off her feet. When she's back on the ground, I take the spoon from her and throw it into the sink, grabbing both her hands. We dance. The music is so loud, I can barely hear my own thoughts, but her laughter cuts through with ease. She spins when I hold an arm up, lowering into one of the messiest dips, and her smile is so wide I think it might actually crack my chest open.

Before Katie, my routine was the same. I came home, I unpacked, and I showered. I ordered or made a boring dinner. I watched game tape. I went to bed.

Now, I come home and I'm with her. That's all I need.

We dance to Whitney until the song ends and changes to something else. Katie wriggles free from me and goes to her phone at the other end of the counter, turning the music down. When she spins back around to face me, the smile is still intact. So is the chocolate.

"What happened to my kitchen, Rockstar?" I laugh as she makes her way back over to me. When she's close enough, I tug her into my arms.

Katie looks around. "What? I'm baking."

"I can see that." I nod, dropping my forehead to hers. "How was your day?"

I feel her stiffen in my arms, but I just pull her in tighter and wait for her to relax again. I know that I likely won't get anything out of her tonight. The baking, the music, the dancing. She is likely trying to forget whatever happened today while she was at the bar, so I don't push.

I gently press a kiss to her lips, murmuring against them, "You destroyed my kitchen. Looks like a flour bomb has gone off."

"The cupcakes will be worth it. Trust me." She smiles and then leans up on her toes to kiss me properly. I sink into the taste of her. Our mouths move in unison, and her arms curl around my neck, hands tangling in my hair.

When we break apart, I kiss a path over her cheek, then I lick the leftover chocolate that she missed. Katie giggles, and I swear to god, it makes me hard.

Fuck.

My fingers dig into her hips, and I drag her around, pressing her against the island bench. She squeals when I grab her ass and lift her onto it, fitting myself between her legs. She tightens her thighs around me and lifts her ankles, crossing them behind my back and locking me in place.

I smile against her lips, biting down on her bottom lip.

"What flavor are they?" I say, pulling back and sinking my hands into her hair.

"Chocolate and gingerbread," she replies, smiling widely. "It's Christmas soon. I want to get in the spirit."

"They smell delicious. How long have they been in the oven?"

"Almost done, maybe another minute?"

I reach around and gently uncross her ankles. Stepping away from her quickly, I bend to turn off the oven, leaving the cupcakes inside. When I step back between her legs, I don't give her time to think. My hands cup her cheeks, and my mouth devours hers.

She tastes like chocolate, ginger, and sugar. It's sweet, and she's right, it tastes like Christmas. Our hands explore one another's bodies. Mine settle on her thighs, still wrapped around me, and I pull her to the edge of the bench. She's in shorts and a long-sleeve tee, a V-neck in the fabric showing a peek of her breasts. I run my tongue down her neck and over her collarbone, and moan when I realize she's covered herself in icing sugar.

"You're the messiest baker in the world," I say against her skin as I lick, and suck, and kiss any exposed spots. "You have icing sugar dusted all over you."

"I may have had trouble opening the bag," she replies breathlessly.

"Mm," I hum. Her fingers tighten in my hair, and she tugs, guiding me back to her mouth. My tongue dives in, and I immediately get another hit of the chocolate. "I think I might have to fuck you on this counter, then I can cook you dinner."

"Yes. *Yes*," she moans as my fingers tug her shorts and panties to the side. I run a single finger up through her folds, finding her soaking. Her mouth opens, and I bite down on her lip as I push inside her. Immediately, she clenches around me.

"Fuck," I groan, feeling her tighten. "You're so ready for me. Already."

"I have been thinking about this all day."

"Oh, yeah? Was I a distraction?" I suck on the base of her neck as I slowly push in and out of her. She moans, stretching her neck to allow me more access.

"Uh-huh. I dropped three glasses today because I couldn't get you out of my head." She squirms on the counter, inching closer and rolling her hips in time with my fingers, chasing more friction.

"You did?" I smile as I pull back, my pace slowing. Katie whines and sets her gaze on me. Her hair is a mess from my fingers, her cheeks flushed, but her eyes sparkle as she nods at me. "Maybe I should stop. I don't want to cause you any more accidents at work."

I pull my hand away, out of her shorts, and I feel her thighs tighten around me. "Don't you dare."

"Say please."

"What?" She leans forward, her arms still circling my neck.

"Say." I kiss her again, a light peck on the lips that leaves her chasing me for more. "Please." I snake my hand back into her shorts, teasing her clit with my fingers. She crumbles, and fuck, if I don't love the way her head rolls against my shoulder.

"Please," she moans. "*Please*."

I've been waiting for this moment. Ever since she knew what she was doing with the ice cream spoon and her tongue, I've been waiting to use these words against her. "I love it when you beg."

I smirk and pull away.

Unlike her that night, though, I bend down and rifle through the bottom drawer, pulling out a box I know I buried in here ages ago. Condoms.

The moment I stand straight, Katie's hands are flying to my jeans, unbuttoning them and pushing them over my ass. With the condom held between my teeth, I hook my fingers onto the waistband of her shorts and tug them down her legs. I step out of my jeans and flick them away, her shorts landing on top.

I run my palms up her warm thighs, over her hips, and under her shirt, pushing it up until she finally gets the point and rips it off over her head. I pull the condom from my teeth, opening the wrapper.

Just as I'm about to roll it over my achingly hard cock, Katie takes it from my hands and does it herself. Her small hands on my cock make me groan.

"Fuck." I hook my hands beneath her knees and pull her toward the edge of the counter, lining up with her opening. "Put me inside you," I demand in a rough voice.

She fists my cock, pumping twice before she obliges. I thrust forward, sinking into her in one go. Katie's forehead drops to my shoulder, and her arms lock tightly around me. My hands stay firmly wrapped around her thighs as I pump in and out, getting as deep as I can.

Her moans are muffled into my skin, but they seep into my bones. Her noises, her breaths. Everything. I tighten my grip, and she does the same. She rolls her hips, seeking every thrust I give her.

"Will you think about this tomorrow?" I rasp in her ear. "Will you think about how good I fuck you while you pour beers for other men?"

"Yes," she says, biting down on my shoulder. She actually sinks her teeth into my skin, but it only spurs me on. I pump harder, faster. I'm practically holding her off the bench now as I thrust deep into her and she clenches around me. "Don't stop," she cries.

"Tell me how good it is. Tell me how good this feels." *How good we feel*, I almost say, but I hold back. I kiss her neck, sucking at the spot that always makes her cry out.

"So good. *Fuck*."

I pump faster, feeling my release begin to build in the base of my spine. Heat crawls over my skin, steaming from the tracks Katie's nails leave in their wake as she claws at my back. Sweat builds between us, our bodies moving together.

"Come for me, Rockstar. Scream for me."

And she does.

Katie collapses against me, her pussy pulsing as she comes all over my cock. No more than a second later, I follow. I kiss her, placing her back on the counter and slowly pulling out. Quickly, I deal with the condom and find myself back between her legs, kissing her as I run my hands up her thighs again. It's my favorite thing to do, feeling the soft skin that's always warm and inviting. I run a finger through her folds, catching some of her cum before I bring it to my lips, sucking the finger clean.

She watches every movement, fire in her eyes. We will definitely be going round two in the shower.

"Such a messy girl," I tease, using the same finger to trace along her bottom lip.

"You're a fucking tease, Reed." She smiles as she leans forward, kissing me senseless. I grip her thighs, lifting her into my arms, and I carry her upstairs.

***

Katie curls into my body, her head resting against my shoulder and her hand on my chest. I trace patterns on the back of that hand, tracing up and down her fingers, over her red nails. Months ago, when she moved in, her nails were red then, too. Then one day, she came home with these bright blue nails. Two weeks later, they were orange, then yellow, then green. Now, they're red again.

I like them red. They look good wrapped around my cock.

After we added to the mess in the kitchen earlier this evening, we showered and dressed in sweatpants and hoodies. Katie in my clothes is a huge turn on. She then curled into the cushions on the couch and turned on some show she'd decided we've got to watch while I cleaned up her baking explosion in the kitchen and made us dinner.

We watched an episode, and then when I fell asleep during the second one, she turned the TV and the lights off, took me by the hand, and led me to bed. I watched her strip out of the sweats and switch them for a T-shirt that she stole from my closet before she slipped into bed.

As I climbed in beside her, she curled into me, and here we are.

It's late, but with no clouds tonight, her face is illuminated by the moonlight streaming into the room. Her hair fans out behind her, covering the pillow. It's her pillow because she's slept in my bed every night since Thanksgiving. Her long eyelashes flutter against her cheeks, and her eyes move as she dreams. Watching her sleep is now my favorite pastime, and some nights,

I need to remind myself that I have to be up for practice the next morning and that sleep is important. Regardless, I'm in no hurry for her to leave my bed.

A buzzing sounds, and I jolt a little as it echoes through the quiet room. The light from Katie's phone brightens the ceiling, and I groan when it doesn't immediately stop. I gently roll her off my shoulder and lean on my elbow, looking at the name on the phone.

Grant.

Fucking Grant is calling her. I squint as the phone illuminates and buzzes again. Eleven p.m. It's eleven at night, and this guy is blowing up her phone. What the actual fuck?

I lean further up, wanting to grab the phone and answer it, and find out what the fucker wants from her. But, as it rings and I lean over Katie, I look down at her, peacefully sleeping, and change my mind. I could answer the phone, have a blow-up with her ex, and then fight with her about the blow-up with her ex.

Or, I could leave it alone.

I could wait for her to trust me enough to let me in on why the guy won't stop calling her. She turns in her sleep, giving me her back, and she shuffles back on the bed toward me. I sigh, dropping back to my pillow and wrapping my arm around her waist. I pull her back to my chest and bury my face in her hair, trying to forget about her shitty ex.

As long as she's here, in my bed and not his, then I'm winning whatever fight I'm in for Katie Murphy's heart.

Chapter Sixteen

Flynn

THE SNOW COULD BE holding her up. It's what I've been telling myself for the last hour and a half while I practically sat in silence and waited for Katie to arrive home from a shift at the bar. The days between Christmas and New Year's are always such a blur. The extra games that are on across the NFL, the NHL, and the NBA mean that the bar is busy at this time of year. She is putting in extra hours to cover some of the staff.

I offered to come with her, keep her company, but she outright refused. She called me a distraction.

How rude.

I thought I would be able to just watch some television, go over some game tape, and then head to bed. She'd eventually just crawl in whenever she got home. I tried to, but when I woke up and saw the time was just past one in the morning, and she still wasn't home, I started to worry.

I fiddle with my phone, my fingers tapping into our text chain and then swiping out of it again, over and over. I texted, no response. Should I call? It could be the snow, sure, or maybe they closed later than usual tonight, and she's still cleaning. It could be a number of things, and I'm sure my mind is just jumping to conclusions.

Fuck it, I'm calling her.

I find her number in seconds and press call. I favorited it a few weeks ago, so even when my phone's on do not disturb at night or while I'm in meetings, her calls will still come through. Call me a simp all you want, I never want to give up the chance to talk to my girl.

I press the phone to my ear and listen to the dial tones.

Once ... twice ... three times. It rings out.

Hi, this is Katie. Good chance I won't call you back, so if it's important, text me.

I drop the phone from my ear and hang up. Before I can even make my mind up fully, I jump out of bed and reach for my socks and a hoodie. Tugging them on, I head downstairs and slip my feet into some trainers by the door, then I swipe my keys off the hall table.

I drive slowly. The weather is shit. Snow falls softly, but enough that the visibility at the moment is awful. When the stadium comes into view as I turn onto the road that Pat's is on, my chest cracks a little.

What if she's been hurt? Someone could've gotten to her as she walked to her car. What if some asshole has hurt her?

Anxiety crawls up my throat. My stomach clenches, and I feel as if I'm going to be sick as I pull into the parking lot. Katie's car is still there, but it doesn't do much to help relieve the pressure building in my chest. The building is dark. I can see a few lights on inside, but they look to be those coming from the signs behind the bar.

I park next to Katie's car and head for the front door. Peering inside, I can't see any movement, or lights, or signs that someone's still inside. I try the door, shaking it with a little more force than needed and making it rattle. The anxiety builds as I head for the alleyway in the back, where I know there's another door. It's locked too.

When I make it back to the front door, I peer inside again. I'm covered in snow now, freezing my ass off, and the anxiety that something has happened to her is quickly turning into panic.

I dial her number again. No answer.

Again. No answer. I shoot off a few texts.

Where are you?

I'm at the bar. Are you inside?

Please just text me back, Katie. I'm worried.

I don't wait for a response I'm sure I won't get, and decide to dial again. This time, with my phone pressed to one ear, I press my other ear to the door and try to hear any movement or a ringtone inside.

"Flynn?" Her voice comes through the line, and I feel like crying in relief.

"Fuck. Thank god. Are you okay?" I ask quickly, standing straight and glancing around the parking lot.

"I'm fine. Still at the bar. What's wrong? You sound weird."

"It's one a.m. You didn't come home, and I hadn't heard from you." I peek inside the bar again as a light turns on all the way in the back. "I, uh, well, I'm here."

"Here? As in here, here?" She laughs. She's finding this funny. I thought she'd been attacked, and she's finding this funny.

I keep my eyes on the back corridor, and my heart starts beating at a normal pace when I see her round the corner. Thank fuck. More lights turn on as she makes her way through the bar and to the front doors. The closer she gets, the more feeling I get back in my body. Fucking hell, I'm freezing. I can't feel the fingers that are clutching my phone, and my trainers are soaked through with water.

"I'll let you in. Hang on," she says before the line goes dead. Her face appears in the glass, and she shakes her head as she unlocks the door. As soon as it's open, I slip inside. It's still warm in the bar, the heating still on.

"Fuck, fuck, fuck." I hop on the spot and shake out my hands. "Fucking cold as shit out there."

"Well, yeah. It's snowing, Reed. What were you doing standing in the snow?" She's got this amused smile on her face, and her eyes shine with laughter as she watches me moving around, trying to warm up.

"You didn't come home."

"I told you I was working tonight."

"Yes, but then it got past midnight, and you didn't come home. I got worried."

"You ... I ..." She looks at her phone, obviously now seeing the texts and calls I'd left for her. "I'm sorry, I didn't see your messages. Or the calls. I was ..."

She pauses, turning back toward the corridor where I first saw the light coming on. "You okay?" I ask when she doesn't start talking again. Katie looks back at me, her eyes searching my face. She's deciding something, like she has something to say, but she's not sure whether she wants to tell me or not.

"Yeah," she says, her face relaxing. "I'm sorry. I didn't see my phone."

Not telling me then. Whatever disappointment I feel by her not sharing with me whatever she was obviously about to, is washed away the moment Katie steps into my arms and presses up on her toes to find my lips. I let her, turning my head and leaning down a little to help. I wrap my arms around her warm body and sink into the kiss.

I could honestly kiss this woman for the rest of my life and die a happy man.

She breaks off and buries her face into my neck, yawning against my skin. I turn my head and press my lips into her hair. "You scared me a little there, Rockstar."

"I'm sorry. I honestly thought you'd go to bed and wouldn't notice I wasn't there." Her words are muffled against my hood-ie.

"Unlikely." I press another kiss to her temple. I look around the bar. It's closed up, clean and tidy. Not a chair out of place or a glass left on the bar. "What are you doing here so late anyway? When did you finish up?"

"I ... I just had some paperwork to finish up in the back. I wasn't feeling tired, so I thought I'd smash it out so I can take tomorrow off and come to the game," she rattles off quickly. A lie. Probably. I think. I'm getting better at reading her every day, but sometimes I can tell there are new walls around certain topics that I shouldn't encroach on.

Her parents, for one. Or the status of our *fake* relationship.

Katie likes to avoid things. She doesn't want to talk about the hard stuff when it comes to her own life, but will immediately throw it back on others. *Thought I would smash it out so I can take tomorrow off and come to the game.* She thinks throwing it back to me and the game will distract me from the real reason she was hanging around here so late at night. I damn well know it wasn't paperwork.

I look down at her. She's nestled against me, her nose buried into the fabric of my hoodie, and her eyes are closed. There's a soft smile on her lips, and it makes my heart ache. So I let it go. I'll wait for her to be ready to give me the real reason she's hiding away in her bar after hours.

Instead, I find the top of her jeans and slip my freezing cold hands down the back of them, squeezing her ass and making her squeal.

"Oh my god!" She jumps in my arms and tries to squirm out of my grip, but I hold her steady. "Get your hands off me! Why are they so cold?"

"You made me come all the way out here," I say, stepping forward and forcing her to step backward with me. I keep a tight grip on her ass, and truly, my hands are starting to warm back up now that they're on her body. "In the snow and the cold."

"I'm sorry. You didn't have to." She laughs, moving with me easily. She presses a hand into my chest and tries to separate us, but I keep hold.

"You had me worried you'd been hurt, or taken, or something." I shake my head at her laughing face.

"What was the plan if I had been? You were going to channel Liam Neeson and go all spy on their ass?"

I smirk when her back hits the bartop, and she helps when I easily lift her onto it. My hands slide out of her jeans and over her hips. "I might have. I wasn't sure what I was walking into."

Her face softens, and she runs her fingers through my hair, leaning down to press a kiss on my lips. "I'm sorry I worried you."

"Promise to text if you plan on staying late again?"

Her brows furrow a little. "Really? Gra—No one used to care when I stayed late."

"I'm not your shitty ex-boyfriend."

"No, you're my devoted *fake* boyfriend." She laughs again, and my stomach clenches at the word *fake*, but I ignore it.

"Promise me, Katie." I lean back, catching her gaze. She stares for a moment before she nods. "Say it."

"I promise," she says easily, using a finger to draw a cross over her heart. She leans forward and kisses me again. It starts so gentle and calm, almost as if it's her way of an apology. Then, she swipes her tongue across my bottom lip before gently biting down, sucking it between her teeth. I groan, massaging my fingers into her hips, over the fabric of her jeans. Her arms wrap around my neck, and she pulls me closer.

Her legs hook around my waist, her mouth devours mine, and I sink my hands into her hair, undoing her ponytail and letting the curls fall down her back. I'm definitely not cold anymore. She pulls back, her breathing heavy, her lips swollen. Her eyes are alight with lust. I know she can feel my hardening cock through the gray sweatpants I wear. As if she knows what I'm thinking, her eyes flicker down. Her hand curls over my shoulder, trailing down the front of my hoodie, over my heaving chest, and to the waistband of my sweatpants. I watch as her red nails play with the fabric for a moment before they disappear, her warm hand gliding down my groin. Then, her fingers wrap around my cock and squeeze.

"Uh, fuck," I groan, dropping my head to her shoulder as she gently pumps me in her hand. As much as I would love to fuck her, right here and right now, I can't help but catch a glimpse at the clock behind the bar. It's almost two in the morning.

"One day," I say, kissing her neck and then her jawline. "I'm going to take you on this bartop." Her hand squeezes me again, and I suck in a breath. I tangle her hair around my fingers and tug, angling her face upwards a little so I can trace a path with my tongue down her neck. "It's going to be so hard, and so rough, that you won't be able to serve anyone without thinking about me and my cock."

She whimpers, her steady rhythm breaking as I bite down gently on her neck. I suck at the spot and release my grip on her hair. Immediately, she kisses me, her hips rolling, seeking some sort of friction.

"And, you're going to love it," I murmur against her lips before kissing her hard again. When I pull back, I gently remove her hand from my pants and smooth her hair down a little. "But, it's two a.m. and I have a game tomorrow. Let's go home."

"Can we fuck at home?" Her words are pleading and desperate. Fuck, I just know she's soaked through her panties and maybe even her jeans. I hold myself back from checking. I know if she is, I won't be able to contain myself, and I might actually rip her jeans off and fuck her right now.

But I can't. I have a game in the morning, the snow is finally letting up, and we need to get some sleep.

"Please?" she begs, almost knowing that my answer should have, would have, been no. As always, though, I cave. When she hops off the bar, looking mighty pleased with herself, I swat her ass.

"You're a brat," I grumble.

"You like me this way."

Fuck yeah, I do.

***

"Flynn Reed, tight end for the Boston Broncos, is here with us now." The reporter looks directly into the camera, the microphone held up to her face as she speaks in a high-pitched tone. "Flynn, hell of a game for you and the Broncos. Seven touchdowns. You were on fire today."

"Thanks, Ash." I smile tightly. I was on fire but running on empty.

"The team has clinched a playoff spot, and you're early favorites for the Super Bowl. Does that add any pressure on the team?"

I scratch the back of my head nervously. The Super Bowl talk has been going around all season. We've been almost unbeatable. We're in the best shape of our lives, and the Super Bowl seems like it might be in the bag for us. But I've been here before with the team, and we always seem to fail at the last hurdle. The conference finals.

"Yes. I mean, I think any team would feel the pressure if they were in our position. We've worked hard this year, and it's paying off. The boys are an absolute unit, and every single player on the team is an integral part of where we're at." I smile at Ash. "But the pressure is a pleasure in this business. We're athletes, so it's what we thrive on."

"And what about you off the field? How's it going with that gorgeous girlfriend of yours? I think half the population is likely jealous of her for taking you off the market!" The reporter's eyes shine. I can't help but laugh. I glance over at Hollie, who's standing off to the side. Another new Louis Vuitton bag, which

I'm pretty sure she bought as a gift for herself from me for Christmas, is tucked under her arm. She rolls her hand, gesturing to me to answer the question.

I shake my head. "She's good. We're good. Thank you for asking."

"You two make the most gorgeous couple. Is she here today?"

"She is. She's up in the coaches' box with Ivy Booker." I point up toward one of the boxes. Flashes of early this morning go through my mind. Katie's hair wrapped in my fist, her back arched, moans muffled into the mattress as I made her come not once, but twice, while fucking her from behind. The little minx is the reason I'm running on empty today. I barely got in more than four hours, and that was with a sleep-in.

"Will you be attending Scott Harvey and Ivy Booker's wedding together? Can you give us any details on how the plans are going for football's golden couple?" Ash pushes the microphone closer to me.

"I can't, but we will both be there, yes."

Ash looks disappointed with my answer, but doesn't let it deter her. "Any plans for you to propose and settle down? You've gone from being filmed punching someone outside a bar to the perfect boyfriend this season. Huge change for someone to make if it's not serious."

"It's serious. I lo—" I stop myself, the words catching in my throat. "It's serious. I like spending time with Katie, but we're not in a rush. We're both still young."

Ash narrows her eyes a minuscule amount, and I glance over at Hollie, begging her with my eyes for help. As if she could sense it, she's already striding—well, striding as far as her small legs will take her—toward us.

"Okay, that's plenty. Thanks so much, Ash." Hollie intervenes, creating some distance between me and the reporter. "You have plenty for your report later."

"Come on, Hollie. That was barely five minutes," Ash whines. Hollie flicks her hand at me, dismissing me quickly as she takes Ash's arm and leads her over to Coach. A few quick words in his ear, and Coach stands straighter as Ash takes her place next to him and the cameraman sets up in front.

Thank god for that.

Not sure the world finding out that I'm in love with Katie Murphy—before I've worked up the courage to tell her myself—is the best way for things to go.

Chapter Seventeen

Katie

"I don't even think Davenport made it home after, either," Flynn says, bringing his beer to his lips as he talks. He takes a sip, and I watch the way his throat works as the liquid slides down. "He was all over the place the next day at practice. Coach sent him off to the trainers' room, which meant he was told to go sleep it off."

"Why didn't Jeff just tell him to go home?"

"We get fined for missing practice if it's not for a really good reason." He places his glass down and rests his forearm on the table. His crisp shirt is tight over the muscles in his upper arms, and it just fits over his broad chest. I'm already thinking about how I want to rip it open later so I can run my tongue over his abs.

"I barely remember New Year's. I vaguely remember laughing with Ivy in the bathroom, and being on the dance floor, but anything after that is a bit of a blur." I take a sip of my wine and shake my head. "If that's what their wedding will be like with most of the team there, I think someone should warn Ivy."

"The wedding won't be as bad. Scott's already warned them they have to behave." Flynn turns his hand over, his palm facing up. I stare at it for a moment before sliding my hand over his. He entangles our fingers together and relaxes into his seat. "So, you're telling me that you don't remember ambushing me in the bathroom on New Year's and asking me to make you come exactly at midnight?"

"Shh," I hiss, feeling my face go bright red. I look around the restaurant, but no one seems to be paying us much attention. We're tucked away at the back of the steak house in a booth, sitting side by side. Flynn told me to take the night off and get dressed up, that we were going for dinner at a place Hollie had booked for us. But when we got here, Flynn used his real name and not the alias Hollie normally books under. They also sat us at the back of the restaurant, in a very private, very out-of-sight booth. My instinct tells me that if this had been a booking Hollie had made, we would be sitting directly in front of the window, and the flashing of cameras would've served as a side.

"So you *do* remember?" He flashes me a grin and leans over, kissing my cheek, then the spot just below my ear. I press my thighs together and sigh.

"Of course, I do. I don't know what you've done to me, but I apparently like sex in public places now." I take another sip of wine as I watch his thumb gently rub the back of my hand.

Flynn laughs, leaning close to my ear as he murmurs, "I bet this place has a nice bathroom. Want to go have a look?"

"Stop it," I say, using my free hand to slap his chest. His eyes drop down my body, again. I pulled an old red dress from my closet for tonight. I don't think I've worn it since college. It's tight, dropping to mid-thigh, but with long sleeves. It's got a low back, with a tie that lies across my shoulder blades, the loose strings falling down my bare skin. The front cuts across my chest in a straight line, and because the dress is so tight, my boobs are pushed up every time I breathe. I've caught Flynn watching my chest rise and fall a number of times this evening.

He looks just as good. Dark gray slacks and a crisp white shirt with the collar open. He wore a jacket as well, but took it off when we got to the restaurant and slung it over the top of the booth when we sat down. The steak house is a pretty fancy place. The low lighting casts a romantic atmosphere over the dining room, and there's gentle music playing in the background.

It's the perfect date.

At least, I think it is. I hope it is. We've been dancing around talking about the whole fake dating thing for a while now. Flynn doesn't believe in it, and truthfully, neither do I. Will I admit it aloud? No way. Do I sometimes throw it out there to gauge his reaction and see if he says anything? Yes. Does it ever work? No.

Both of us have obviously decided that bringing it up is too hard, that it's better to just keep pretending. Like this date. He said it was a booking Hollie made, but all signs lead to him being the one to have booked it. I haven't slept in my own bed for well over a month. I haven't bothered denying it whenever Ivy accuses me of liking him; instead, I just shrug my shoulders and gently draw her attention elsewhere. We act like a couple, a *real* couple.

Except my phone still rings every few days and reminds me that I still haven't dealt with my past. And the notifications on my YouTube channel are still a reminder that I haven't been totally honest with Flynn about what I want for my future, either.

In all honesty, I haven't been totally honest with myself.

"Katie?" Flynn asks again, gently guiding my face to meet his with a finger beneath my chin.

"Huh?" I ask, confused and lost in my thoughts.

"Do you want dessert?" I blink at him and cock my head. What kind of dessert does he mean? I open my mouth, but, as if he can read my mind, he shakes his head and looks to the edge of our booth, where one of the wait staff is waiting. "The waiter wants to know."

My gaze snaps around to them, and I blush. "Sorry. Lost in my own world. Uh—" I look back at Flynn. "Are you having any?"

Flynn studies me for a moment and then smiles. "I will if you will."

"Okay, sure. I'll get whatever you have that's chocolate on the menu. Thank you." The waiter nods and then looks at Flynn.

"Same for me. Thank you." He smiles at the waiter and waits for him to leave before he untangles our fingers and snakes an arm over my shoulder, pulling me closer to him so our thighs press together. I shift, turning into him. He leans down, his free hand dipping beneath the table to grab my thigh. In one easy move, he lifts my legs so they're draped over his under the table. I'm practically sitting in his lap.

"What are you doing?" I ask in a low voice, a smile playing on my lips as the hand draped over my shoulder begins to play with my hair.

"What were you thinking about? You were a million miles away," he asks.

"You. And how you've gotten me addicted to sex." He huffs at my words, looking offended, and I laugh. "You have. I think I've had more sex in the last month and a half than I ever have. Even in college."

Flynn frowns. "Don't talk to me about all the other guys you've slept with."

"Why? Does it make you jealous?" I ask.

"Yes." I laugh again, but he cuts me off with a kiss. He tastes like beer and peppercorn sauce. I smile against his lips. He tastes like home.

"Flynn?" I ask, pulling back from his mouth. He frowns a little again.

"Yes, Rockstar?"

"You know this whole—" I get cut off by my phone ringing in my clutch. Normally, I would ignore it and just call whoever it was back later, but the ringtone is the specific one I apply to all the guys who work for me at the bar. If they're calling, it's for a reason. "Sorry," I say as I lean across the table a little and reach for my clutch. I fish out my phone and answer.

"Justin? Are you okay?"

"Hey, Katie. I'm really sorry to call," my youngest bar staff says into the phone. He's twenty years old. Old enough to work in the bar but not to drink. He's a good kid, trying to save money to go back to school next year to study engineering.

"It's okay. What happened?"

"It's, uh—" He pauses, and I press the phone to my ear hard. I can hear something going on in the background. Someone is yelling, then someone else yells back. I flinch when I hear a glass shatter. "Grant is here. He's kind of … Well, he's drunk and he's demanding we call you and get you to come and see him."

"What?" I sit up straight, and the arm Flynn had around my shoulders falls down my back. He catches himself, and his hand presses into my hip as he sits up with me.

"What's happened?" he asks from my other side, but I just shake my head.

"How drunk is he? Have you served him?" I ask, already sliding out of the booth. Flynn follows me, even with the confused look on his face.

"I don't know. He turned up here, tried to order a beer, but we refused him service. He's pretty messed up already," Justin explains down the phone. "Then he just started demanding to see you. We tried to tell him you weren't here, but he didn't believe us."

"Okay. It's okay. Just tell him to calm down and drink some water. I'm on my way," I say as I stand up. "If he breaks anything else, call the police."

"Okay, thanks, Katie."

"See you soon." I hang up the phone, and my hand drops to my side. "Fuck. *Fuck*."

"What is it?" Flynn's hands cup my cheeks, and he bends a little, trying to catch my eye.

I shake my head and close my eyes. A vision of Grant, drunk and angry and stomping around my bar, fills my head. "This is all my fault. I should've just answered his fucking phone calls."

"Is this about Grant?" Flynn asks, and I open my eyes to find his green ones waiting.

"He's at the bar, drunk out of his mind and demanding to see me."

"No."

I sigh as I sag in his hold a little. "Flynn, I have to. He's putting my staff at risk. The least I can do is go over there and back them up."

"Call the police. They will be there faster than us, and I'm sure they're great at backing up staff," he says, his thumbs gently stroking my cheeks.

We stand by the table in silence, only breaking when the waiter appears with two molten chocolate cakes in hand. He looks between us, confused, and I just shake my head at Flynn.

"Sorry, can we get these two to go? There's been an emergency. I'll need the check and the car brought round if I can," Flynn says, not looking away from my face.

"Of course, sir." The waiter disappears, and I collapse into Flynn's chest. His arms encircle me, and he rubs my back gently.

"I think I might go to the bathroom before we go. Then, we can go home, and I'll get my car to head over there." I sigh, pulling away from his chest and wrapping my arms around my stomach. I feel sick.

"Like hell," Flynn grumbles, stepping into my space again. "There is no way I'm letting you go to the bar alone, knowing that douchebag is there waiting, drunk and probably aggressive."

"But—"

"No, Katie. We either both go, or you come home with me and call the police." He steps into my space again, gently kissing me on the lips. "Go to the bathroom. I will meet you at the front."

I watch him take his jacket from the back of the booth and head for the front of the restaurant, where he meets the waiter, waiting with our dessert, now in a bag, and the bill.

I turn the other way, taking a right down one of the corridors off the kitchen, and head for the bathroom. Flynn was right—they are fancy. As I wash up, I look at myself in the mirror. You can't see the bruise anymore. Months have passed since it finally cleared up, and I was able to stop piling on concealer just to get through the day. I still see it, though. The yellow and purple bruising he left the last time I saw him. The split lip, the blood trickling down my chin.

I didn't even cry when he did it. I was just in shock. I remember the way it felt so distinctly that when I reach up to brush the space just below my left eye, I flinch as if expecting it to still hurt like it did the days directly afterward.

I take a deep breath, holding it in while I count for seven seconds before releasing it. Tears sting the back of my eyes, but I refuse to cry. Grant lost the right to my tears the day I walked away from him for the last time, the day he decided slapping me across the face was a good idea.

***

Flynn pulls into the parking lot of the bar twenty minutes after we leave the restaurant. His hand rested on my knee the entire time, and as I wait for him to come around the truck and open my door, a shiver rushes through me. I started working at this bar when I was eighteen. I looked forward to earning my own money, even if it was my parents paying my wages, and I couldn't wait to finally give the ideas I'd gotten from years of watching them run the place a go.

Not once in the last eight years since starting here as an employee have I ever wanted to run the opposite way. Not once have I been scared of the daily challenges that await me inside those doors, not once have I ever been nervous to stand toe to toe with a drunk man and tell him he has to leave. Usually, I enjoy it.

But almost a year ago, I walked away from the man waiting inside and vowed that I would never speak to—let alone see—him ever again. After we broke up, I saw a counselor for a few weeks. I never admitted it to anyone, but I knew it was probably for the best. I didn't go into the details of my relationship, nor did I tell her about the slap, but we just talked, and she gave me some breathing techniques to help with the anxiety that came along with the change.

Then, I went to Italy.

After Italy, everything seemed to go back to normal. I felt better, stronger. I just wanted to move on and get back to my life. Of course, the whole falling into bed with Flynn, then hearing how much of a playboy he was, put a little damper on the trip, but if I'm truly honest with myself, the months of playful banter, the little love-hate friendship we formed, healed me a little. I've felt like the girl I was in college, before Grant. Headstrong, opinionated, free.

The car door opens, and Flynn holds out a hand to me. I take it and step out of the truck. He doesn't let go of me as we make our way to the front door. Again, he steps in front, leading us both inside.

The place is almost empty. The kitchen staff are standing in front of the bar, Justin and Maria behind it. Doug and a few other locals stand off the side, speaking quietly amongst themselves. There's glass all over the floor and a cracked plate, the food that was obviously on it when it dropped, lying nearby.

Jesus Christ.

I look around, spotting a man sitting in a booth across from the bar. He stares at me, his eyes glazed over, and he sways even though sitting down. His tie is half undone, his hair is a mess, and his shirt, from what I can see, is covered in beer.

Grant.

Fuck, he looks awful.

Flynn squeezes my hand, letting me go as he moves to stand behind me, his chest against my back and his hand on my hip. He's letting me handle it, but not alone.

"Everyone okay?" I call out, and my staff all look up, relieved.

A few of the chefs nod. Doug and his friends hold their pints up, still half full of beer, in greeting. Why he's still here, I have no idea. Well, I do. The man's the biggest gossip I know. Justin races around the bar and comes over, stepping carefully over the glass. "Sorry about the mess, Katie. I tried to clean it, but every time we got close, he started up again. Thought it best to just leave it until you got here."

"That's okay." I glance at Justin. His face is as white as a ghost. "Roscoe?" I call out to my head chef. "Will you take Justin for some food out back? And a drink, yeah?"

"Sure, boss." Roscoe, my tattooed, six-foot, forty-year-old chef, nods and motions for Justin to follow him. The rest of the kitchen staff turn and face Maria, who's been a bartender here for years.

"Grant?" I ask, taking a small step toward the booth he's sitting in. "What are you doing here?"

"You won't answer any of my calls. Had to come. Had to see you."

"It's been months, Grant. We're over."

"I never wanted that." He shakes his head, still swaying in his seat. "I never wanted to be over. You walked out without giving me a chance."

"I gave you four years," I say carefully.

"What do you want? Do you want a ring? You want to get married like your friend? I'll get you a ring," Grant slurs.

"You know that isn't what I meant."

"I didn't do anything to deserve you leaving me."

I take a deep breath. Suddenly, I wish I'd asked everyone to leave, not just Justin and Roscoe. "You cheated on me. Multiple times. I'm not sure what else you expected me to do."

"You forgave me."

"I was wrong to do that." I feel Flynn's hand tighten on my hip. "I should have walked away the first time I found out."

Grant gets to his feet, shuffling uneasily our way. He points his finger at me. "You told me you loved me."

"I did." It was true. I did love him. Just not in the right way, and not anymore.

"I miss you," he slurs. "Please give me another chance." He takes another few uneasy steps and gets too close for Flynn's liking.

"That's close enough," he growls, tugging me back. He takes a step back but stays behind me. As if he only just notices I'm not alone, Grant's eyes flash, anger firing up in them as he stares at Flynn.

"Stay out of this."

"Then stay back. You can have a conversation without getting in her face."

Grant's gaze lands back on me, his lip snarling. "How long did it take you to replace me? Or were you fucking him before we broke up? Is he the reason you walked out on me? *Slut.*"

I flinch at the word but don't react. He's called me this before. He's called me every name in the book before, whenever he drank too much and then picked a fight.

"That's enough," Flynn growls. This time, he does move in front of me. His hand on my hip tugs me backward, and he steps around me in one motion, placing himself between Grant and me. "We came here to have you removed. You wanted to see her, you've said your piece, and nothing's changed. Time to go."

"Fuck you." Grant spits on the ground at Flynn's feet, and I cringe. Ew.

"Back off."

"Katie," Grants says, his voice now pleading. "Come on. You know I am the only man who knows how to take care of you. Come home. Please?" There's a beat, and I rest my head on Flynn's back, sighing as I don't respond. His next words, though, make me want to laugh. "I'll even get you those good bagels you like, and the flowers you always begged me to get whenever we went past the stall. Come on, babe."

I laugh out loud. It's hollow and full of disappointment. "I'm not begging for the bare minimum anymore, Grant. Go home."

"Katie—"

"You heard her. Time to go." Flynn takes a step forward. It's the wrong move.

In one go, Grant curses at him and then rushes him, aiming a sloppy punch at his jaw. Flynn reacts on instinct, blocking Grant's sloppy attempt and hitting him back. Square in the jaw.

The crunch echoes through the bar. No one dares to take a breath. Grant hits the floor, knocked out.

"Oh, shit," Maria curses.

"Atta, boy!" Doug cheers, holding his pint up as his friends all clap.

I just stare at Grant, groaning and moaning on the floor as he comes round. His eyes roll back, and he coughs, moving onto his side as he tries to get up. A finger gently drags my gaze away from my ex-boyfriend on the floor. Flynn studies my face.

"Are you okay?"

"Yes." I nod. "Are you?" I look down at his hand, hanging by his side. It's already red, likely going to bruise all over his knuckles. "Oh my god, Flynn. Your hand."

He shakes it out, flexing his fingers as I stare at it. "It'll be fine."

Behind us, Maria calls the police and asks for the ambulance as well. Grant will likely spend the night in a police cell or a hospital bed. As long as it's not at my bar, I don't care.

They take less than five minutes to arrive.

I watch from the front door as the medics bend over Grant, asking him questions and checking his jaw. Not broken, thank god.

The police talk to Justin and Maria, getting their story of what happened when he first showed up. Doug and his friends are told to go home, and the chefs help clean up the remaining glass and broken plates on the floor. Flynn stands behind me as I watch them roll Grant out on an ambulance stretcher. Flynn broke his nose.

Good.

As they pass us, Grant's eyes open, tears filling them. "Katie. I'm sorry. I am. For everything. For cheating—" I don't say anything, but I also don't look away. God, what a sad excuse for a man. To think, I used to believe I would be happy with this guy. "For never treating you right. And ... I'm sorry for the last time we saw each other. I shouldn't have done it." I close my eyes and plead silently with Grant. Please, please don't say it. Please don't say it.

"I never meant to hit you. I'm sorry."

I feel Flynn's arm around my waist tighten, and his chest freeze. I let out the breath I'd been holding since I walked into the bar tonight to deal with Grant and the mess he made. Goddammit. He fucking said it.

"He what?" Flynn says in my ear. I can only shake my head, keeping my eyes closed and hoping that maybe Flynn will just leave it alone. Of course, he won't. He's not the kind of guy to leave it alone. He never was, and he never will be. Flynn spins me around to face him, taking my face in his hands. "He hit you?"

CHAPTER EIGHTEEN

KATIE

"You can't do that."

"I can. I'll just call Coach and tell him to shove it."

"Flynn, I am fine. I have been fine for months." I rub my temples as I sit cross-legged in the middle of his bed. He paces back and forth at the foot, his overnight bag half packed between us. "If you don't finish packing, you'll be late and miss your flight."

"Fuck it. I'm not going." He pulls out his phone and starts typing furiously. I sigh and get off the bed, stopping in front of him and putting my hand over the screen.

"Who are you texting?" I ask.

"Scott. I'm telling him that I won't be coming."

I take the phone from his hands, gently placing it on the bed beside his bag. "You are going. I am fine." I lift his hands in mine and inspect the bruising that has well and truly formed on his knuckles. I kiss the injured hand and then look up at him through my lashes.

He's been overprotective since we came home from the bar a few nights ago. At first, we argued about me not wanting to formally report him. Grant is a lot of things. He's selfish, a drunk, a cheater. But, he's not a hitter. The slap was a one-off. We'd been circling the drain for a long time, and if he were going to resort to physical violence to get me to stay, he would've done it long before he did.

I also walked out as soon as it happened and cut off contact.

Flynn, though, wanted to report him. He wanted it on Grant's record. So we compromised. I reported him to the police the next day when I went to finalize my statement about the damage to the bar Grant caused, but I didn't press charges. Flynn wasn't thrilled, but he respected my decision.

Ever since, the man's been hovering like a bad smell. Well, a good smell, but still hovering. He's made me breakfast in bed, he's brought me fresh flowers daily, he's been extra attentive at night. It's been ... nice.

My parents and I talked over what happened the next day. They agreed to put in some hours at the bar so I could take the week off. Since I became their unofficial manager, they've taken a step back. But Mom was beside herself when she showed up at the house the next morning. Maria had called her.

We had a long talk about the future, and I honestly think they might be coming around to the idea of me taking over the bar full-time. Maybe. Dad, more so, but Mom is getting there.

Flynn took a personal day from practice the day after, but, to his annoyance, he had to go back to training the day after that. The playoffs are well and truly here, and the Broncos are favorites for a conference win and a Super Bowl slot.

I drop his hands and press my palms into his chest, not pushing him away but simply feeling the warmth under his T-shirt.

"You know what would make me really happy?" I say, staring up at him.

His hands curl around my neck, brushing my hair over my shoulder. "What's that?"

"You, winning your playoff games. You, winning the conference. You, winning the Super Bowl." I smile widely, trying to show him that I'm just fine and he doesn't have to worry.

"Me winning a football game would make you happy?"

"Uh-huh," I say, nodding as I use his chest to balance and rise up on my toes. "You're always so horny after you win." I kiss his neck, then graze my teeth along his ear.

He groans, the hands he still has around the back of my neck tightening a little. "Murphy. Are you teasing me?"

"I might be." I laugh as I drop back to my toes. He stares at me for a while, studying my face. He does this a lot. Like he's looking for something that isn't normally there, a way into the deepest parts of my soul. Little does he know, he's dug himself quite far down already. "You're going on this trip. You're going to win this game, and then you're going to come home and fuck me so hard in celebration, I'll have to take another week off work."

He shakes his head, smiling as he leans down and kisses me senseless. I'm about to say fuck it, and drag him to the bed, but his phone rings. He rips his mouth away from mine and curses. "Fuck."

I smile, watching him pick up the phone and place it to his ear. Through the small speaker, I can hear Scott's voice. *Time to go.*

I turn back to the bag on the bed, peeking inside and then tossing another pair of Flynn's underwear and sweatpants in the bag. I go into the bathroom, take his toothbrush and the face wash he swears by, and put them in a toiletries bag. I walk back into the bedroom and throw it into his overnight bag.

A strong arm wraps around my waist, and I lean back into his chest.

"Are you sure you'll be okay?"

"Flynn"—I turn in his arms—"it happened months ago, not the other night. I am fine, I promise."

"Can I call you when my flight lands?"

I smile softly at him. "Sure."

We make our way down the stairs together. When I open the door, Scott's black Mercedes G-Wagon is parked on the side of the road, and I wave to him. They're riding together to the airport this weekend. During the playoffs, the team closes ranks. The guys hang out together. They train, eat, and play video games whenever they can. They get in sync. It's been quite wholesome to watch over the last week, actually. Flynn kisses me once more before heading down the front steps and getting into the passenger seat. I wait until Scott turns at the end of the road before closing the front door and locking it.

Padding down the hallway toward the living room, I shiver. It's cold now, without him here.

Fuck, I think I miss him already.

He's been going away for games every other weekend since I moved in at the start of October. I used to love it. I had free rein of the kitchen, I could watch whatever I wanted—although Flynn never chooses what we watch anyway—and it was quiet. Now, and for a little while, I've started to hate it.

In the living room, I reach down in front of the electric fireplace and switch it on. Ivy has this great big traditional fire, and her Pops would try to teach us both how to light it and keep it going. We never succeeded. Luckily for her, Scott knows how to light it now, and luckily for me, Flynn has an electric one.

The room starts to warm up, heat washing over me as I head for the kitchen and dig out a packet of popcorn in the cupboard. I spin it around in my hands. It's an extra butter, extra salty popcorn packet. One of the ones you put in the microwave for them to pop, and it's warm when it comes out. It's my favorite kind. I smile, about to close the cupboard, when something else catches my eye.

Bagels.

From the good bakery, not the crappy supermarket ones. There's a whole bag in the cupboard. There's also a new jar of Nutella, and a box of my favorite cereal that I could swear I ran out of last week. He's filled his pantry cupboard with all of my favorite things.

I rub the heel of my palm against my chest, trying desperately to soothe the ache. This man is going to kill me. Or, at the very least, make me let him in.

I blink away the tears I feel forming and shake my head. I'm not going to cry; that would be ridiculous. He's a man, doing the bare minimum to impress me. Getting me flowers? Bare minimum. Filling the cupboard with all my favorite things? Bare minimum.

I've almost convinced myself of this fact when the doorbell rings. Who the hell?

I head down the hallway, unlock the door, and pull it open.

"Oh my god, Ivy? What are you doing here?" There's a bag over her shoulder and another in her hand, but it's definitely my best friend. Her eyes light up when she sees me, and she rushes inside, dropping both bags and throwing her arms around me in a hug.

"Flynn called. Said you weren't feeling the best and we should have a sleepover," she squeals excitedly into my ear. I go still, and she pulls back. "Was that wrong? What's happened?"

She stares at me. I stare at her. The longer I look at her, I realize that inviting my best friend over to stay with me while he's gone, knowing I would need her, isn't the bare minimum.

Flynn fucking Reed has raised the goddamn bar.

Oh god. Now I'm going to cry.

The tears fall over my cheeks, and Ivy immediately snaps into action. She shuts the door, locking it behind her, and picks up both her bags in one hand and takes one of mine in the other. She leads me back to the living room, where she dumps the bags and pulls me onto the couch.

"You never cry," she says.

"I know. I hate this." I swipe desperately under my eyes, trying to catch the tears as they fall. My face is hot and sticky. I pull the sleeve of the hoodie I'm wearing over my hand and wipe my eyes.

"What happened? Did you and Flynn have a fight? Did he call me because he's trying to get back in your good graces?" I shake my head and try to calm my breathing. After a minute of counting my ins and outs, the tears slow.

"We didn't have a fight." I shake my head. "A few nights ago, Grant showed up at the bar. He was drunk. He said a bunch of stuff to the staff, threw some glasses around, but refused to leave unless I came."

"You weren't already there?"

"No, Flynn and I were in the city at that new fancy steak-house."

"You were? Like on a date?" Her eyes light up, and she sits on her knees. "Like a real date or a fake date?"

I give her a watery laugh and smile. "Honestly, Ives. I have no idea what's real and what's fake anymore."

"What do you mean?"

"I don't ... I don't think it's fake anymore." She squeals again, and I can't help but smile. "Neither of us will say it aloud. I think we're both scared it'll ruin it."

"Like the bubble will burst." She nods, knowingly. "So, what happened when you turned up at the bar?" I dive into the play-by-play, telling Ivy everything that happened. When I come to the end, I take a deep breath. She's going to murder me for keeping this from her for so long. We've never really kept secrets, not since we met on the first day of college as roommates.

"A few months ago, when Grant and I last broke up and I moved all my stuff out overnight..." She nods, remembering the time. "I left so quickly because he slapped me across the face. Gave me a black eye and split my lip on his ring."

Ivy's face falls. "He what?!"

"It was a long time ago. I went to see someone after it happened to talk it out—"

"Katie." I look up at my best friend. Heartbreak is written all over her face. "Why didn't you tell me?"

"I—" I shrug. "I think I was embarrassed."

"You have nothing to feel embarrassed about." Ivy leans over and wraps her arms around my neck. "I'm so sorry. I'm so, so sorry."

I hug her tightly. "It's okay. I'm fine. Really, I am." Ivy sits back on her heels and gives me a disbelieving look. "Promise. I went to see a counselor afterwards, and we talked about it, and I was going to tell you, but you got engaged, and I honestly just wanted to move on."

"You sure?"

I nod. "Yes, I'm sure."

"So why the tears?"

"I have no idea. I think maybe I'm realizing I wasted four years on a guy who never bothered to learn a thing about me, and within a couple of months, Flynn has learned it all. He got the good bagels, Ivy."

Her eyes widen, and she laughs. "Oh my god! I knew he wasn't asking for no reason. A few weeks ago, when you guys came round for wedding planning and football, he was bombarding me about all your favorite foods. Said he just wanted to make sure you had things that felt like home."

"Yeah, well"—I swipe my sleeve under my eyes again—"he remembered. All of it."

"He's a simp for you, Katie. I'd say even maybe worse than Scott."

I scoff and roll my eyes, pinning her with a look. "No one is worse than Scott."

Flynn

I toss in the sheets for the fifth time, rolling over to check the clock on my phone again. Almost midnight. Fuck, it's late. I'm going to be wrecked tomorrow if I don't get some sleep. A text pops up on my phone, just as I tap the screen again.

> **Katie:** Thank you for the popcorn. And the Nutella. And the bagels.

> **Katie:** Don't forget to win for me tomorrow.

I smile, snatching the phone off my nightstand and hitting the call button on her contact. She answers halfway through the first dial tone.

"Hello?" she whispers.

"Hey, you," I rasp, my throat scratchy after a few hours of not speaking. Scott and I called it an early night, eating with the boys, but not staying for the FIFA tournament they wanted to start in Cooper's room.

"What are you still doing awake?"

"I can't sleep," I tell her, pressing the phone to my ear and rolling onto my back. The room is pitch black except for the light from the screen, and I can't see a single thing. "Can you talk? Why are you whispering?"

"Hang on." I hear the rustle of covers and the quiet click of a door before she says, "Okay, now I can talk."

"Where were you?"

"In the guest room, with Ivy."

"You were sleeping with Ivy?"

"Duh, it's a sleepover."

"But you don't sleep in the guest room anymore," I say. This only makes her laugh.

"I know, but I thought it would be weird if we slept in your bed."

I pause. "Why would it be weird?"

"I don't know, it just would be."

I listen again as I hear sheets rustling. "What are you doing now?"

"Getting into your bed, Reed. Happy now?"

"Very much so." I smile into the darkness. "You should stay there. I like knowing you sleep in my bed even when I'm away."

"How do you know that?"

"Because you never, ever make the bed. You're messy, Murphy. You leave evidence behind you wherever you go." She laughs, and the speaker muffles for a moment. I imagine her burrowing into my sheets, warming herself up under the heavy cover that she always accuses me of stealing.

"I won't change my ways. I haven't in twenty-six years, and I won't now."

"Wouldn't dream of it."

"So..." She hums over the phone. "What's keeping you up?"

"Are you okay?"

"I'm fine, Flynn. I promise."

"You'd tell me if you weren't, right?"

There's a beat of silence and then a small, "Yes." She's lying. Of course, she is. I may have gotten through many of her tall, thick walls, but there's still more to break through. More like wait for her to build a door and open it for me. Grant did enough breaking of her boundaries for a lifetime.

"Good. I miss you."

She's silent again, but this time, when she speaks, I know she's telling the truth. "I miss you, too."

"Do you want to watch something together?" I fumble around, feeling for the remote on the other side of the bed where

I threw it earlier. The TV screen lights up the room instantly. "Oh, I want to show you something. Turn on YouTube."

Her laughter rings down the phone and sends a warm jolt through my veins. I wish I could bottle that sound. The sound of her laughing, happy and free. "Okay," she says. "I'm on YouTube."

"Type in *secretsongsboston*." I type in the name of the channel as Katie goes quiet on the other end of the line. "It's this girl, woman, I have no idea how old she is, but I found her a few weeks ago. She posts these incredible covers of all these songs, and lately, they've all been these ones that I love. It's incredible."

"You ... you don't know who it is?" she asks quietly.

"Nah, the channel is completely anonymous." I flick through the tracks. "Have you found it?"

She sucks in a breath before answering. "Yeah. Yeah, I have."

"They just posted a new one the other day. 'I Don't Want to Miss a Thing' by Aerosmith." I flick across until I find the video I want. "It's got to be one of my all-time favorite tracks."

"I-I know. The vinyl is hanging on the wall on the staircase." Her voice is a little shaky. The reception must not be the best in the hotel.

"Will you listen to it with me?" I ask her, hovering over the play button.

I can hear the sounds of the TV back in my bedroom, the small clicks as she searches through the videos on the screen. "Okay, I found it."

"Ready?"

"Go," she whispers.

The voice coming through the phone and the one playing on the screen are in perfect sync. We stay quiet, listening to the singer's soft voice as it turns every lyric into the most beautiful melody. The video is trained on her fingers as they play the keyboard that accompanies her voice. She's got red nails.

"Katie?"

"Yeah?"

"Will you get the red nails back if I win tomorrow?" I ask, smirking as I remember how good they looked. She lets out a watery laugh and then sniffs. Is she ... crying? "Hey, what's wrong?"

"Nothing, nothing." Another sniffle and a ruffle of sheets as she turns over. "It's just a nice song. What's another of your favorites?"

I name track after track on the YouTube channel, and we listen to them all. Sometimes twice. Eventually, I hear her breathing go steady, and she's been quiet for a while. I realize she's fallen asleep on the other end of the phone. I turn the TV off, listening to whatever sound comes through the phone, and close my eyes.

I'm asleep within minutes.

Chapter Nineteen
Katie

My emotions are all over the place. One minute, I'm fine, the next, I feel like crying. It's all utterly and completely Flynn Reed's fault.

The man has no idea how he makes me feel or what he's done to my brain chemistry in just a few short months. In college, I felt strong and independent, but I was also still growing. With Grant, I felt like I had settled. Settled with him, with my career choice, with my decision to give up playing music whenever I wanted.

With Flynn ...

With Flynn, I feel free. Free to make a choice, a mistake, a rash decision. He takes every change of mind in stride, adapts to the mood, and runs with whatever plans are changed in the moment. He's charming and funny, and likes his routine, but he still broke it for me. He continues to break it for me.

Now he's somehow stumbled upon my secret music channel and has fallen in love with my covers? Well, I suppose if I wasn't falling in love with him before, I am now.

My heart pounds every time someone new comes through the bar's doors. The day after an away game is the worst. I only have a rough idea of when he'll be back. They get off the plane, collect their bags, and then head home from the airport. Since he normally carpools with Scott, he gets dropped off here, and then he'll stay and distract me until the end of my shift.

I tap my fingernails, back to being painted the bright, fire engine red he liked so much, on the bartop.

Why the fuck am I nervous?

I try to shake myself out of it and move around the bar. Doug stands at the end, his pint almost empty.

"Do you want another, Doug?"

He nods, his eyes on the highlights from yesterday's game. Ivy and I watched from home, curled up on the couch with hot coffee and popcorn.

"Your man isn't half bad," Doug comments as I take the empty glass from in front of him.

I smile, dropping in on the back of the bar and grabbing a fresh glass from the fridge. I twist the pint under the steady stream of beer. "Not my man, but thank you. I guess."

"They make a good team, he and Harvey. You and Ivy are lucky girls."

"Are we?" I'm regretting this conversation already.

"Course you are." He takes the pint and hands me a twenty-dollar bill.

I roll my eyes as I take it. "How's that? Because they're million-dollar football players?"

"No, because they're friends too. Just like you and Ives." Doug sips his beer, and I place his change in front of him. "You'll see when you start having kids of your own. When you have friends in the same place as you in life, you feel lucky to get to do all those milestones together."

"Did you have friends like that?"

"Oh, yeah. We all lived on the same street. Half of us got married in the same year, and then twelve months later, we started popping out kids. Now, most of us have grandkids all the same age. One of my grandsons was in Ivy's kindergarten class two years ago. Connor. Such a sweet lad."

I just nod, my eyes flickering back to the door, waiting for Flynn to appear. Doug goes back to his table, so I go back for the dirty glass that I put aside and take it over to the dishwasher. Bending down, I place it inside and turn the thing on. It's only half full, but what else can I do to waste time?

I glance back at Doug, now back among his friends. I wonder if he's right—if it's easier going through all the milestones with friends by your side. I'm sure it is.

But Ivy wants kids. Scott wants Ivy to have his kids. I have no idea what Flynn wants, but, judging by the way he talks about his relationship with his dad, he wants kids, too.

They were never on my radar. Grant never talked about what he might want in the future, and I think after some time, I stopped thinking about it, too. I settled into the life I'd chosen and was content, on the surface, to just live through it.

When I stop now and think about what I want, I'm not so sure anymore.

I thought I wanted to be a teacher, but I don't.

I thought the bar was a temporary stop, but it isn't.

I thought I wanted to be with Grant, regardless of whether I ever got the ring or the kids. I couldn't have been more wrong.

My stomach turns over as I try to imagine what my life would be like with kids. I try to imagine my wedding, see myself in a white dress, walking down an aisle. I try to think about anything beyond the next six months.

Completely and utterly blank.

I think over the last four years. I stopped thinking about what I wanted. Maybe that's why I'm struggling to define whatever Flynn and I have. It's certainly not fake.

People in real fake relationships don't fuck as much as we do. Is it real? Is what we have one of those lasting things like Ivy and Scott? Do Flynn and I have this inevitable thing tying us together, or am I setting myself up to settle once more for whatever is just in front of me?

Surely not. The man stocks his pantry with my favorite food. He cooks for me. Watches the shows I like with me, and he doesn't complain. He respects my boundaries but also isn't afraid to let me know when I'm not respecting his. He's protective but in the 'I'll watch you fight it out, but I'm here if you need me to tap in' sort of way.

That's not nothing.

"Katie Murphy?" I spin at the sound of my name. A tall, skinny man in a blue suit stands on the other side of the bar. If a corporation had a poster boy, this guy would be it. There isn't a wrinkle in sight, and his hair is perfectly styled with what looks like half a jar of hair gel. He carries a soft briefcase by his side, and he smiles at me like I'm his next big paycheck.

I look around, picking up the towel sitting on the side of the bar just to have something to do with my hands. "Who's asking?"

"Mark Madison. From Legends Entertainment." He digs a hand into his briefcase, then holds a card out to me. I stare at the block letters. Legends Entertainment? As in the record label? That Legends?

I take the card without saying anything and turn it over in my hands. Sure enough, yep. It's *that* Legends. I look up, confusion written all over my face. "How do you know my name?"

"We discovered your YouTube channel. You're a hard woman to find, Ms. Murphy."

"You discovered … I'm sorry, what?"

"We at Legends pride ourselves on being up to date with new, up-and-coming talent. We are constantly on social media looking for hidden gems. We found *you*." He leans on the bar, gesturing at the card still in my hand. "We want you to come and record a demo for us. Do you do original songs?"

"Yes—I mean, yes, but not since college. I don't—" I shake my head, trying to clear my thoughts. "I don't understand. How did you even find me? My channel has been up for years, and not a single person has ever even noticed. My mom doesn't even know."

"You're a true hidden talent, Ms. Murphy. I recognize that." He nods at himself, a hand planted on his chest. God, this guy is an idiot.

"How the hell did you find me?"

"Oh," he says, his shoulders falling. "Well, someone sort of, tweeted you."

"They ... what?"

"I logged in last week, and they had DM'd me every single one of your video links on YouTube. Nothing else. Just all your video links and your name, Katie Murphy." He rubs a hand on the back of his neck.

My heart stops beating. Someone knows it's me. I run through all the possibilities in my head. My mom and dad haven't paid enough attention, and definitely don't know how to use Twitter, let alone know how to share all those links. Ivy thinks I gave music up in college.

Flynn?

No. It was only two nights ago that I was curled up in his bed, surrounded by his scent as he told me about the channel. He found it on his own. He would've just asked if it were me if he had known. Right?

So, it was someone else. Someone else knows and has taken it upon themselves to send all my videos to a label? What the actual fuck?

"Can I see the messages?" I ask, my hand stretching out and placing the business card on the bartop between us.

"Oh." Mark Maidson digs in his bag again and pulls out his phone. He swipes on the screen a few times, then turns it around to face me. "Here you go. Some account called *fantastyaccountant11*."

Oh my god. My chest feels as though it's cracking in two. Like my world and all those careful walls I built have been taken to with a wrecking ball. I spent so long building a place where I was safe and myself. I didn't let anyone in. Except him. I let him in—by accident—in the early days.

He remembered.

He ruined it.

Grant.

***

"I'm quitting teaching," I say as soon as I walk in, placing my bag on the kitchen counter and my hands on my hips. I take a steadying breath and fortify my emotions. Today has been ... well, uneasy. But I chose to leave it behind in the bar, and I will think about it later. When I feel like it.

Now, it's replaced the memories of Italy in the small box in my mind.

It's locked up. And, for good measure, I used an extra padlock.

Now is not the time to be confessing to Flynn or my parents about the channel or about the music producer that wants me to record a demo.

Now is the time to finally make a decision.

And I choose the bar.

My mom, who's cooking what looks like the biggest pot of pasta anyone has ever seen, jolts and turns around. "Hi, to you too."

"Sorry." I rush around the island and kiss her cheek. "Hi, Mom."

"Hello, darling." She smiles gently at me.

"I-I've made my decision. I want to take over the bar. Full-time." I rehearsed these words over and over in my head as I was driving over from the bar. "Which means that I won't be teaching anymore. I just wanted to let you know."

"Oh." Mom turns the stove off and faces me, wiping a hand down the apron she wears. "Well, we can talk about it."

"There isn't anything to talk about. I don't like teaching," I say. Just as she opens her mouth to reply, Dad walks in, holding a newspaper in plastic wrap and a football.

"Sammy's arm is getting stronger and stronger," Dad tells Mom as he stretches his shoulder. He spots me, and his eyes light up. "Pumpkin, what are you doing here?"

"Just thought I would come by, and I wanted to talk to you both."

"She's giving up teaching, Sam," my mom says sharply. She clicks her tongue and turns back around to the pasta sauce on the stove. "All that energy you put into getting your degree, and you're throwing it away to run a bar."

"You guys did it," I argue.

"So you didn't have to." She throws her hands up as her voice rises. My dad springs into action, moving to her side instantly and placing a calming hand on the small of her back. She sniffs, her head hanging low as she clutches the countertops. "I didn't want you to have to do the three in the morning finishes, or clean people's vomit. I wanted you to have a nice job, a nice life."

"Honey," my dad murmurs in her ear, "she likes the bar. We should be happy she wants to take it over. Saves us from having to go through the motions to try and sell it."

"You guys are going to sell?" I ask, my frown deepening.

Dad looks up, his eyes a little sad. "We were thinking about it. Your mom and I aren't interested in going back to full-time work. After the debacle with Grant the other week, we were sure you might decide to walk away from it as well."

"Oh." I glance down at my hands, my fingers tangling together in front of me. I didn't even think about that. It never crossed my mind that I wouldn't go back to the bar even after Grant's tantrum, throwing my glassware—and our past—around the place.

"Is that not the case?" Dad says gently.

"No." I shake my head. "I like working there. I have lots of ideas to build the clientele and make it more than just a sports bar."

"I thought you liked being a teacher?" Mom says, turning in my dad's arms and sniffling. "You did all four years at college to become a teacher, and now you've just decided it's no longer for you?"

"I like teaching, I just don't want to do it full-time." I sigh, leaning against the counter. "I appreciate all the effort you guys went through to put me through college. I'm grateful for your support and for the things you've done for me. But the bar is like a family business."

"It is." Dad nods. He squeezes Mom's shoulder as her eyes fill with tears. "And, if you want to take it over, then we will be happy to pass the reins."

"Thank you," I murmur.

"Are you sure?" Mom presses. "Are you sure this isn't just a reaction to what happened with Grant? And what about this new boyfriend of yours?"

"He's not—we're just seeing each other. It's not ... that ... serious." The lie falls from my lips before I can stop it.

"Does he know that?" Dad raises an eyebrow. "He seems very serious about you."

I blush a deep red. They met at the police station the other day. Flynn almost fell over in his attempt to shake my dad's hand. It would've been funny if it hadn't been so damn endearing. "We're friends. I don't think it will ... we probably won't last."

The lie tastes so sour in my mouth, I feel like gagging a little bit. When I look up into my dad's face, he just smiles at me like he knows I'm lying through my teeth.

"That's a shame," Mom says as she pushes away from Dad and goes back to her pasta sauce. "He seems like a very nice boy."

Dad just winks at me and pulls me into a one-armed hug. He kisses me on the forehead, and I lean into him. "Are you sure this is what you want?" he whispers to me.

"Absolutely." I nod. "I have some big plans for the place. I think I'll make you proud."

"You already make me proud." He kisses my hair again before letting me go. "Are you staying for dinner, pumpkin?"

"I—no, thank you." I shake my head, grabbing for my bag. "Flynn's waiting for me in the car, so I better go."

"Katie Murphy." I immediately flinch at my mother's scolding tone. "Are you telling me you made that boy stay in the car while you came in here, intending to have a conversation that could've gone for hours?"

"I—"

She spins around, pointing the sauce-covered spoon at me. "You go and invite him in for dinner. Right now."

"Yep. Sure." I swallow hard and make my way to the front door, Dad's laughter echoing behind me. I throw it open and wrap my arms around myself as I head for the car sitting at the end of the driveway. Flynn's head snaps up when I open the passenger side door.

"We're having dinner with my parents," I say, grimacing.

"Are we?" He sets his phone down on his thigh.

I nod. "And if my mother asks, you insisted you would stay in the car."

Flynn laughs as he steps out and comes to stand by my side. He throws an arm over my shoulder and pulls me closer to his body. I curl into his warmth. "So, did you talk to them?"

"Yep." I nod, craning my neck to look at him. "I'm going to be running a bar."

"Fuck, yes." He leans down, eyes shining. "Does this mean I can eat for free now?"

I laugh and smack his chest as we climb the steps up to my parents' front door. "You wish."

CHAPTER TWENTY
FLYNN

Life is good right now.

The team made it to the conference finals—we've been practically undefeated this season. We're going up against New York on our home field in just a few days. Every time I think about it, the adrenaline pumps through me. This season, it feels like I've fallen back in love with football again. I felt old last year, run down, stuck in my routine. Something about this season has completely changed the way I've been playing, the way I've been seeing the game.

I have no doubt that the *something* is more of a *someone* with blonde hair and blue eyes.

Katie sits next to me, my arm draped over the back of our booth seat, my fingers fiddling with a piece of her hair. I never expected the harmless flirting on that eight-hour plane ride to Italy last summer would end in me finding the love of my life.

Sure, she has no idea I love her. Nor do I think she quite understands exactly how much her presence affects me, but she'll get there. I'm learning very quickly with Katie that things will need to be slow. There'll be no ring within six months. No kids within a year. She's only just decided that she wants to take on the official role of venue manager for the bar. I suspect this will be our lives for a while.

If she agrees to stay. Getting her to agree will require me actually asking her, though. Something I have chickened out of doing about once a day since we had dinner at her parents' a week ago.

Instead, I've let her distract me with sex and football.

The two go well together. I fuck her before practice, I have a killer day on the field, then I get to fuck her again when I get home. I have been playing at my best, and Katie is a huge part of that.

"When are you getting your suits done?" Ivy says from across the table. There's this twinge of panic that sets into her voice every time we speak about the wedding now, and it gets more and more prominent as the date they've chosen gets closer.

"Baby, relax," Scott soothes, his hand snaking over her shoulders. He tugs her closer to his side and smiles down at her. "We will get them after this weekend. We'll either lose and be done for the season, or we'll be on a bye before the bowl. It will get done."

"Promise me you'll go next week?"

"Promise." Scott leans down and kisses her. Katie makes a gagging noise, and I snigger into my water glass.

"You two are no better," Scott growls, glaring at me for laughing along. He asked me for help today with keeping Ivy's stress levels down, but as Katie has already said, they will get worse. Then, she'll likely have a big cry to get all the emotions out before she snaps out of it.

"We aren't nearly as gross as the two of you." Katie scoffs. I tug on the piece of hair that's tangled around my finger, warning her not to go too hard on my friend. The man is under the most intense amount of pressure with leading the team right now, and while I think the banter between them is hilarious, Scott's fuse is shorter than normal.

"My wedding dress is ready, but they're only open during the week. Who only opens a bridal boutique during the week? Do they think people don't—"

"I'll pick it up, Ives. Send me the address and just let them know. I'll collect it."

"Oh." Ivy slumps in her seat. "Are you sure?"

"Of course. Anything you need." Katie reaches across the table and pats her friend's hand.

"Thanks. You're the best."

"Are you getting excited? Or just too stressed to think at the moment?" Katie smiles knowingly. I tangle my fingers further into her hair, finding the back of her neck and massaging lightly. I love touching her. The moment I feel her skin, her hair, the moment I kiss her lips, a calm settles over me. I smirk when she shivers under my touch.

"Too stressed." Ivy rolls her head against Scott's shoulder, closing her eyes. "I can't wait, but also, I kind of just want it to be over."

"Just what I want to hear from the woman I'm marrying. She can't wait for it to be over," Scott murmurs, a smile playing on his lips as he looks down at Ivy.

She slaps his chest. "Oh, hush. You know what I mean."

His reply is cut off as Justin appears and drops a few plates of food onto the table. Ivy leans forward. "Oooh. New menu?"

"Uh-huh. I sat down with Roscoe the other day, and he's already started ordering ingredients for it. Try the blue cheese sauce with the wings. It's probably the best thing I've ever put in my mouth."

I raise an eyebrow at her, turning in my seat. When she looks at me, her eyes shine with mischief, and I squeeze the back of her neck where I still hold her.

"I said what I said," she says, winking at me. I pull my hand away from her neck and dig my fingers into her waist. Katie squeals and laughs. The sound sends a jolt straight to my heart. She swats my hands away and faces Ivy again. "What will you wear to the game on the weekend?"

"Uh—" Ivy shrugs. "What I normally wear. Jeans and a jersey. Why, what were you thinking?"

I rub my palm over Katie's thigh as she shrugs. "I thought we could dress up. I know heaps of other girls make a big deal out of it."

"*You* want to dress up?"

"Why not?"

"You haven't wanted to dress up in, well, forever," Ivy says carefully.

Katie only smiles, dipping one of the wings into the blue cheese sauce. "If you're up for it, it could be fun?"

"Whatever gets you out of your black hoodie, I'm in." Ivy laughs.

Justin brings over a few burgers, and we dig into the new menu items that Katie designed with Roscoe. Everything is classic bar food, but, unsurprisingly, it's fucking delicious. Even Scott moans when he takes a bite of the burger. We're laughing, going over details for the wedding, and completely distracted from the game coming this weekend, when I look up at the entrance and my blood starts boiling.

I'm out of my seat in a flash, my hand slipping off its permanent position on Katie's thigh as I head for the man who just walked in.

"Leave," I snarl.

Grant puts his hands up. "Whoa. I promise I'm not here to make trouble. I just—" His gaze drags behind my shoulder to where Katie is sitting.

"No way."

"Come on, man. I just want to apologize," he pleads. I widen my stance, my arms crossing over my chest as I place myself firmly between Katie and this piece of filth. I feel a small, warm hand press gently between my shoulder blades and, when I look down, I see Katie coming to stand at my side.

"I really don't want to have to order anymore glassware, so if you could leave without smashing up half the bar, I'd appreciate it," she tells him, her words dripping in venom.

"I'm sorry—"

"It's a bit late to apologize."

"Yes, even so, I am sorry." Grant takes a step forward. My hand shoots out, hitting the middle of his chest and causing him to step back in surprise.

"You had no right to barge back into my life. Not after everything you did to me." The hand still on my back squeezes the fabric of my shirt into her fist. "You cheated on me so many times, I think I lost count. You told me time and time again I was too much and too loud, so I dampened myself for you, and you still cheated, still hurt me. You fucking slapped me, Grant."

He flinches, and I have to hold back a smile. Fuck, but I'm proud of her right now.

"I was selfish and wrong to come here the other day."

"Yes. You were." Katie nods. "This is my family's business. This is my workplace. You caused distress to my staff—you berated them and scared them. You threw a tantrum because I didn't answer your fucking phone calls. How fucking childish are you?"

"I know—"

"You could have just left it. I walked away. I didn't ruin your life by pressing charges for slapping me, and I didn't tell all your friends about the cheating. I didn't even tell your mom, who kept calling me for weeks, asking what happened to the two of us, by the way. I let you off, for free." Katie releases her hold on my T-shirt and steps forward. She's only a little shorter than Grant, but right now, you'd think he was about two feet tall.

I step back, standing behind Katie as she gets in his face. "You should've just walked away. Instead, you did something even worse. You told someone about something that wasn't yours to tell."

Huh? I look at her. She's seething. Anger is written all over her face. Grant gulps, taking a step back and putting his hands up. "I was drunk. I'm sorry. I really am—"

"It's too late. You ruined it. You took yet another thing away from me, and this wasn't yours to take." Katie launches forward, but I catch her around the waist and pull her back. Her back lands against my chest, and I grunt. "Let me go, Flynn."

"Uh-uh. No way, Rockstar," I say against her ear. "You'll hurt your hand and your license if you get caught fighting."

Katie fights against my hold, but I keep my arm locked around her waist. "You had no right."

"I know. I'm sorry."

"They're going to expose the channel. My safe space."

"I'm sorry, Katie. I am."

"You—" Katie struggles, then goes still. Silence fills the bar, and I feel myself holding a breath. When she hiccups, a sob falling from her lips, I spin her around in my arms.

"Katie, baby." I grasp her cheeks, watching her eyelashes soak with tears as they leak from her eyes. "Talk to me."

"I can't apologize enough." I glance up to see Grant retreating, heading for the door. He gives Katie one last, apologetic look. "I'm sorry."

What the fuck is going on?

She didn't cry last time he was here. She barely batted an eyelash when he called her a slut or admitted that he hit her in front of her staff. He comes back—sober, thank god—and starts apologizing again, and she's brought to tears?

Fuck, I'm confused.

I tuck her into my side, walking her to the back corridor. Ivy watches us as we pass, blocked in her seat by Scott, who, I'm guessing, was caught between getting up to stand behind me and keeping Ivy in her seat so she didn't get up and stand beside Katie. I get it. If the roles were reversed, I would've kept Katie in her seat, too.

I shake my head at Ivy, silently asking her to stay in her seat. Another sob rolls through Katie's body, and I tighten my hold on her. When we're out of sight of the main room, I gently release her, leaning her against a wall and crowding her in. Before she can hide her face in her hands, I cup her cheeks, using my thumbs to wipe her tears.

"Hey, hey," I say softly, catching what I can as they fall down her cheeks. "You're okay."

Katie shakes her head, her eyes jamming shut as if she's physically trying to stop the tears. "He sent them. Every single one. He had no right."

"I don't—" I take a deep breath and restart. The last thing I want is to sound panicked or push her. "I can't help if you don't tell me what you mean. Is this about what happened the other night when Grant was here?"

"No," she says, her voice trembling.

"Do you want to tell me what's wrong? You don't have to." I swipe her cheeks again. "We can just wait here until you're ready and then go back out and pretend everything is normal."

Katie huffs, and when she looks up at me, even with a few stray tears still running over her cheeks, she gives me a watery smile. "Thank you."

"Of course."

"I—" Katie looks down the corridor. There are a few doors, the bathrooms, and the door leading into the back alley. "Can I show you something?"

"Yes. Of course, you can." She hesitates but only for a moment before she takes my hand and leads me down the corridor. There's a fancy code lock on the door, and she taps in four digits. It beeps, and the door clicks open.

The room isn't bright. Katie switches on the light overhead, but it's dull, likely in need of a change. I expected it to be an office, and maybe she was going to show me her plans for the bar. It's all she's been talking about since we came home from her parents' house last week.

Instead, it's full of musical instruments and recording equipment. There's a laptop on the desk, a camera, and a microphone plugged into a sound board. There are wires along the ground, connecting the keyboard and the two different guitars on stands in the corners.

"What the—" I step into the room behind her, taking it all in. "So you *do* play more than occasionally?"

I smirk, snaking a hand around her waist and pulling her back against my chest. She sniffles but lets me.

"Yes. More than occasionally." She taps my arm, and I release her. Moving over to the music station, she lifts the lid of the laptop and, once it loads, steps aside to show me the screen.

It's a YouTube page. Not just any YouTube page, but the one I showed her the night I called from my hotel. The one that's been posting all my favorite love songs.

"But that's—" I look over at Katie. She's wrapped her arms around her middle like she's protecting herself from whatever my reaction is going to be. "Is this you? This channel?"

She nods.

Chapter Twenty-One

Katie

So, everyone knows.

Flynn, Ivy, and even Scott.

They all know about the channel, the music producer, and the fact that Grant was the one to spill the beans by sending all my videos to said music producer. Instead of spending the night eating dinner and talking about the wedding, Ivy grilled me on the music and the channel. Flynn stayed quiet, but his hand also stayed under the table and firmly on my knee for the whole evening.

The house is dark and cold when we get home. I slip off my shoes, not bothering with the hallway lights as I head for the living room and the fireplace. All I feel like doing is curling up under a blanket, with the fire on, and watching a show. I want to forget about Grant. I want to forget about the channel.

I feel Flynn following me.

We didn't really speak in the car. He drove one-handed, his other hand on my knee, his fingers squeezing my leg every few minutes. I rested my head against the window and prepared for the conversation I knew was inevitably going to happen between us.

I wish I could delay it. I wish I could live in the bubble Ivy talked about for a little while longer.

Flynn flicks on a lamp, but leaves the rest, as I kneel in front of the fireplace and turn it on. It heats up quickly, and I shiver as a fresh wave of warmth floods me. I strip off my jacket and lay it over the back of the couch, heading for my favorite corner.

Flynn watches me sit down, right in the corner, before smirking. One knee at a time, he lowers himself almost directly on top of me and starts crawling.

"Excuse me," he says, trying to wedge himself behind me and into my favorite corner. "Sorry—I just need—excuse me. One second. I just—there we go."

When he's finished, he's completely wedged himself into the corner of the couch, forcing me to sit up. I glance over my shoulder. "You're not funny."

"Liar." He pats his chest. "I'll curl up in the corner, you can curl up on me."

"You're not as comfortable as the couch." I pout, but he just smiles wider.

"You're lying again, Rockstar."

I frown, giving in and finally lying back against his chest. His arms immediately encircle me. A calm, safe feeling rushes through me as I settle into him. I close my eyes when I feel him press a kiss against my hair.

"So," he says after a minute or two. "All of my favorite songs, hey?"

Thankfully, it's too dark in the room to really see it, but I feel my face heat up with a blush. I hum. "I've been staring at the records on these damn walls for months. It was an unconscious decision on my part."

"Uh-huh." His hand slips onto the waist of my jeans.

"Besides, in my defense, I didn't expect you to find it on your own and then show it to me," I say, angling my head to see him. The low light of the room casts his face in shadows, but they don't stop me from seeing the way he stares at me, into my soul. I used to think it was intense, that maybe he stared a little too much. Now, I hope he never stops.

"Why didn't you tell me that night on the phone?"

"I-I don't know." I bite down on my lower lip, chewing for a moment. He slips his hand from my jeans and uses his thumb to tug my lip free. "I wasn't ready. It was my safe space. It had been for a long time. Grant made me feel so casual about music, like I wasn't any good. In college, for a while, I thought maybe I could do it professionally. Sing, write songs, something."

"You still can."

I shake my head a little. "It's not my dream anymore."

"Because of what Grant said?"

"No." I stop myself. "Well, yes. But, not just him. I love the bar. I do. I was always good at music, all my teachers thought I had talent, but honestly, I love pouring pints for Doug and his friends all day. I love Roscoe, and I love trying to figure out if he's actually from Russia or not."

"Huh?"

"Oh, I have this theory that Roscoe used to be in the mafia and he's lying low at a small sports bar in Boston because he's being hunted."

Flynn snorts. "That's ridiculous."

"Yeah, yeah. We'll see. When they find him, I'll be the one to say I told you so," I say, my heart feeling lighter with every word. I sigh. "I think if maybe I had never met Grant, I might have gone down a different path, but I did. And I can't say I'm that disappointed."

"So you're not going to call the music executive guy?"

I lean back, meeting his eyes again. "No. I'm not going to call him."

"Are you sure? This could change your life. You could be the next Taylor Swift."

"No one will ever be the next Taylor Swift," I say. "She's an icon."

"She really is," Flynn says on a dreamy sigh. I smack his chest and he laughs. "You're an icon too, don't worry."

"I think—" I take a deep breath, wanting to voice an idea that's been forming since I started singing more and more. "I think I want to get a band, maybe on a Saturday night, and just sing at the bar once a week. We could host different themes, and during the summer, we could do afternoon sessions, maybe."

Flynn lifts my chin with his finger, leaning down at the same time to press his lips to mine. When we break apart, he smiles at me. "That's a great idea."

"You think?"

"Hell yeah." He kisses me again. "I'm going to be fucking the singer in a band."

"As opposed to who? The owner of the bar?"

He groans, the hand that's tucked into the waistband of my jeans dropping lower. "Fuck, that's hot too."

"You're an idiot."

"Uh-huh. Your idiot." Silence engulfs us, and blood pounds in my ears. I feel a lump form in my throat. This is the moment. If I am going to tell him how I feel, how I really feel, this would be the time to do it.

"Katie, I have feelings for you."

"I—"

"And I know that all the stuff with Grant is still fresh. That you went through a lot with him, and four years is a long time to be in a relationship with the wrong person. But I think I'm the right person."

I sit up, moving off his chest and turning around, facing him as I tuck my legs beneath me. "Flynn, I—"

"This isn't fake. It was never fake. Not since the moment I saw you in that airport lounge and realized you were single. Not since I spent my entire summer trying to make you laugh just so I could hear the sound again. I have no idea what I did to piss you off after that night, but—"

"You gave your number to another girl," I blurt out.

"What?" Flynn's eyes snap to mine, and he sits up. "No, I didn't."

"You did." I nod. "We were at dinner the night after we were first together, and you went to the bar. You were talking to these girls, and then you hugged them. Later, in the bathroom, I overheard her tell her friends that you slipped her your number. Told her to call you when she got back to the States."

Flynn shakes his head, his eyes wide and unfocused. "No. No, that's not—"

"So you didn't give her your number?"

"Fucking, of course not, Katie! I had just spent the night with you. I was *obsessed* with *you.* Why the actual fuck would I give my number to some random girl?"

"Because you're a flirt." I feel my voice rising, the resentment bubbling under my skin. "Because you play professional football and get photographed with a different girl on your arm every other night. Because you take girls like Heather to charity balls and then never see them again. What was I supposed to think?"

"Oh, I don't know, maybe not to believe everything you hear in the media?" Flynn sits forward, throwing his legs over the side of the couch and resting his elbows on his knees. He looks at me, pure disbelief in his eyes. "Do you seriously believe I would do that to you?"

"I—Not now. I don't think that now."

"But you did? Back in the summer?" I nod, and he scoffs, hanging his head. "Fuck. You didn't even know me then. We'd barely scratched the surface, and you passed a pretty big judgment."

"I know—"

"I think I've had maybe five, six, sexual partners in my life. I dated a lot of girls, but I was never a player. I wanted—*want*—a future with someone. I want marriage, a nice house, to come home and tell each other about our days. I want kids, a few of them." He shakes his head, keeping his eyes firmly trained on the floor. "I know I come off as one of those cheeky, charming players that would love to mess around in the media, but I'm not. I'm not that guy."

"I know." I wrap my arms around my legs. "I'm messed up from Grant. I know it was wrong, but I saw you with those girls and I just ... freaked out."

"How many times did he cheat on you?"

"You say it like there was a time he didn't." I try to laugh it off, but thinking about it again just makes it hurt. Not necessarily about the cheating, but the effect it had on me. Especially now, with Flynn. I can't even begin to know how to trust him fully, and he's the perfect gentleman.

The perfect fake boyfriend.

"Jesus Christ, why did you stay so long?"

I shrug, tightening my hold on my legs. "I don't know. I thought maybe it would get better. Then it didn't, but I was ... I settled. I settled for it."

"You deserve more."

"I know that now."

"You deserve me." Flynn looks at me, pain all over his face, the shadows jarring the lines in his face. "And I deserve you."

A lump forms in my throat. I open my mouth, trying to find the right words, but I get stuck on them every time. Instead, I just find myself whispering, "Flynn. I want to be with you, but I just ... I ... "

Silence surrounds us again. We stare at each other, the electric fire washing over us and warming the room, a single lamp casting jagged shapes all around us. It's dark and messy, and hot. Like us, really.

"Are you going to move out?" he asks quietly when I don't finish my sentence.

I blink, that annoyingly familiar sting of tears coming back. "Do you want me to?"

"No."

"Neither."

"But you don't want to be in a real relationship?" he asks.

"I don't—Do we have to label this? What we have right now is perfect. It's as real as it gets." I sigh, inching forward on the couch. "You make me laugh and feel safe. And, we're really, really good in bed together. What is the point of defining this when we are perfect already?"

"So you just want to keep doing what we're doing?"

I lean forward, slipping my fingers between his, my hands taking both of his, and I pull them into my lap. He watches our hands, letting me move them easily and turning his body toward me at the same time. "Are you okay with that?"

"I want to be with you, Katie," he says. He squeezes my hands. "I want you for the long run. If you need time to come to terms with that, then I can wait for you to be ready."

The tension in my chest releases, my lungs inflate, and I squeeze my eyes shut.

Thank god.

In one move, Flynn leans over and wraps a hand around my waist, pulling me across the gap between us and onto his lap. I squeal, smiling as he settles my legs over his thighs and wraps his arms around my waist to lock me in place.

"Thank you," I whisper, running my fingers through his hair. "For being patient with me."

"Of course." He leans in, pressing his mouth to my jawline, kissing a path to my ear. His fingers splay on my back and press my hips into his. "You're my Rockstar. I would do anything for you."

I lean back, keeping my hands around his neck. "Why do you call me that?"

"What?"

"Rockstar? You called me that at the airport. Why?"

"I guess the first time I met you, I just got the feeling you were made for bigger and better things. You had this energy about you, like someone could offer you the world and you'd say, 'No, thank you, I'll take it for myself.'"

The lump is back as I try to swallow his words. "That's—that's how you saw me?"

"Yeah."

"It sounds like the girl I used to be."

"You'll be her again." He kisses me on the lips, lingering close as he murmurs his next words against my lips. "I'll be right next to you while you figure it out."

Chapter Twenty-Two
Flynn

THE HUDDLE'S QUIET, ELECTRICITY sparking between the guys. You can feel it in the air. No one's joking, no one's laughing. We made it. Finally, the fucking Super Bowl.

We scraped through the conference finals, winning by the skin of our teeth, but we did it. New York put up a good fight, but we'd been on fire all game. For every play they threw at us, we had the answer. Scott almost cried. So did I.

He came to Boston to get a ring.

We've dreamed of the ring since college. Both of us, together on the field when the confetti releases. Every player wants to feel it at least once. If they're lucky, if they're good, they will.

Now is our time.

Scott looks each of us dead in the eye. "One play. Gun Spread Y Corner. We go now or we go home." He looks at me last. "You ready, Reed?"

All eyes are on me. This is what we train for. What we live for. What we sacrifice for. I give a sharp nod, the movement minimal. Adrenaline rushes through my veins. I'm on the high again. As we break the huddle and spread out across the line, I flex my hands. The sharp pain I felt in those early regular season games is nothing but a memory.

I can't regret it. That bar fight brought me Katie. If it weren't for that douchebag in boat shoes, I would've probably just kept staring at her from afar, never having the guts to find out if we were anything more than a one-night stand on a holiday.

We are.

So, so much more.

My heart pounds as if it's trying to match the game clock. I split off, wide off the line, advantaging the wide receiver's position and lining myself with a smaller defender. I'm quicker. I can outrun him. It's fourth and goal, the ball's on the eight. The end zone is in sight, and my blood rushes from the pressure cooker that is this final play.

I glance at the safety. Too shallow. The corner's inside leverage. If I go wide, he'll miss me. Mistake. They're weak. *We're going to do this.*

Snap.

I burst off the line, exploding into my route with every inch of power and speed I can muster. I make a quick jab to the outside, leading the cornerback out of position. He bites, taking the bait as he shifts his weight to the outside line. I plant my foot into the turf and use the leverage to change my direction, heading for the corner of the end zone.

It's a clean route. No stumbling, no contact. I feel open before I even look back.

When I do, I see it. The ball, hanging like a gift as it sails through the air. I stretch out my arm, but ... fuck, it's short. I make the decision on instinct. I dive.

Arms stretched, fingers splayed, I feel the ball hit my hand.

I got it.

Before I can curl my fingers, before I can pull it in to my chest and secure the win—

Bam.

A helmet crashes straight into the side of my head. I hear a deafening crack. My ears begin to ring, the sound of the stadium disappearing as my cleats hit the turf and my knees buckle beneath me.

It's a blindside.

Helmet-to-helmet contact. The defender didn't mean it. He just couldn't stop in time. It's not malicious, it's just football.

Just bad luck.

I feel as if I'm falling, but it's infinite. I don't hit grass or another body. I just keep falling. Then, it goes white. Everything brightens in the space of mere seconds, blinding me.

Then black.

Then nothing.

***

I come to on the turf, flat on my back and unfeeling. My ears still ring, and it sounds like someone is screaming through a broken radio. Everything is muffled even as I strain to make out the sounds around me. My arms won't move. My head feels as if it's caving in on itself.

A pulsing deafens my ears, traveling through my nerves and down my spine. My vision's a tunnel. Everything is blurry, and when it begins to clear, the stadium lights stare down at me like a judgment.

I hear my name, over and over. Someone's shouting for my attention. Teammates? Trainers? Fans?

A face hovers over me, then a bright light. On instinct, I follow it.

"What happened?" I try to say. I can't be sure that it comes out. My mouth is dry, my muscles numb. I can't move. Nothing is working right.

But then I feel it. Someone lifts a finger, and I twitch as they let it drop.

I feel the ball.

It's pressed against my chest. Still there, still tucked in. I never let go.

I held on.

Above us, on the screens that shine around the stadium, one word flashes.

Touchdown.

The whistle's blown. The clock's run out. It's game over, and we won.

We're champions.

Confetti falls like rain around us, but my teammates aren't celebrating. I jostle and realize they're moving me onto a stretcher. I want to walk off. I *need* to walk off.

Katie's face flashes through my mind, and I feel like screaming, just so one of the medics will hear me. She's watching right now with no idea what's happened or where I'm going.

Scott's face comes into my line of sight, covered in dirt and grass from the game. His helmet is off, his hair sticking to his forehead with sweat. He looks distraught. I want to tell him I'm fine. I want to ask him to make sure Katie knows I'm fine.

But I can't.

The truth is, something is definitely wrong.

Chapter
Twenty-Three

Katie

Panic crawls up my throat and suffocates me every time someone in a pair of scrubs walks past the waiting room. It's full. People are everywhere. Trainers sitting on the plastic seats, coaches huddled in the corner, Scott pacing in front of the doors leading to wards, waiting for news.

We're all waiting for news.

Flynn scored, ball clutched to his chest as the defending player took him down. It was too late, though. He got the touchdown. The confetti exploded from the canons, covering the crowd and the field. The Broncos won the Super Bowl.

People in the box screamed, cheering along with the thousands of fans in the stadium, elated to finally get the ring. My brother shook me, euphoric, and my parents cheered happily.

I could only feel Ivy's hand in mine, only see the body still lying on the field, players surrounding him. Silence enveloped me then, as it does now.

He went down, and he didn't get up.

It's been a blur, from that moment to now. I watched from afar as the trainers carefully moved him to a stretcher, carrying him off the field. Scott was right next to him. The celebrations for us were done before they began.

I sit next to Ivy, her hands covering one of my own. Her thumb slides from side to side over my skin in irregular strokes, the only evidence that she's also freaking out. She doesn't show it, though. She's holding strong on this one, for me.

"You don't have to be here," I whisper. "I know you hate coming here, after everything. If it's too hard—"

"Absolutely not." Ivy shakes her head, inching closer to me and wrapping her arms around my own, drawing my hand tighter into her grip.

"I—" I glance at the doors again, checking for the hundredth time that no one is coming through them with an update on his condition.

"I know," Ivy murmurs. She leans her head against mine. "He's going to be okay, though. Promise."

A sob inches up my throat, and I swallow it down. I can't cry. I won't.

Even though the last words I said to him this morning were, "Go get 'em, tiger."

I'd wanted to tell him I loved him. That I was proud of him. That even if they didn't win today, he should be so proud of himself because he is a big reason the team made it this far. I wanted to remind him that he's good, really good, at catching the stupid ball, and no matter what anyone says, he deserves to be there.

Fuck.

My eyes sting as I think about the way I made him leave things. The way I could tell in his eyes when we spoke about what we were. When I lied through my teeth and told him I didn't want things to change.

Of course, I was lying. Of course, I want things to change.

Namely, the fucking label I told him I didn't want.

I glance around the room, at all the people from the world he adores. At the trainers, the teammates he's close with, the coaches he boasts are geniuses. What the hell was I so afraid of?

Grant's face flashes in my mind, and I feel the anger bubble under my skin.

Fuck him for ruining my trusting nature. For taking me for granted and breaking down my self-worth with his gross words and lies.

I wish I had walked away years ago.

I wish I had never allowed him to break the person I was, the person I loved, down into these tiny little pieces. I hate that he made me into this complicated jigsaw that I've been struggling to put back together ever since I finally walked away.

I realize now that Flynn has been the one putting those pieces back together. Healing something he never broke in the first place, all while wearing a smile like it's his favorite pastime.

And I was too chicken shit to tell him how I really feel.

Of course, it's more than a fling, more than one night in a foreign country.

It was months of him smiling at me while I scowled at him. Weeks of him trying to start a conversation with me and persisting even when all I did was shut him down. It's the charity ball, and him seeing me so clearly. It's him standing at my back, letting me handle my past, protective but only if I call on him. It's the dinners he cooks for me every night now, overruling any takeout options. I close my eyes, a tear finally falling down my cheek. I don't bother wiping it away.

It's the way he kisses me, like I'm the one he needs to breathe properly.

It's the way he stares at me in bed.

It's the way he listens.

What if I never get to tell him? What if something's happened and he thinks all I wanted from him was a good time? A short time.

My throat closes, and I struggle to breathe. Another few traitorous tears fall over my cheeks, and I feel like I want to claw at my throat, stop the sobs creeping toward the surface. Ivy lifts her head, her body turning toward me and her arms wrapping around my shoulders, drawing me in. I bury my face into her shoulder, and my body wins. I cry.

Because, for fuck's sake, I love the man and I didn't even get the chance to tell him.

Flynn

I wake up to the rhythmic sounds of a steady beep. As my vision comes into focus, my eyes stinging and sore, I take in my surroundings. A hospital room, tubes coming out of my forearm, machines surrounding me, reading for signs of life.

There's a heavy weight on my legs, and before I look down, I internally prepare for a cast or two. Did I break a leg? An arm?

Something was wrong, and my head hurt like hell after the contact with the defender. Getting hit directly by someone's helmet is never fun. It's how we break ribs, get bruised bodies. It's part of the game. But contact with the head … it's downright frightening. Dangerous.

I glance down and smile.

No cast or broken legs, but Katie. Sitting in a chair by my bedside. She's leaning over the bed, one arm stretched over my legs and the other curled underneath her head. She's asleep, but the tear tracks are clear, her mascara having run down her face. She looks a little like a raccoon. She's going to hate that.

I laugh, and the gentle shake jostles her.

Her bright blue eyes, blinking away the sleep as she opens them, stare right at me. "Oh my god, you're awake."

"Hi," I try to say, but my voice is scratchy and raw. Katie jumps into action, hurrying to the table at the other side of my bed and getting the water cup from it. She holds the straw up to my mouth, but I refuse, trying to lift my arm.

"You have a cracked bone in your shoulder and a very bruised collarbone. Let me fucking help you," she commands. Is it wrong that her bossing me around turns me on? In the context of me lying in hospital, probably yes. I lean forward and take a sip of the water.

The liquid slides down my throat, and I immediately feel better. "Thank you."

"You scared the shit out of me," she says, her voice breaking a little.

"It must have been a scary thing to watch." I stare up at her, wishing I could lift a hand to touch her. I will my fingers to move and they do, thank god. I lift the arm that isn't in the sling very carefully, but Katie stops me, slipping her hand into mine.

"You shouldn't move too much. The doctors haven't come in yet, but they will now that you're awake."

"Is it bad?" I ask.

"Well, they won't tell me anything." She rolls her eyes. "Scott got pretty mad. They wouldn't let any of us in."

"Why?"

She gives me a sad look and gently squeezes my hand. "We're not family. Eventually, Ivy pulled a string with a nurse she knows."

"Oh." I want to kiss her. I want to take that pained expression away.

"But..." She takes a deep breath. "It's not good. I saw them talking to Jeff. He looked distraught."

Fuck.

I don't know what to say. I've had football injuries before, but nothing quite like this.

There's a knock at the door, and a doctor pokes his head in. He must be from the hospital because the team doctor follows him in, along with Coach, and then they shut the door.

"Reed, you okay?" Coach says, nodding at me.

"Just a little banged up. Nothing a recovery in the off-season can't fix."

"It's a little more serious than that," Danny, the team doctor, says. He looks at Katie. "Will you give us the—"

"No," I tell them, keeping a firm grip on her hand. "She stays."

Danny smiles a little at me and throws up his hands. "You got it, Reed."

The doctor then pulls something out of a large envelope and places it on the back-lit wall behind them. Both Danny and the doctor move to either side. Coach stands by the door.

Doc tells me gently, but he doesn't sugarcoat it.

"You have a severe traumatic brain injury." He switches on the backlights, and images of my brain light up. The rest of the conversation blurs. I don't ask questions, but Coach does. Katie cares about what I need to do to get better. But all I hear is: Concussion. Career-ending. No contact sports. Ever.

It's over.

It's all over.

When they leave, the doctor tells us they will let our friends in the waiting room know that I'm awake, but I just stare at the ceiling. The afterparty has likely started, and the boys are probably knee deep in beers and celebrations.

We did it.

We got the ring. I got a ring. I scored the game-winning touchdown at the fucking Super Bowl, and now...

It's over. My career is over.

Football and me? We're done. But I made the catch, and I'd do it again. Even now, knowing the outcome, knowing what it would cost me in the end. I look over at Katie's face. She's staring right back at me, searching for any sign of how I'm feeling about it all. I don't know if she expects me to cry, to rage. I bet she won't expect me to smile.

And that's exactly what I do.

"We won," I say, my face breaking into the widest smile.

"You're insane." She sniffs, her eyes shining. She sits on the edge of my bed, keeping my hand in hers. "They just told you that your career is over and you're smiling?"

"I won a Super Bowl, baby. I think I'm allowed to be happy."

"What about football?"

"Everyone's time eventually comes. The clock runs out on us all at some point, even the legends. We don't always get to choose how we leave, but I'm glad I went for it to get the win."

"It was a hell of a catch."

"Thank you, Rockstar."

"You're a Super Bowl-winning football player. That's pretty damn cool." She sniffs again. "My brother lost his mind when the confetti rained down."

"I'm glad everyone could come."

"Are you sure you're okay?" she whispers. "You were carried off the field unconscious."

"I promise you, I'm okay. A little sore, but it'll heal. They're bones, they heal."

"And the football stuff?"

"I will find something else to do with my time." I squeeze her hand. "Maybe I'll come work for you." I gently lift our hands and tug her forward. She rolls her eyes, but shuffles toward me. "I can be your bar bitch."

She laughs, and for the first time since I opened my eyes, it's a true laugh. "No way. You'd be too much of a distraction."

I pout, which only makes her laugh more. I nod my head at her. "Come here." She obliges, leaning forward and pressing her lips to mine. When she does, the pain drains from my limbs. I don't need football. I just need her.

"I love you," I murmur against her lips. I watch as her eyes shoot open, and I instantly find the panic in them. I smile. "You don't have to say it back. I meant it when I said you should take your time to learn to trust me, and that I will wait. But I wanted you to know that I lo—"

"I love you too," she says quickly, pressing her lips back on mine. I almost don't catch her words as they're muffled against my mouth, but I feel her smile. My chest cracks. I wish I could touch her properly. I wish I could pull her into my arms and bury my hands in her curls. I wish I could spend the next week showing her just how much I love her, and just how much I needed to hear those words. Especially today.

I can survive without football, as long as I have her.

She presses her forehead to mine, her breathing uneven and her smile so wide, I feel like tracing the shape with my fingers. "I want the wedding. The house. I want all the kids, and the life you picture," she whispers. Tears shine in her eyes again. "I want it with you."

"Yeah?"

"Yeah." She wipes her face again.

"You've been crying a lot lately." I reach out, trying to cup her face, but groan in pain as my shoulder sears with the movement. Fuck, that hurts. Katie leans over, bringing her face to my hand. I curl my fingers over her cheek and swipe my thumb across her bottom lip.

"It's been a rough couple of weeks. Falling in love is really fucking emotional," she says, rolling her eyes and trying to smile through the tears.

I chuckle. "It's not as fun as they make it seem in the movies, huh?"

"Worth it, though." She leans into my hand and closes her eyes.

Yeah, it's fucking worth it.

"So, we're the real thing?" I say, brushing my thumb over her cheek.

"You were a great fake boyfriend." She nods gently. "And I know you'll be a better real boyfriend. But you have to promise me—"

"I promise," I say immediately.

Katie laughs and swats my chest. "I'm serious. Let's just … be us for a while, okay?"

"Who else would we be?" I say, a smirk creeping over my lips. I know exactly what she's going to say.

"I don't want a ring, not straight away." She bites down on her bottom lip.

"But you do want one, eventually?"

She shrugs. "If that's what you want, too." I watch her chew on her lip as she looks at me. "I just took over the bar, and you're injured. Let's just be us, okay?"

"So not tomorrow?" I say, holding back my laugh.

"Not tomorrow."

"Next week?"

She groans, shuffling closer to me on the bed and dropping her lips on mine, and I smile widely at her. Of course, I'm kidding, but it's fun to make her squirm. "You're infuriating."

"You love me."

Chapter Twenty-Four
Flynn

"Please join me in welcoming the new Mr. and Mrs. Scott Harvey."

I bring my fingers to my mouth and whistle loudly as Scott practically carries Ivy into the ballroom. His arm is wrapped so tightly around her waist, holding her so close to his body, that she's barely touching the floor. They make their way through the crowd of people, everyone smiling and cheering.

It's not a large wedding. Scott's parents invited a few friends, and the rest of the guest list is mostly teammates and a few teachers from Ivy's school. There are no more than a hundred people here, but I think that's exactly what they wanted.

The woman standing directly in front of me leans back, her shoulders pressing into my chest, her head rolling onto my shoulder. She sighs, a smile painted on her lips, aimed at the couple.

When her eyes flicker up to mine, dark lashes showcasing the brightest blue, my heart seems to skip a beat. I've come to realize that the heart skip, the racing pulse, it's all going to be normal from now on. It's the effect Katie Murphy has on me.

One I know she'll likely have on me forever.

"They're happy, right?"

"If they were any happier, they'd be taken away to be studied." I drop my head, pressing my lips onto the exposed skin of her shoulder. My hands find her hips, and I tug her back into me. Her surprised squeal makes me smile, grazing my teeth over her skin. My palms slide around her waist, fingers slipping over the satin fabric wrapped around her body. The light blue creases under my touch, and Katie lifts her hands to stop my movements.

"Don't play with my dress, it's expensive."

"Did I pay for it?" I say, turning my head to look at her. Her eyes sparkle, her lashes painted and surrounded by makeup. She's stunning. I haven't been able to take my eyes off her since the moment she walked down that aisle earlier.

"Obviously."

"Well, it's mine to ruin then, isn't it?" I lift an arm, trapping her chin in my fingers and angling her head so I can drop a kiss on her lips. She sinks into me. Her mouth moves with mine, and we get lost in the feeling. But, only for a moment.

"Stop it," Katie says, pulling her lips away. I pout and lock my arms around her tighter, keeping her from stepping out of my orbit. "We're supposed to be watching their first dance."

"Who cares," I murmur, leaning in to kiss the corner of her mouth. "They're swaying back and forth in the middle of a room. Not much to miss."

"These are our friends."

"But I don't like kissing them the way I like kissing you."

"You're annoying." She shakes her head but doesn't pull away when I kiss her again. When we break apart, she sighs and leans back into me, resting her head on my shoulder, and looks up at me.

"I missed you last night," I tell her quietly, not looking away from her face. "And this morning."

"It hasn't even been twenty-four hours. We only slept in separate rooms down the hall from one another."

"Too far," I say, my thumb dragging back and forth across the satin fabric of her dress as I hold her. "How was this morning? Manic?"

"Actually." Katie's gaze flickers back to the dance floor, where Scott and Ivy are wrapped up in one another, swaying from side to side. Just like I said. "It's been the calmest week of my life. I expected Ivy to be out of her mind stressed, but Scott's made it pretty damn easy."

"He's a simp."

"He's in *love*." She playfully hits my hand. "He organized a driver to take her to all the appointments this week. Organized a spa day. This morning he had breakfast delivered to the suite—"

"We," I interrupt. "*We* had breakfast delivered. I was a part of the ordering."

She narrows her eyes at me before rolling them and smirking. "Fine, *you* as well."

"Thank you." I kiss her hair.

"As I was saying." Her hands drop, fingers curling over my forearms as if she's silently telling me not to let her go. As if I would. "Ivy's been so calm. This morning was a dream. Everything was on time, and she was ready with plenty of time for photos. There were a few tears about her parents and her grandparents."

"Wouldn't be Ivy without a few tears," I say gently, squeezing my arms around her. Ivy loves to cry; at movies, at books, at commercials. If it's even the smallest bit sad, she'll have a tear in her eye.

"I think it helped having the empty seats in the front row. The spaces for them."

"That was a nice touch," I say, lips pressing into her hair again, just above her ear so no one else knows. "It was a good idea, Rockstar. Proud of you."

Katie flushes a deep shade of pink, and her eyes drop to where her hands are covering mine. She wriggles her fingers. Her empty fingers. Particularly one. On her left hand.

I so, so badly want to give her a ring.

Ever since she told me she wanted to just be us, to wait for a little while before making any major, life-changing decisions, it's taken everything in me not to rebel and ask her anyway.

But I suppose it would be wise to take her home first. Introduce her to my folks and show her where I grew up. I also need to ask her parents for permission.

I remind myself for the thousandth time that we have time. There's no working around the season, no wondering if our plans will be messed up because I'll be out of town. We just get to be us.

"Have I told you how gorgeous you look?" I whisper into her ear.

She smiles softly. "About a hundred times."

"It's true." I duck, pressing my lips to the spot just beneath her ear. "You're stunning."

"You don't clean up too badly yourself, Reed."

I hum, ghosting my lips over her skin as I pull her in tighter. "Don't tempt me, or I'll drag you out of this ballroom right now. I don't care. I'll make you come in the hallway again."

"What is it with you and wanting to fuck in public places?" She giggles as she swipes a glass of champagne from a passing waiter. People are starting to move about now, the crowd watching the happy couple disperse as they look for their seats.

Katie taps my arm, her signal that she wants me to let her go, but I just hold her tighter. I can't help myself when I whisper in her ear, "You make me horny."

"I haven't done anything."

"You exist." With that, I uncurl my arms from around her body, freeing her. She lifts the glass of champagne to her lips, smirking, but her eyes don't leave mine. They shine, the challenge and heat evident, swirling around.

When she turns, her hand reaches back behind her as it looks for mine. I slip my palm against hers, my fingers locking around them, and I let her drag me across the room toward the bridal table. I take my seat next to Katie, Ivy next to her. At Scott's side, his parents sit, chatting quietly to one another.

"You good?" Katie asks Ivy as I slip my jacket from my shoulders.

Ivy's face lights up as she leans away from Scott to hug her best friend. "Perfect. I'm perfect."

"You look perfect." Katie grins. When they lean back from one another, I scoot my chair closer to Katie's, my thigh pressing against hers.

I stretch my arm back, pulling it behind me so I can lean it across the back of Katie's chair. Her hair falls down her back in loose curls, and my fingers are itching to get amongst the silky strands. I love playing with her hair.

As I'm stretching, a nerve pinches and I groan, quickly pulling it in and cradling it against my chest. Fuck. That hurt.

"What?" I glance over at Katie when she speaks, her voice low and dripping with concern. Her body is completely turned toward me now, her hands hovering over the arm cradled against my chest. She's staring at me, her eyes flickering between my face and my arm.

"I'm okay."

"You groaned. Is it hurting?" She shifts closer. "Damn it. I knew you shouldn't have taken it out of the sling for today."

"The doctor said I was fine to go without." I slowly stretch my arm, allowing the tight and healing muscles to ease into the new position. I rest it on the back of Katie's chair, my finger hooking around a curl immediately.

"Are you sure?" Her hand drops to my thigh, and she squeezes her fingers. "I packed it. I can go and get it for you from upstairs."

I smirk, rolling my eyes. "Of course you did." I lean in, crowding her as I put my face right in front of hers. "I promise, I'm okay."

"You're absolutely sure?" She glances around my face as if she's desperately trying to find a sign of the fleeting pain that went away the moment I slowed my movements down.

"Yes, baby. I'm good." I lean in, kissing her gently. I sink the hand leaning over her chair into her hair, cupping her neck and keeping her lips on mine.

Since my injury, Katie's hovered. She hovered beside me at the doctor's appointments. At home during the recovery. At the back of the crowd during the press conferences, as we told the world about the injury and that the Super Bowl game was going to be my last. At home, she fusses and clicks her tongue whenever I do something that takes it too far. Like rearranging furniture in one of the spare bedrooms to turn it into a home recording studio for her to keep singing. Or, getting on my knees in the shower and throwing one of her legs over my shoulder.

But, then again, she's also been attentive. Loving. It's strange because before her, I thought the end of my career would destroy me. After her, it seems like it's come to a natural end, like I was waiting for something that meant more to me than playing football, until I admitted to myself that maybe I've been done with playing for a little while now.

Not the game, not altogether. I love the game, but playing? I think I've been done for a while.

"Love you," Katie whispers as she pulls back. My hand drops, but I keep it on her back, my fingers tangled into the ends of her hair.

***

"You married that."

"I know."

"Did you know she was like this?"

"After some wine? Yes, but I thought she wouldn't do this in the dress."

"One thing I've learned about these girls is that they will hype each other up until they both do something dumb. If Ivy suggested a few wines and then a bungee jump off a bridge, Katie would ask how many bottles," I say as I watch my girlfriend sing into the microphone Ivy holds up for her. An hour ago, the DJ gave them a microphone to make some announcements. They announced the party was starting, both lifting a bottle of wine each over their heads and laughing hysterically. Since then, the

DJ has played pop song after pop song that both Ivy and Katie have screamed the lyrics for.

We started in the middle of the dance floor with them, Scott and I. Scott, who has never been much of a dancer, tried his best to keep up, but he bowed out by song number five, taking up residence on the edge of the dance floor. He hasn't taken his eyes off Ivy since.

I lasted a little longer, but after a full straight minute of Katie grinding her ass against me during some Justin Timberlake song, I needed a break.

A server places two bottles of beer down on the table Scott and I lean against, and I give him a nod. It's been a pretty decent night. Scott looks completely and utterly in awe of his new wife, and I couldn't be happier for the both of them. I tell him as much, bumping my shoulder gently with his.

"Thank you." He takes a swig of the beer, never taking an eye off Ivy. The girls are now screaming the lyrics to 'Baby' by Justin Bieber into the mic.

"I'm glad you guys found each other. You're meant to be. She's good for you. Has been since you met her," I say, tipping my beer in Ivy's direction. "Plus, she kept you in Boston, and we won the ring we've been chasing since freshman year training camp."

"You were a scrawny shit, running your mouth about how the school had never seen a QB quite like you."

"And they still haven't." I smirk. "You never let me show them."

"You are a talented tight end. Fucking one with the ball, you know that." Scott turns a little toward me, taking his eyes off Ivy for the first time in hours.

"Was," I say quietly. "I *was* a talented tight end. Now, I'm just another retired NFL player with serious brain damage and a bogus degree in business."

"It's not bogus. You graduated."

"I have no interest in using it."

"Are you sure you don't want to get a second opinion? Lots of players have come back after concussions." His words wash over me like cold water. Suddenly, I'm wide awake, and the hair on the back of my neck is standing up. For a second, his words pump adrenaline through my veins, and I feel the anticipation crawl under my skin, giving me the slightest of buzzes.

"Sure, but none from a severe traumatic brain injury." Scott flinches at my words, and the adrenaline, the anticipation, that was just humming through my body ceases.

"Fuck." He runs a hand through his hair. "I guess I just can't believe it's over."

"We got our ring. We did what you came here to do, with me."

"I know, but—" Scott takes a deep breath, his eyes flickering back to his new wife and avoiding my gaze. "You're so calm. I would be freaking out."

"I—Oh, well, I guess I am calm." I shrug, swigging at the beer again. The amber liquid slides down my throat, and I expect to feel something at Scott's words. I expect disappointment, panic, maybe even anger.

But I don't.

He's right. I'm calm.

"The injury, the way I had to go out, it was shit. I'm disappointed the choice was made for me, but—" I lift a hand to his shoulder and squeeze. "I'm not disappointed that it was made. It was my time. That's that."

I remember the beginning of the season, when I spent all my free evenings sitting in a booth in Katie's bar, staring at her from across the room while she wouldn't even make eye contact with me. I remember the conversation with Hollie after the video got leaked. She was worried I wasn't going to get re-signed, but I was worried Katie would be even more pissed that I started a fight in front of her bar.

I think, deep down, I knew my time on the field as a player was coming to an end. I just didn't know when.

"Have you thought about what you might want to do now?" Scott asks, speaking over the music.

I shake my head and shrug. "Coach? I don't know. College ball could be fun. High school might be good too, if any of the local colleges or high schools are hiring."

"Would you coach pro ball? You'd make one hell of an offensive coordinator. You know your shit."

I think about his words as my eyes travel over the small crowd that's still left. It's nearing the end of the night. Most of the guests filtered out the moment the girls took to that microphone. Some of our teammates and Scott's parents remain, looking over the dance floor with amusement.

Katie's blonde hair is a mess of curls. She's holding her dress up in one hand and her shoes have been tossed to the side. She's laughing, her face flushed and her eyes bright. She's happy.

I want to see her happy every day, for the rest of our lives.

"I think I'll stick close to home for a while." I smile as I watch her, and when her eyes lock on mine and I watch her bite down on her bottom lip, the air gets knocked from my lungs. "Maybe I'll learn how to pour beers and spend all day staring at my girl."

Beside me, out of the corner of my eye, I see Scott grin and shake his head. "You're fucking worse than me."

I'm about to dispute his comment when I hear a squeal over the music and then cheering from the teammates that are left on the dance floor. They've been egging on the girls all night.

I look up, my eyes finding Katie immediately. She's standing on the fucking bartop, dress hitched up, microphone in her hand. She laughs, catching herself just before belting out the chorus of the song playing at the top of her lungs.

I watch, completely entranced as she throws her head back and sings. Her voice isn't in key, she's not trying very hard, and she keeps stopping to laugh. But she's having fun.

That is, until I see her slip a little, looking like she's more unsteady on her feet than I realized. I move at the same time as Scott, because Ivy's decided she wants to join in on the bartop fun.

"That's it. Calling it," he grumbles as we head toward the bar.

"Yup, one of them is going to break a bone." I swipe Katie's shoes from the ground as we walk past them. When I reach her, I look up, my hand shooting out to grab her ankle in an effort to help keep her upright. "Let's go, Rockstar. Time for bed."

"No," she whines, crouching down on the bartop so she's almost face-to-face with me. "Don't be a party pooper, Reed. I'm having fun."

Next to me, Scott is gently coaxing Ivy from the bar. She gets down willingly.

"You're going to break a bone if you're not careful. Then who's going to be the breadwinner of the house?" I point to myself and wink. "Unemployed, remember?"

"NFL money, remember?" She pushes a playful hand against my chest. I grab it, tugging her toward me. She comes willingly, letting me pull her off the bar and into my arms.

Chapter Twenty-Five

Katie

June

THE SUN BEATS DOWN, blue sky stretching above us with not a cloud in sight. I sip on an iced-cold strawberry soda, my legs kicked up and ankles crossed on the curved bar at the back of the cart. The club's cart girl just left, serving us these soda drinks and restocking the snacks that Ivy and I brought along for the day. She sits next to me, her Kindle on her lap, and she sips gently.

I stick my arm out, the warm sun heating my skin as I turn my arms over. The bracelet Flynn gave me for my birthday sparkles in the sunlight, and I smile. My eyes dart over the green to where the boys stand, both in shorts and polo tops, leaning on golf clubs as they discuss something in quiet voices.

Flynn was cleared to work out and play low-impact sports a month or so ago. He immediately decided golf, where he's swinging a club back and forth in a repetitive motion, was going to be his new thing.

I lost my boyfriend to the golf course, and it hasn't given him back, so the only logical option was to join him. Naturally, as Scott was being dragged along with Flynn in his new sporting venture, I dragged Ivy along.

"The sun feels nice today," I say, my sunglasses sitting low on my nose.

Ivy doesn't look up from her Kindle, taking another small sip of her drink as she gives me a non-committal hum.

I look back at the boys. Flynn is waving an arm around, pointing out towards the course and the hole they are currently trying to aim for. They're both terrible at golf, but bless them, they try.

"What do you think they talk about all day while they're out here?"

"Scott says Flynn just babbles about all the jobs he thinks he might try."

I sigh. "He still keeps saying he just wants to be a bartender."

"That would be hilarious." Ivy snorts, finally laying her Kindle down in her lap and looking over at me. Her hair is tied into a high ponytail and she's wearing a matching golf skirt to mine, just in white where mine is blue. Of course, we had to dress the part. "I think he should coach."

"Me too." I nod, glancing over at them as Scott swings, and the sound of the club coming in contact with the ball, sending it sailing through the air, echoes. I put my fingers to my lips and whistle loudly. "Nice shot, Harvey."

"Hey!" Flynn turns immediately, holding his arms out. He's got a cap over his blond hair, his polo shirt is tucked in, and his shorts are almost too tight against his thick thighs. My eyes run down his body, and I tip my head forward, obviously checking him out. "What about me? I'm a great shot, too."

"You're doing great, baby," I call out with a smile. He tugs his sunglasses down his nose so I can see his eyes and winks.

"So." I turn back to Ivy. "Are you wearing the black or the green dress tonight? Did you decide? And, should I bring a bottle of champagne in the car? I wonder how long it will take to get to the hotel?"

"Ah," Ivy says, hesitating as she glances around me and at the boys. Flynn is now lining up his shot. "I don't think I'll drink tonight."

"What, why?"

"I-I, uh." She sighs and places her cup in the small holder between us. "I don't think I can."

I shake my head, confused. "We have been talking about this night for ages. It's ring night. We said we were going to drink lots of free champagne and dance the night away."

"I know, and I'll still dance the night away with you, but I just won't have a drink."

"Why the hell—" I sit up suddenly. I rip off my sunglasses and scan Ivy head to toe. Her cheeks go a deep shade of red, and she sinks into her seat. "Oh my god. *Oh my god.*"

"Shh." Ivy waves her hand. "I haven't told Scott."

"What? Why the hell not?"

"Because, he would make a big deal and then not want to go tonight." She shakes her head. "Besides, I only took the test this morning. I'm late, but it could be anything. I want to get tests done. And the dress. I want to wear the dress before I get too big for it."

"Ivy... this is, like, huge news." She nods but I notice the tears springing to her eyes. I reach over and grab her hand. "Are you—are you not happy about this? Do you not want kids?"

"No," she whispers, her free hand resting gently on her stomach. "I do. With him. It's just ... scary."

"I bet." I glance over at the boys just in time to see Flynn take his swing. He whoops when it goes straight and does a happy dance. I smirk. He's such a fucking dork sometimes. I look back at Ivy to see her watching Scott, her hand still on her stomach. I squeeze her hand. "He's huge. That baby is half him. Oh my god, you're going to get ripped apart."

"Stop it." She laughs, sniffling the tiniest bit, but no tears.

"Well, if it's for real, and you are, then I'm so happy for you." I squeeze her hand again before letting go, settling back into my seat as the boys make their way back over to us. "I'm going to spoil the shit out of your kids. It's going to be so fun."

Ivy just smiles, shaking her head a little before her eyes flicker over my shoulder. Seconds later, I feel a hand dive into my hair and tug. My head falls backward, and a smile forms when I see

Flynn's face hovering closely over mine. He smirks and leans down further, lips pressing to mine.

"Did you see my shot?" he asks between kisses.

"Yes." I reach up, my hand finding his newly healed shoulder and tracing the fabric of his polo up toward his neck. I pat him gently. "Don't beat yourself up too much about it, you're still improving."

He growls, tightening his grip and tugging at my hair again. "Rockstar. You're being a brat. You're supposed to hype me up if you come to golf."

"I never said that."

"You said you'd watch me play."

"And I did." I smile, watching his eyes flash with playfulness and cheek. "My feedback is that you have time to improve."

"You're lucky I love you." He gives me one last kiss before retreating. He leans his arms on the top of the cart. I look over to find Scott in a similar position, except he has one hand on Ivy's neck, his thumb gently stoking down her throat as she lifts her strawberry soda for him to try.

"How much longer is left? We need to head home and get ready for tonight," I ask, eyeing Ivy suspiciously again. The deep flush she had only moments ago has suddenly drained from her face. She takes a couple of deep breaths, and I nudge her knee a little.

"Only one more hole." Flynn wraps my ponytail around his fingers, toying with my hair. "You'll have plenty of time."

"Okay, well, let's hurry up. Perfection takes time." I reach up and tug my hair from Flynn's grip. He lets go but dips down again, pressing a kiss to the corner of my lips.

"Scott and I were just talking—"

"How dangerous of you both." I smile.

Flynn leans down and nips at my ear. "Behave or I won't wait until after the ring ceremony to ruin your nice new dress."

Scott groans. Flynn's whisper obviously wasn't so quiet after all. I readjust my sunglasses and glance at him. "Payback."

"Anyway," Flynn interrupts before I settle into a verbal sparring match with Scott. "We were talking and, if you can swing it, we thought we should head back to Italy again. Get the same villa. Make it a summer thing. Maybe every year."

I smile at the hope in his voice. This isn't the first time he's mentioned Italy to me again, or proposed another holiday with the two of them. He loves living so close to Scott. They see each other daily, training at the gym, going running. I know he's getting nervous about camp and pre-season, and Scott going back when he won't be.

They've always had football in common. It's been the foundation of their friendship for so long, I think he's worried now that he can't play, he might get left behind.

"Oh, that's a great idea," Ivy says, looking between the boys.

"I agree. Making it a yearly thing would be fun, too. I loved it there."

I look up at Flynn, still standing over me with his arms resting on the top of the cart. He smiles brightly, his eyes full of excitement. He'll be over the moon about Ivy, excited for Scott, and just like me, he'll be itching to spoil the new addition.

I think about what Doug told me, about having friends to do life with, how it makes a difference.

My brother is so much younger than me. My parents are retired and enjoying their hard work. They're thinking about traveling for a few months when Sammy graduates, getting out to see the world. Flynn's parents are the same as always, supportive but uninterested in being involved.

Scott and Ivy have become family. They're the ones we celebrate the wins with, who are next to us through the hard times. The milestones seem bigger and brighter, getting to cross them off with them by our sides.

I'll never tell him this, but thank god for Scott and the day he decided to gamble on me giving Ivy a coaster with his number scribbled on the back.

Epilogue

Katie

Three years later

"Fuck, fuck, *fuck*." I chew on my lip, my fingers tapping on the benchtop as I stare at the white sticks laid out in front of me. There are six of them. Two boxes worth. All with two dark blue lines. Clear as day. Can't miss them.

I'm pregnant.

Holy fuck.

My eyes glance at the clock hanging on the wall across the room, and I wince. It's almost six and Flynn will be walking through the front door any minute. He took some time off after his career with the Broncos ended. He wanted to make sure the next step was the right one, so he stepped back from football, tried his hand at a few things. He even tried bartending, which he lasted a day doing before promptly telling me the magic he thought was in bartending was actually in his watching me do it. Of course, he swears up until this day it has nothing to do with the fact he was shit at it.

By Christmas that year though, he was getting itchy. Restless.

So, when Boston Metropolitan University called and asked if he wanted to join them as their new head coach for the spring season, Flynn knew it was the right decision. I must say, the man was meant to coach. He was a great player, but he sees the game, understands its players, like no one I've ever seen before. Even Jeff commends him for his achievements in the short time he's been there. They're getting closer and closer to a bowl game.

Flynn also just loves it. Deep down, I think there is a part of him that is grateful the injury happened. It all worked out. He took the time off he wanted, and we traveled a little. Spent a few months jetting off whenever we felt the urge, since he wasn't tied to a training schedule or games. He found his peace, and then the job at the university dropped in front of him, and he stepped up like it was always meant to be. I have never been prouder than the moment he won his first game with those kids. They'd been on a bad streak, he turned them around, and now he's well and truly building a championship team.

I'm still at the bar. I laugh and joke about how much work it is but secretly, I love it. I love the hustle and bustle, I love the ever-changing challenge it poses. We now have open mic nights and it's been a hit. One of the country singers who played a few weeks at the bar over the summer just got signed by Mr. Suit himself, Mark Madison. And on Friday nights, with a regular crowd, I get up on the makeshift stage and get to perform. I never wanted to be a singer, not one that traveled and toured and had to push album after album out. I just wanted to love singing and have a place to do that while having fun. Now I do, even if it is only at the bar that my family owns.

Sammy graduated from high school and went to play football for Texas State. He's a quarterback, and he's a damn good one. I actually think Flynn is a little upset that he didn't pick BMU to play at. I fly out with my parents whenever we can to see Sammy play, and whenever he's home and comes round, he and Flynn are in the backyard, passing a ball back and forth while rambling about different stats. It's sweet.

Our lives haven't really changed all that much. We still live close to Scott and Ivy, and their cheeky little boy, Matty. We still holiday in Italy every summer together. The boys still play golf, and they're still terrible at it.

I glance down at my left hand. I'm *still* just a girlfriend.

I thought a year, eighteen months max, would be the time it would take for Flynn to crack and propose. In fact, I was so confident that he would that I was waiting for it by our first Christmas together. It never happened. Then, our anniversary passed. My birthday. Another summer holiday in Italy.

At every event over the last three years, I have been holding my breath for the moment he decided to get on one knee and give me a damn ring.

I know what I said. I know I told him that I just wanted to be us. But I meant for like, a few months. Not years.

And now I'm fucking pregnant and we're still just playing house, skirting any mentions of a ring or a wedding. I try to drop hints, but either they're not obvious enough or he's ignoring me.

Maybe I should just tell him I want to get married?

I groan, dropping my head to the kitchen bench and shifting on the stool. I should've just told him I wanted to get married a year and a half ago. If I had, I wouldn't be having anxiety about what my very Italian mother and very Irish father are going to say about me having a baby out of wedlock.

They'll be over the moon for a grandchild, but I can just see the flash of disappointment my mother will throw my way when we tell them.

"Urgh, what am I going to do?" I ask myself.

A deep chuckle echoes down the hallway, and a shiver runs down my spine. I sit up, glancing over my shoulder to see Flynn coming through the front door. He's wearing a deep red polo shirt and black running pants. He toes off his sneakers and drops the BMU backpack he takes to work by the staircase.

"What have you done now?" he says, a smile painting his lips as he pads toward me.

I swipe the white sticks still lying on the counter into a pile and stand from the stool. I keep them bundled in my hands, hidden behind my back. Flynn approaches me, looking a little tired but still smiling. His eyes are bright, the mix of blue and green swirling as he takes me in. He smirks, gaze dropping down my body as he checks me out. God, he's so sexy it makes my stomach clench and my heart skip multiple beats.

When he nears me, he bends, dropping a lingering kiss to my lips. Instantly, his hand reaches for my ponytail and pulls at the elastic wrapped around my hair. The curls fall free, and he sinks his hands into the strands, gently massaging my head as I look up at him. I try to smile, but looking at him, having his hands in my hair, makes me feel like I'm going to cry.

Fucking hormones.

"Hey," he murmurs, noticing what I can only guess is the glassy look in my eyes as the sting of impending tears overwhelms me. "What's wrong? Did you have a bad day?"

He steps closer as I shake my head, my lip quivering. Fucking hell, I think I might lose it.

What if he doesn't want to marry me anymore? What if I made him wait too long, and now he's bored? What if he's changed his mind and doesn't even want kids?

"I—" I gulp in some air, trying to get the words out without completely allowing my internal, irrational meltdown to take over. It doesn't work, and a fat tear drops down my cheek.

Flynn immediately wipes it away.

I revel in the feel of his hands on me and use the calming strokes of his thumb across my cheek to even out my breathing. I take a step away from him, pull my hands from behind my back, and show him the numerous white sticks I'm holding.

His expression goes from concern, to amusement, to confused, to downright shock.

"Is that—" he stammers.

"Yes."

"Are you?"

"Yes." I nod, my heart pounding in my chest as I watch him take in what they mean.

He takes one of them from my hand and turns it over, eyes gazing down at the clear as day, double blue lines. "When?"

"I felt off last week." I shrug, turning to place the remaining tests back on the kitchen bench. "And I'm late. Very late."

"How late?"

"A month, maybe six weeks."

Flynn blows out a breath and shakes his head. "How did you not notice?"

"I ... haven't really been tracking. We've been busy getting ready for Italy, and you're in the middle of recruiting. I just ... didn't notice that I missed a period." I wring my hands in front of me, twisting my fingers. I wish he would touch me. Or tell me that he's excited. Logically, I know he loves me, but today's been one hell of a rollercoaster, and I don't have the energy to play mediator with my own emotions.

"What made you think about it?"

"Ivy's pregnant again. She told me this morning." Flynn's eyes snap to mine, widening.

"She is?" I nod and he laughs. "Fuck, yeah."

I frown, my stomach twisting. Happy for Ivy? Happy for us? Fuck, I need to lie down.

"Flynn," I say, gently taking the test from his hands and placing it with the others. "Are you ... do you want this? Are you happy?"

Silence envelops us as we stand there, staring at one another. His eyes are darting over my face. He's searching. He's reading my emotions, tapping into my thoughts, like he does so well. I'm his open book.

He steps forward again, his hands cupping my cheeks and his thumbs swiping gently over my skin. "I don't think I have ever felt happier in my entire life. This feeling? It's pure bliss. It's euphoric."

"It is?" I ask weakly, sagging in his arms. He holds me steady, wrapped in his arms.

"Nothing makes me happier than knowing I'm the one you chose to procreate with."

I scrunch up my nose, trying to hold off the sob that crawls up my throat in pure relief. "Procreate?"

"You and me, Rockstar." He leans down, kissing me gently. When he pulls back, he whispers against my lips, "We're having a baby."

"I thought you might not want one with me."

"I see the hormones are already kicking in." He smiles, not letting go. "Because I know you know that's a wild thought to have when it comes to me wanting you. Babies with you, a future with you. I'll take it all."

"You will?"

"Fuck, yes I will." He kisses me again. "You're never getting rid of me now, Murphy."

The heavy weight I felt earlier as I stared at all the blue lines lifts, and the euphoria that he spoke about settles into my skin as though he's transferring it to me through his touch. His hands drop, tracing the lines of my neck and over my shoulders, down my body until they settle on my waist.

He touches his forehead to mine. "Can I ask you to marry me now? Give you my ring to wear? Or do you want to wait a little longer?"

I rear back as though he's shocked me with a low current. "What?"

"I mean, I will drop to my knee right this second, but if you want to wait, that's okay too."

"You have a ring?" I ask, pushing out of his arms a little and staring at him. What the fuck? "Since *when*?"

"Since, like, two weeks after you told me you would be my girlfriend for real." He nods his head like what he's saying is common information. He smirks, his eyes darting over my face as I shake my head.

"Why the fuck haven't you given it to me yet?" My voice pitches as I throw my hands, my heart racing. I'm going to kill this man.

"You wanted to wait," Flynn says, laughing and taking a step toward me, trying to pull me back into his arms. I shake my head and slap his hands away. "Rockstar, you told me you wanted to wait, so I waited. I was just waiting for you to be ready, for you to say you wanted the ring."

"I—you, what?"

"I would've married you that day in the hospital, concussion and bruised bones be damned."

"I meant like a year." I throw my hands up. "I meant like eighteen months. I meant like until we had some time to settle in, until you had figured out what was coming after football. I didn't mean—" I press my hands into my stomach. "Wait until I was pregnant."

"Oh, baby." He laughs, shaking his head. He grabs for me again, and when I try to push him away, he doesn't let me. Instead, he pulls me around, spinning us so he can sit on the stool and position me in between his legs. His fingers find my waist, and he digs in, holding me there. "I'm sorry."

The fight drains from me instantly, and I sag into him.

"If I'd known you had a time frame in mind, I never would've missed it." He leans forward, his hands coming around my front and resting on my stomach. He splays his fingers over the non-existent bump, his hands warming my body.

"Okay." I sigh. "I'm sorry for freaking out."

"You're allowed. You're growing my little girl in there."

"Girl?"

"I'm built to be a girl dad, don't you think?"

I give him a watery smile, the tears burning behind my eyes again. "You're ridiculous."

He only smiles. "Do you want your ring now? Or would you like a big fancy proposal with the flowers, and the string quartet playing, and the hidden photographer?"

"Now, please."

Flynn gently pushes me back so he can stand from the stool. I watch as he rounds the kitchen bench and pulls open one of the many junk drawers we have around the house. He hates them, but they balance out my messiness to his over-the-top cleanliness. He rifles through the contents, finally pulling out a red velvet box and turning to face me.

I stare at him, my jaw on the floor and disbelief in my eyes.

"You kept it in the junk drawer?" I exclaim as he comes back to me. He holds the box out and shrugs.

"You never found it. In fact, I'm surprised you never did. I guess those junk drawers really do hide treasures when you need them to." He flicks open the lid of the box. A diamond the size of a small boulder sits nestled into small velvet cushions. The gold band glints from the lights above us. Simple, understated but still fucking huge. I stare at the ring, completely dumbfounded that he kept it in a drawer for three years. A drawer I toss things into every day.

"So, Rockstar, will you marry me?"

I blink up at him as he takes the ring from the box and holds it up, turning it a little between his fingers. A smile spreads across my lips.

"Fine, but keep a piece of my jewelry in the junk drawer again, and I'm throwing out your golf clubs," I say, trying my best to have the fake threat come out convincingly. I fail, and my voice shakes with emotion. Flynn feigns shock for a moment, his face falling in horror before a smile cracks and he lifts my left hand, sliding the ring onto my finger. He leans down, kissing me hard and leaving me breathless.

We were never very good at faking it anyway.

Acknowledgements

Thank you for reading Play The Last Track! It has been a labour and a half but it's here. This has been the book that I have learnt the most lessons about being an author and self-publishing during it's process. It's been a battle, but one that was one worth fighting.

As always, thank you to my family and my friends for being by my side every step of the way.

This book wouldn't have been possible without my incredible editor, Laura. Thank you so much for everything and I can't wait to continue working together. To Ellie at LoveNotes for being so supportive with the campaign to get this book into your hands early.

To Bec, as always you have kept me grounded and sane and off the emotional cliff. The day to day of being author would be 100% harder without you.

And finally to you, my readers. You make every single word worth it.

About the Author

Olivia is a romance indie author living on the east coast of Australia with her miniature spoodle.

She's been writing since high school and is doing her best to live out her dreams in becoming a published author. Her hobbies are snuggling with her dog, reading all sorts of romance books, and hanging out with her family.

She's currently working on her new series that is set in her favourite country in the world, Scotland!

OTHER TITLES

The Boston Broncos Series

Play The Last Card
Play The Last Track

Standalones

A Misstep Of Fate

WANT MORE?

Turn the page to read the first chapter of *Play The Last Card*, which follows the love story of Scott Harvey & Ivy Booker.

Chapter One

Ivy

Fingers tap against the rounded edge of the bar. Despite the large hands and the long fingers, the tapping is soft, and gentle, and completely out of rhythm. It makes the hairs on the back of my neck stand up. A slight shiver trickles down my spine as I eye the man who seems to be studying the bar top with great interest.

The tapping stops and he lifts his head. With the cap pulled low over his eyes, a shadow falls across his features and I can't quite make out the color of his eyes from my spot by the beer taps. I force myself to look down, eyes back on the taps as I twist my wrist and switch out the glasses in my hands. A steady stream of beer flows eagerly and the second pint glass fills to the top.

"Won't be a moment," I call out, my eyes falling on the man again. He hasn't called me over since sitting down, nor has he really shown any indication that he is ready to order, but I call out anyway. Still, there is something in me that can't resist trying to get his attention. He gives a slight nod without meeting my gaze and his fingers take up tapping again against the lacquered bar top.

The man's disinterest bothers me.

Why?

No idea. But it does.

"Here you go, Doug." I push the two overflowing pint glasses in front of the older gentleman.

"You should pour yourself one, darlin'. On me and the boys," he replies as I add the drinks to his tab.

"You know I can't drink on shift, Doug. Stop trying to get me in trouble."

He laughs, heartedly and with his whole body. He gives me a fake pout and shakes his head, telling me, "I'm just waiting for the day you quit this place and run away with me. You know that."

I can't help but laugh right along with him. Doug is good natured, sweet, and madly in love with his high school sweetheart. I've heard the stories about him and his wife enough times to know that he is only kidding about running away with him.

Doug is my favorite regular customer by a mile. I'm only here casually to help out but during the quieter hours when Doug and his buddies are the only ones around, they like to regale me with stories, talk nonsense, and dissect any football game that happens to be playing on the bar's televisions. I remember the time I'd asked Doug if he'd ever played before—a passing comment after I'd first started working shifts at the bar—and the rollercoaster of a story that had followed ended with him breaking his ankle in high school and ruining any chance of him going pro. I laughed, commenting that it was a damn shame because he looked like he could have been an American All-Star. That had earned me the brightest smile from Doug who'd been quick to agree.

That story remains my all-time favorite of his.

"You're a gem. Thanks, Ivy." Doug is missing a tooth but his grin hasn't suffered from it. The faded, over worn Broncos jersey stretches over his large beer belly. I can't help the smile that grows again and I wave him off.

When I turn, the man in the cap has raised his head a little and I can see more of his jawline. Sharp. So sharp.

He's been watching the exchange with Doug but when our eyes meet, his gaze drops and his fingers resume their out-of-rhythm tapping. I approach, moving slowly down the bar to his seat.

"Hi," I say, resisting the urge to clear my throat first. My mouth is suddenly dry and I practically feel my nerves pulsing under my skin. Why the hell am I nervous? "Can I get you something to drink?"

"Water." He pauses as his chin lifts slightly. His rough voice raises goosebumps on my arms when he adds in a low grumble, "Please."

"Sure. Nothing else?" My hand is already moving toward the chilled glasses in the fridge next to where I stand.

"Just the water. Thanks," he adds quickly.

At least he has manners. I fill his glass with ice, eyeing him as he whips the cap off his head and runs a hand through his hair.

My stomach turns over with a pang of familiarity.

I know him.

He looks so familiar, it's as if I recognize some of the features of his face but can't place them clearly in my mind. It's a blurry, pixelated version. My mind screams at me, positive that I have seen this man before. I try to school my features though; I don't want to scare him off while my brain tries to put the pieces of this puzzle together.

"You from around here?" I ask before I can stop myself, letting my easy and well-rehearsed customer service smile slip into place. I slide a coaster under the glass of water and place it in front of him.

Green. His eyes are green.

My gaze drifts over his strong jaw, and up to his hair, taking note of the way his hair curls at the ends after being trapped under his cap. I glance down, following the trail of corded muscles down his arms. His biceps stretch the cotton, the t-shirt he wears hugging his shoulders, his chest, his stomach. I swallow. I would bet good money that he has an eight pack under that shirt of his. My gaze darts around his impressive form and my fingers twitch, wanting to reach out to feel how solid he is.

God, I need to get a grip.

Finally, he meets my gaze. Another small shiver rolls down my spine as a chill spreads up my arms and I fight off the urge to shake them out.

"No."

"So, you just moved here?" I ask, studying him. My eyes linger on the shadow of a beard growing. I wonder what he looks like with the beard fully grown out? I imagine it only adds to the appeal. The ruggedness of him. A tall, wide man with a full beard. I think he would look good with a full beard. Although, it would probably hide that jawline of his, and that would be a shame.

His eyebrows crease, long lashes framing the green of his eyes and deepening the color just a little. He cocks his head to the side and frowns, clearing his throat.

Shit.

I'm staring.

"Yes. That would be the definition of me not being from around here," he replies in the same low, gruff tone.

"You could be just visiting." I shrug. I could walk away, I *should* walk away. There are a few glasses that could go through the wash, missing bottles of beer to be refilled in the fridge. I have things to do before we close. I don't have to stay and chat with this guy.

Yet the puzzle pieces still aren't making sense and I can't shake the feeling that I know him from somewhere. I hesitate for a second. "You look familiar."

It's his turn to study me and with his gaze the beginnings of a flush burn at the nape of my neck. I take a subtle deep breath, willing the heat to stay off my face. The corners of his eyes begin to tighten, fingers reaching to clutch the untouched glass of water in front of him before he says, "Hazard of the job, I guess."

"Oh?" I shuffle through my memories, searching for him. He isn't a teacher at the school. Unless he is new? No, I don't think they've hired this year for the junior school. I haven't seen him around the bar before, nor around the hospital and I don't spend my time anywhere else these days. I press on, my curiosity winning out over my politeness.

"What do you do?"

"I—" He goes to answer but something in his eyes shift as if he's only just realizing what I'm asking him and a gleam of joy flashes through the small cracks of his stoic mask. "Nothing important. I work across the road."

"For the Broncos?" I lean on the bar toward him, wanting to figure him out and trying my best to do so before I scare him off.

I'm curious. Sue me.

He's a mystery and the only thing I want at this moment is to figure him out. Eagerness be damned.

"You could say that," he answers. My heart skips a little as his fingers drum along the bar top again.

"Oh, well, you'll be a new regular then I expect. They all come over here during the week from what I'm told. And during home games, the bar is packed with fans." I wave a hand lazily around the bar.

"You're told? This is your first shift?" he asks. I bite down a smile. Good, I've got him curious too. Curious about me, maybe. Hopefully. My stomach flips and something flutters lightly in my chest.

I ignore the feeling though, tugging the cloth from my back pocket to run it over the bar.

It's cliché as hell but whatever.

I need a distraction from the butterflies suddenly roaming around inside me.

"My friend's parents own the bar. I only really work on weekends when they need help." I drop my gaze to the mahogany bar top, the flush creeping even higher up my neck without permission. "I'm actually a kindergarten teacher."

"Bit of a change. Toddlers to drunk adults."

"You'd think so, but not so much in my experience." I curl my fingers into the cleaning rag, sweeping it across the bar top again. "They're more similar than you'd think."

As if on cue to prove my point, a bunch of rowdy guys stumble through the door. One of them wears an off-white, stained with beer wedding dress. The others don t-shirts with a drunken photo enlarged—of what I assume to be the groom—and printed on each one. *Great.* I drop my head, rolling my shoulders back. So much for an easy, quiet afternoon. I was hoping for a story or two with Doug, an opportunity to pull out my school work and plan some lessons for the kids so I was well and truly ahead before the school year starts.

"Ah." The familiar man's eyes follow mine, his jaw tightening as he watches the group loudly decide on a round of shots. He shoves the cap back onto his head, pulling it as far down over his face as it will go. "I'll leave you to it."

"Oh." My chest tightens. I didn't want him to go. "Well, it was nice to meet you ..."

"Scott." He fills in for me.

I beam, holding out my hand across the bar. "Ivy."

Scott stares at my hand for a moment before wrapping his fingers around mine. His hand is calloused, rough, and uneven. It dwarfs my own. Yet as I settle into the shape and feeling of his fingers curled around mine, it's as if the two fit perfectly. As if each is carved out purely for the other.

He drops my hand, brows pulling together and a frown tugging at his lips.

"See you round, Ivy."

Despite the fact there isn't a hint of a smile on his face and his features are still set into what I'm beginning to think is probably stone, his eyes flash with something else. The green of his eyes swirl under the shadow of his cap. They're intense but a spark takes hold and lights a small fire in the pit of my stomach.

I swallow the lump in my throat, losing the war with the unwanted flush heating up my face. I give him a small wave, calling after him, "Welcome to Boston."